Dark Soil

DARK SOIL

Fictions and Mythographies

Edited by Angie Sijun Lou

with Stories by Karen Tei Yamashita

COFFEE HOUSE PRESS
Minneapolis
2024

Coffee House Press books are available to the trade through our primary distributor, Consortium Book Sales & Distribution, cbsd.com or (800) 283-3572. For personal orders, catalogs, or other information, write to info@coffeehousepress.org.

Coffee House Press is a nonprofit literary publishing house. Support from private foundations, corporate giving programs, government programs, and generous individuals helps make the publication of our books possible. We gratefully acknowledge their support in detail in the back of this book.

LIBRARY OF CONGRESS CATALOGING-IN-PUBLICATION DATA

Names: Yamashita, Karen Tei, 1951– author. | Lou, Angie Sijun, 1994– editor.
Title: Dark soil : fictions and mythographies / edited by Angie Sijun Lou; with stories by Karen Tei Yamashita.
Description: Minneapolis : Coffee House Press, 2024.
Identifiers: LCCN 2023043691 (print) | LCCN 2023043692 (ebook) | ISBN 9781566896870 (paperback) | ISBN 9781566896887 (epub)
Subjects: LCGFT: Short stories. | Creative nonfiction.
Classification: LCC PS3575.A44 D37 2024 (print) | LCC PS3575.A44 (ebook) | DDC 813/.54—dc23/eng/20231113
LC record available at https://lccn.loc.gov/2023043691
LC ebook record available at https://lccn.loc.gov/2023043692

PRINTED IN THE UNITED STATES OF AMERICA

31 30 29 28 27 26 25 24   1 2 3 4 5 6 7 8

Contents

Dark Soil

Editorial Introduction

Angie Sijun Lou

The project began when I approached seven writers with a simple prompt: to write a prose piece that illuminates the hidden history of a place, a history that would not be obvious with one's first visitation to the site. The word *mythography* did not come to me until much later, when I looked over what we had made together with a retrospective eye, trying to find a word that could coalesce the different elements of the project: history, biography, geography, and mythmaking. As I read and reread the pieces, these fields blurred into indistinction. I thought of Audre Lorde's *Zami: A New Spelling of My Name*, a biomythography of Lorde's life. Much like Lorde teaches us how to wield speculative narration as a correction to history, the stories in this anthology unearth as much as they reimagine. They look for what has been omitted from the geographical record of a place, and they resurface that layer with a new sense of exigency.

The first ten stories in this collection, authored by Karen Tei Yamashita, are set in the city of Santa Cruz, California, the city where she has lived since 1997. Each of the stories features a guided tour of a hidden landmark: the lost Santa Cruz Chinatown after it was flooded by the San Lorenzo River due to racist city zoning laws, the Santa Cruz Mission where a neophyte murdered a Spanish missionary and buried his testicles in 1812, the gravestone of a formerly enslaved man who became the godfather of Santa Cruz public education. As signature in her writings, Yamashita gives us characters filled with incisive humor and blunt desire, enlivening them until they subvert their static contexts and exhort themselves into the present tense. At the heart, these stories are driven by an urge to animate and reconstruct liminal histories, textual interplays that defamiliarize familiar landscapes. She outlines the vanishing points of a city that is always making itself over anew.

After her methodology was outlined, we believed that this way of mapmaking could expand beyond Santa Cruz and into the greater United States, into its territories and borderlands. We wanted to experiment with broadening the project to see if this form of witnessing could take on a more comprehensive political valence. The writers I chose were already attentive to spatial processes and accumulated histories in their writings, poets and lyric prose writers who had cultivated an ekphrastic approach to geography. Their work engaged critically with unknowability in the historical record, looking for lacunas as speculative openings for narrative possibility.

By dilating the scope, I watched as the constraints outlined in Yamashita's stories morphed and evolved, creating new variants across time. Every writer gravitated toward their existing obsessions and ruminations. They returned to sites they had visited once or more in the past, sites that said something inexplicable to them. All the pieces in this anthology reconsider how space is conceptualized, but they attend diversely to the ecological, colonial, racial, and patriarchal structures of domination that inform our experiences of the present. By using Yamashita's mode of inquiry as our listening device, we wanted to retrieve the past from its immaterial haze. This anthology is our attempt to constellate a memory field, a field that comes to us resounding with spectral voices. As the writings took form, I watched this field become connected with subterranean networks—like mycelium, they converse with each other through electrical impulses. Maybe they are oracles through which the past can speak.

By beginning with a spatial intimacy, the constraint asked us to reimagine what constitutes archival work. What happens if we explore deserts or school-yards or parking lots as memory spaces? The soil is dark everywhere we once believed it was exempt. Each author's supra-sensuous experience of this soil acts as the point of departure. They eliminate the illusion of the static objectivity of the researcher, instead textually embedding the writer directly in history's line of fire. They show us the potential of moving us away from an event-based model that centers an original act of violence, and toward a cartography of active processes, layered and rhizomatic. By performing what Saidiya Hartman calls "critical fabulation" of the past, using literary narrative to redress historical omissions, these writers also give us a field guide for understanding our future and its terrain of struggle.

The pieces in this anthology are invested in polyvocal forms of storytelling, each voice eclipsing one another. There is dissonance as much as there is unity. They are invested in using language as the primary instrument of our excavation, uncovering layers of hurt and desire concealed in the land. In the words of the South Korean poet Kim Hyesoon, "I thought to myself that I needed to excavate the faceless face with language . . . I came to think fervently more than ever that someone involved in such idle labor is a poet." Like metamorphic rocks, we sought to break open existing historical narratives, subjecting them to refraction and assemblage into new forms. The language of pastness feels deceptive—we have to illustrate our memory field as something alive, in flux.

The eight pieces in the second half of this collection vary in scale. Some are very place-based, while others use the location only as a launching point, ending somewhere else entirely. Juliana Spahr writes a poem about an unnamed lot on the bank of the Ohio River that is only locatable with its GPS coordinates, while Craig Santos Perez's personal essay points to the entire island territory of Guam. Saretta Morgan gives us an essay in fragments, each coordinate charted with precision, while the landscape in Thirii Myo Kyaw Myint's piece is painted with intentional obliqueness, receding from particularity into universality. Ronaldo V. Wilson's poetic script unearths a mythic geography of a Bay Area shoreline rendered by the passing of his father, and Brandon Shimoda's piece follows the history of Hom Wong Shee, a woman who committed suicide while detained on Angel Island in 1941. Sesshu Foster uses family photographs to tell a story about the Fellowship Hostel, a former hostel in Los Angeles that once housed Japanese people returning from concentration camps, and my own piece concentrates on the site of Theresa Hak Kyung Cha's murder. All these pieces illustrate how the shadow of history percolates into our private lives in strange and discursive ways, how it is transcribed with circular and lateral recordings.

Instead of historians or geographers, I chose poets and storytellers, writers indebted to the beauty of the lyric. This aesthetic propensity has forced me to consider the role of the language artist in a time of crisis and decline. We've seen the way art acts as a pressure-release valve when tensions could have escalated into a full-scale riot or strike, how art has the illusion of being outside of the circuit of capital while still being enmeshed in its logic. I could go on about the ways I wish our energies were being channeled into destabilizing the premise of literary production under these forms. At the same time, I also believe that the page can be a location where we enact the collective being-together before the material conditions of possibility are here, a place where we can exercise our imaginary before we enact it, so that when the time arrives, we can say that we have been practicing for this.

In the spring of 2019, Karen asked if she could take me on a tour around Santa Cruz. I thought it was strange because it is a small coastal town whose main attractions I could finish seeing within a day, and I had been living there for two years by then. It was blistering hot in the afternoon. The sun subdued us. What should have been experienced with the slow leisure of a walking tour was instead experienced with the time-space compression of Karen's air-conditioned SUV. We cruised through banal sites I had passed through so many times before without a second glance. She took me to the saffron dragon archway in the floodplain where the Santa Cruz Chinatown once stood, the parking garage whose intercom vibrates with white static and the voice of London Nelson, finally ending on the Evergreen Cemetery, which is less of a cemetery and more of a patch of grass that grows on the periphery of a parking lot. Only after reading her half of this anthology did I realize that she had taken me on the tour that was the foundation for this project. In the cemetery, we shared the umeboshi onigiri she had prepared, and told stories of our families and how we were raised. I remember the sound of Highway 17 as it bled toward us, and what it felt like to look at the detritus of what once was somehow being made new.

Santa Cruz Nori
Karen Tei Yamashita

For my students

Contents

Mystery Spot: 95065

This is someone's paradise, but it's not mine.
RONALDO LOPES DE OLIVEIRA

Santa Cruz is someone's paradise. Funny thing for a Brazilian to say. Don't those handsome, naked bronzed people from the Southern Hemisphere live in paradise? What about *their* paradise? And what about the Surfer Dude and the Lighthouse, beacons guarding our looking-glass world, long ago left to us by the Hawaiian Duke Kahanamoku. Our looking-glass paradise. Paradise Lost. Paradise Regained. Paradise Central, California. Throne of the most regal female khalifah, Calafia.

In the sixteenth-century Spanish novel, Queen Calafia of the mythical island California fights with her virgin army of Black Amazons, their golden weapons and terrible griffins, to regain Constantinople for the Moros, only to be defeated and converted to Christianity. And to marriage. This mythic history was lovingly remembered in the documentary, *Golden Dreams*, featured until a few years ago at the Anaheim Disney California Adventure Park, with Whoopi Goldberg narrating as Queen Calafia with her mythical griffin, the great extinct Grizzly, at her side. In twenty-five minutes, you got the Chumash, the Spanish missions, Japanese picture brides, the Mulholland water scandal, freeways, and Steve Jobs. Whoopi California. This is someone's paradise. And now where are the Amazons?

Children. Neófitos. Bestes. *And still it is the same sky, the same night arched like a reed house, the stars of their birth.*
LOUIS OWENS, *BONE GAME*

A birthing ground. A burial ground. Sacred or haunted? Profaned. What happens when you plant a Holy Cross on an ancient Indian burial ground? Layers upon layers of slaughter. Indian author Louis Owens wrote about the curse of mixing blood, churning the earth with dismemberment that produced an appropriated New Age, a new white ecology with its literal pundits and new savage practitioners. New blood to appease an old age. Some hippie dude migrating in from the Summer of Love couldn't get laid for the next decade. It's not that weed slows things down; could be it just makes everything stop. Stop in the name of Love. The next decade after the Summer of Love contained a cycle of murder and dismemberment. Serial murders, meaning this murder is like that murder is like that last murder. Three men killed a family of four, and twenty-one women in three years. Seven of the murdered were Asian Americans. A serial poem to death. And before that, Alfred Hitchcock got wind of a newspaper report about thousands of crazed seabirds, sooty shearwaters, that crashed into homes, broke windows, pecked residents, regurgitated anchovies before flopping dead onto the streets. Thousands of stinking dead dark birds were shoveled into trucks the next morning. Talk about ecology for a new age. To continue, Hitchcock put a psychopath in one of the Victorians on Beach Hill. This is how the dark cloud of noir blackened the sunlit California seacoast. But some hippie dude who couldn't get laid said it was an old Indian curse.

> *Yet here's a spot . . . Out, damned spot! Out I say!*
> LADY MACBETH

Cruz marks the spot, the oracular crossroad, sanctified in these parts because at the cruz, Oedipus fulfilled his destiny to kill the patriarchy. Whatever happens later (incest) happens somewhere else, but at the sainted Cruz under the shadow of the fog that slips in and out with the moon tides across the mountains, that's the legacy we get left. Cruzians become fatherless Munchkins. *Ding-dong!* they sing, and they query: *Are you a friend of Dorothy's?*

It's Mother's Day, and the grande mother of everyone is Asako, who's made it to ninety. We celebrate at the hillside Chaminade's festive all-you-can-eat brunch at a long table of maybe twenty. The only guy there is our neighbor, the historian David, but Asako, who's seated at the head of this table, still asks about the twenty guests, *Now, who are all these men?* She's ninety, so she gets to be confused. It's the weekend of the Feminist Studies Conference. How to tell Asako her Mother's Day has been hijacked by the Dyke Ladies Society. *Oh,* she says, but then, quick recovery, *I wasn't born yesterday, you know.* The Chaminade proceeds to take a hit since our table out-eats everyone, prime rib to made-to-order omelets, three to one. And how many gallons of mimosa we talkin'?

Overlooking Chaminade's valley with the sweep of May sunshine, feminist scholar Anjali remembers that the Mystery Spot is somewhere nearby. It's the tourist attraction featured on bumper stickers. *You'd better not take Asako there,* Anjali says. *It's not advisable for older people or anyone with a heart condition.*

What are you talking about? For godsake. It's an optical illusion.

No, seriously. I looked it up on the internet. It's one of eight magnetic spots on Earth. Anjali must be one of the smartest intellectuals we know. Scientific and geographical, internet research reveals this is apparently about a 150-foot-in-diameter time-space antigravity vortex. Or it could be UFO activity. Go figure. *Le Cigare Volant.*

At the Feminist Studies Conference, someone might have given a talk on female ejaculation. There's even a documentary film that goes with it. When you learn about this, you're sitting between two South Asian sisters, Pratima and Prarthana. They might be twins, but their names are differentiated, they tell you, by an M and an N. *Oh yes,* they agree. *When we were growing up, we identified as Caucasian.* Asians from the Caucasus. *But then we came to Philadelphia, and there was all that dotbuster shit.* Now, this Indian lore jams into Cruz.

Spots and dots. Magnetism and ejaculation. Titter titter.

But back to ding-dong. Every night for seven nights at about three am, some car out there goes berserk with honking. At first, it's just a beep-beep, so you turn over and think, *Get out and catch your damn ride.* But then it goes off like a car alarm, and you snarl into your pillow, *Steal it. Steal the fuckin' thing.* This goes on nightly with a pattern. Serial car orgasms. You check the clock; it's three am, plus the heating system always goes on. Even the house knows it's too cold to get out of bed to be a witness. The next nights you dream about dead bodies fallen, or invasive vermin pouncing on the wheel. Maybe it's the neighbor's cat that's jumped on the car. Could be a coyote or a raccoon or a barn owl. You call faculty housing and complain. Anjali says, *You look tired.* Then, *Dude!* she exclaims. *That's my Mazda. We can't do anything about it. For some reason, the horn just goes off. It's a mystery.* Her partner Lucy says, *Don't tell anyone. It's so embarrassing.*

Years later, make a choice to see this film *Albert Nobbs,* in which Glenn Close plays a nineteenth-century Irish male waiter, and sit in the Nick Theater between two colored homosexuals, in the broader sense of the word, who groan over you like call and response. God knows Close could have done some Cruzin' first before she turned Nobbs into a pathetic simpleton. No relief. Not even the tattered endearment of Charlie Chaplin. Plus, the colored homosexuals are scholars of critical theory. Yammer yammer. The most exciting moment is when Janet McTeer pinches a rolled cigarette between her lips to free her hands to unbutton her shirt to reveal her gigantic bosom. Nobbs gasps the same gasp that the white audience gasped at *M. Butterfly* when the Chinese butterfly exposed his penis. It's a mystery, cruising for a bruising. What the fist?

Some mysteries get punished: serials killers go to prison; Oedipus blinds himself; M. Butterfly's Frenchman commits ritual suicide; Glenn Close is only nominated for the Oscar. Some mysteries get solved. Turns out the Mazda Protegé has her quirks. When the temperature dips, the horn freezes, which triggers the honking spasms. The mechanic explains. *It's sensitive, see. You got to keep her warm. I suggest a hot water bottle and a blanket.* Is someone studying this? You bet. This is that queer technology stuff interrogating the cyborg versus the goddess. Check it out, Queen Calafia. This is your dark paradise. This is your mystery spot.

The Missing Testicles of Padre Q
Los Compañeros Ausentes del Padre Q

Our walking tour might begin at the clock tower. The original location of that clock was actually down the street in the tower of the Odd Fellows Lodge on Pacific, built in 1873, damaged by fire in 1899 and rebuilt. With the remodeling of Odd Fellows in 1964, the great clock was removed and stored in the basement of the city museum in Seabright until the current tower was erected over the Fred Morris Memorial Fountain on Water Street in 1976 to celebrate the American Bicentennial. Next to the clock tower, we walk around a bronze sculpture of an embracing family, Guernica-like, facing skyward, rendered by a local artisan of bronze works, E. A. Chase; it's entitled, *Collateral Damage: A Reality of War*, in memory of civilians killed in wars and dedicated in 1995 on the fiftieth anniversary of the atomic bombing of Hiroshima and Nagasaki. Getting close to the inscriptions on the metal plaques and ceramic tiles surrounding the sculpture or the clock tower might not be so easy, as this plaza is a sunning area for local unhoused folks, who congregate to smoke, sip coffee, and rant at passersby. One of the plaques remembers the three local people who died in 1989 in the Loma Prieta earthquake, its epicenter only ten miles northwest of the clock tower in the redwood Forest of Nisene Marks State Park near Aptos Creek.

Looking from the clock tower across Pacific Avenue, there's a yellow building with red doors, ivy almost covering the painted signage for the shop Serpent's Kiss, housing a spiritual gift and witchcraft shop said to have the largest crystal selection in California and supplying all paths to the mystic life (European, Celtic, Wicca, Faery, Feri, Stregheria, Norse, Ifá, Native American, Hoodoo, Voudou, Afro-Cuban, Lukumí, Santería, Palo, Jewish, Christian, etc.). Inside, the saints and crystals are backlit in glass cases and glow. Next to the magic shop is Los Pinos Mexican restaurant. We peer into the windows of Los Pinos, lined with posters for The Catalyst and Moe's Alley, past the neon featuring Bud Light, Victoria, Modelo, and Corona, to see scattered customers forking plates of enchiladas and burritos. Now, turning from the windows to the end of the building's yellow stucco corner, it's possible to miss the narrow cement stairway pressed between Los Pinos and the Arrow Beauty Bar salon, but this is the Mission Hill staircase.

We count seventy-three steps to the top of the hill, supported by handrails of lead plumbing pipes, and approaching the first landing, we look back over the downtown cityscape, spreading brick and foliage following the San Lorenzo River to the bay. The last twenty steps turn up the hill, past a gracious stucco home decorated in blue tile, likely the original site of Elihu Anthony's house. Preacher and blacksmith Anthony arrived in Santa Cruz around 1848 at the beginning of the Gold Rush and made his initial fortune forging the picks and shovels that miners used to dig up the California landscape. Finally, walking past this house, we reach the end of School Street and the site of the adobe remains of the old Santa Cruz Mission. A giant avocado tree, marked by a gaping hole in its old trunk, spreads its great branches skyward. They say it's the oldest avocado tree in California, and this is where our story begins.

My Trip to the Santa Cruz Mission
by Edgardo Asisara

My teacher Miss Bailey is really nice. I'm not saying this to get a good grade. I'm just saying. She planned this field trip to the Santa Cruz Mission for our fourth-grade class because we are learning about early California history, about the missions, Indians, and Californios. To be honest, I wasn't that interested. Panning for gold, weaving baskets, mapping the El Camino Real. But then, stuff happened. One thing I need to say at the outset is that none of this was Miss Bailey's fault. I boarded the wrong time machine, not the fourth-grade app like I was supposed to, not even the right date.

When our class got to the mission, we took the tour of the long adobe house, what's left of the original mission. You could see the adobe bricks in the walls and the way the roof is made of sticks tied with leather straps holding up bundles of straw. We went from room to room, looking at the exhibits, the old tools, bones, baskets, and one of those birds-eye 3D remakes of the old mission. There were also picture posters of the real Indians and then the ones converted to the church, what they call *neophytes*. When we got outside, Miss Bailey wanted us to look at an old clay oven and the stove where you can make candles, but then we started to chase each other around in the grass, around the big redwoods and a giant avocado tree, but like usual, they never chase me. It's not like I don't try, but I got no friends. So I stuffed myself into a hole in the trunk of the avocado tree, and that's when the rest of the kids got into the fourth-grade app and left, probably for the correct date. Who knows what date? Maybe 1795. Go figure. I haven't met up with them yet.

When I got out of the tree hole, everyone was gone. I went back into the adobe house, searched the exhibits for a good date, googled some app, and punched it in: 1812.

When I got here, the big trees and the grass and the adobe house were all gone, just the weedy earth was here, plus it was raining. I was standing in the mud getting soaked. I looked down at my new Nikes. Mom would be really mad. I turned around and around and saw a guy pulling a wooden cart. He wasn't an old man. He was maybe my brother's age or older. Rain was dripping from his hat over his face. When he came toward me, I froze. He could see me. I thought I would be invisible, but he could see me. He said something. What did he say? Then he spoke again. It was Spanish. I answered. You speak funny, he said. Where do you come from? I didn't know what to say. From the future, I said. Where is that? he asked. I don't know, I said.

So I got into the cart and went with this guy named Venancio. Even though I told him my real name, Edgardo, no one ever calls me that. They all call me Futuro, little Futuro, like it's a big joke. Venancio is certain I am from his tribe, the Awaswas. Maybe from Sokel. That's why he first spoke in his language to me. I told him I was Mexican from Watsonville. He shook his head. No. It's a lie. Look into your heart.

Venancio took me to live in the mission with Fausta the cook and her husband Julian. Julian and Venancio are both the mission gardeners. Julian is the older head gardener and maybe Venancio is his second. Fausta and Julian have no children. Every time Fausta had a kid, it died, so they kind of adopted me. They told Padre Q that I was a nephew who came from the other mission in San Jose, and pretty much that was it. This is good because otherwise I would have to work in the fields with the other Indians. At first maybe it seemed like a good idea to be converted to the ways of the church where you could get something to eat. Things were never easy, but after Padre Q, they went from bad to worse.

By the time I arrived, they said Padre Q had beaten two people to death. Fausta goes every day to their graves and puts flowers there. If Padre Q is around, she makes the sign of the cross, but sometimes, at night, she secretly burns herbs. Julian and Venancio make the garden around there pretty. And they make sure to plant the herbs that Fausta wants. Julian knows everything about plants, and Venancio is learning. You might think something is a weed, but it's not.

At first I didn't believe the stories about Padre Q because he was always coming around to be nice to me. If he asked me to do something, Fausta was always following behind, stalking us. I followed Padre Q into his rooms, and that's how I stole this paper and ink to write my report. I thought of telling Padre Q my story about being from the future, but then Venancio said that if I ever said that, Padre Q would have me burned alive like a witch. And when Venancio caught me writing this, he really got afraid. Futuro, he said, you can't let anyone know that you can read and write. He made a wood box for me to hide my report, and we hid the box under the floor, under the straw mat where I sleep.

Okay, you might be wondering why I didn't just phone Miss Bailey or my folks to let them know what happened, but typically, the phone died. Maybe all the data using that app fried it. Then Fausta washed it. I mean washed it in a tank of water. It was the cheapest phone my mom could find at Best Buy, so no big loss. It went into Venancio's box with my report. Anyway, who in 1812 would believe me? If my mom or dad or Miss Bailey ever read this, they just need to know I miss them. The food is okay. I'm not complaining. Fausta doesn't have much to work with. Her tortillas and bread are pretty good. No one is getting fat here.

Venancio likes this girl. She gets locked up in the ladies' rooms every night, but then the guys get locked up with the guys. I found out that one of the guys tried to escape with a girl, but then they got caught, and Padre Q beat the guy to death. The girl got sent away to another mission. That's why Venancio and the girl he likes don't talk to each other much. They don't want Padre Q getting any ideas. But I know Padre Q already has ideas because he takes Venancio's girl to the vestibule behind the chapel and has her pray with him. One day I saw the girl come out of the vestibule. She looked messed up. Maybe Venancio found out, but I'm not telling him. If he tries to escape with that girl, he'll get killed too. This is no joke. Practically everyone has been beaten by Padre Q. Julian and even Lino, Padre Q's most trusted butler.

I ran out of paper, so I snuck into Padre Q's room to get some. I should have been more careful. Padre Q found me there. At first, he looked mad, but then his face got slimy, and he said, My son, what are you doing here? I backed out of the room with the paper tucked in my shirt. What do you have there, son? I wanted to run, but he saw the paper slip from my shirt. Ah, he said. Stealing? I shook my head, and he said, Come. Sit here. He patted his bed. I kept backing out, but he said, Do you want a whipping? If you sit here, I promise. No whipping. I sat down, and he pulled the paper from my shirt. What do you want with paper? Who wants this paper? If you tell me, God will spare you. Tell me the truth.

What happened next is pretty gross. I scratched and kicked him and yelled like crazy. And Lino the butler, and another guy named Donato ran in. Padre Q got up off me and yelled, The boy was stealing! I caught him. Hold him. Lino, get the whip. Donato said suddenly, Padre, it's not his fault. I sent him to steal from you. I don't know why Donato said that. Maybe it was because his little brother was whipped the other day by Padre Q. He didn't want to see that happen to me.

Padre Q made everyone come out to the courtyard to watch Donato get whipped, but whipped extra because the strap was tipped with a fish hook. The strap came down on Donato's back and buttocks again and again. It tore his skin in bloody cuts, and Donato cried and cried. I cried too because I felt every cut. I watched Padre Q's sweaty face, staring at me, whipping Donato. Padre Q's face got puffy, his mouth foamy, panting like a horse. He stared at me and beat Donato, and then his eyes went glassy. The whip fell from his hand. I don't remember what happened next, but when I woke, Fausta was washing my face.

After that, they planned to kill Padre Q. Fausta went to tell Padre Q that her husband Julian was sick and he should come to see him. Padre Q went back and forth to see Julian, who pretended to be sick. Finally, Fausta went to tell Padre Q that Julian was dying, and this time, they grabbed old Q in the dark, held him down, and stuffed his mouth with his own clothing until he suffocated. Then they took his dead body to his room, dressed him for bed, and tucked him in like he was always sleeping. I didn't see them do this. I just know because Venancio told me everything.

The night they killed Padre Q, they had a party after. Lino got the Padre's keys and unlocked the ladies' rooms and the guys' rooms, and they partied. So when it got noisy, I got up to find out what was happening. I bumped into Venancio. He had a piece of bloody cloth in his hands. He looked anxious. He said, Futuro, take this over to the privy and throw it in. Yuk, I said. What is this? I asked. Padre Q's compañeros, he said. Then he smiled. I need to find my girl. Help me out. Okay, I agreed. The privy was kind of far, so I walked out there. The moon was hanging there in the clouds like a happy white banana. I peeled back the cloth. Inside were two sacks of wrinkly skin like chicken kidneys, two big slimy lima bean things hanging by veins inside. I walked to the privy, peed into the smelly poop, and walked back.

In the next days, they found Padre Q's dead body sleeping in his bed. I was up in the rafters spying through the hole, so I could see them cut open his stomach to see if he had been poisoned. They said, No poisoning. Good, I thought, or they might accuse Fausta of feeding him bad food. Someone pointed at his penis, dangling there with no compañeros. They covered him up quickly. No one must know this secret. Then, they buried Padre Q somewhere under the stone floor of the church. We know his ghost is there. He can't go to heaven or probably hell because he's looking for his missing compañeros.

Everyone pretended to be sad, but now it's been a couple of years, so people might think it's safe to talk. Some soldiers hanging around heard that maybe Padre Q was killed. And that's when Donato, Julian, Lino, Venancio, and others got arrested and taken away. They let Venancio go, but Julian, who really was always sick and not just pretending, got sicker in prison and died. When Fausta heard about it, she went to get his body in San Francisco. Before she left, she gave me the zipper she tore out of my old jeans. Futuro, she cried. You are growing so big. I will bring Julian home and we will bury him properly. But I never saw Fausta again. The rest of the guys got something called a novenano which means that they got whipped fifty times every day for nine days. Lino got sent to the mission in Santa Barbara to work in chains. He must have died there.

When Venancio returned from prison, he showed me how to make an avocado seed sprout. I put my tree in a basket and made it grow. The tree grows, and I guess time moves on, but it is never going to move fast enough for me to get back home again. Venancio got married to his girl, and they had a baby boy they named Lorenzo. Lorenzo is like my little brother. A new padre arrived to replace Padre Q, but he is just as bad. I got used to my life here. Venancio and his wife Maria are always good to me, raising me the rest of the way.

Today, Venancio ran in, all out of breath. He said, They say the pirates are coming, so we must leave. He looked at me with sad eyes. But if you come with us, it will be more of the same for you. We are slaves to the padres, and if we try to leave, they will catch us. But you can escape. You know already that this new padre is bad for you. You cannot follow him. You are a man now. You can leave. How many years has it been since I arrived? Six years? Maybe I can be a pirate, I said. Maybe.

I gave Venancio my box. In this box is the zipper from my jeans that Fausta saved. Also the shoelaces from my Nikes, the useless phone, and two gold coins Venancio gave me when they found Padre Q's hidden money. And, don't forget, Padre Q's shriveled up compañeros. I gave Venancio my avocado plant. Please, I said, you must do this for me. Remember where we first met? Bury this box there and plant this avocado tree in the same place to mark it. One day, I will return to find it. Go, said Venancio, go quickly. Go find your future.

The Brother's Parking Lot

Please take your ticket and proceed forward.

The voice is melodious to my ear. I can't help but respond, Yo Brother, don't mind if I do. I wait for my ticket, but it doesn't appear.

The machine hesitates, then: *That's some car you have there. Candy-apple red BMW 230i 248 turbo-charged four-cylinder, zero to sixty miles per hour in 5.3 seconds.*

I stare at the machine, then look around for the surveillance cameras.

The machine continues impassively: *Of course, you could have gone for the M240i turbocharged 3.0 liter inline-six; that babe lightning rockets to sixty mph in a second less, but that would be another ten thou. What's another second? I'd say, Brother, this is a good starter package for the newly tenured.*

I could be hallucinating. It's been a difficult morning. Ah, do you think you could give me my ticket and raise that arm?

Now hold on a minute. You started this conversation. You can't just drive on by and park.

But this is a parking lot.

So it is. So it is. But didn't you call me out?

Call you out?

You know, call me "Brother." I certainly appreciate it.

I think, okay, this must be like that Alexa thing. It responds to "Brother." I say with authority, Brother, open the gate now.

Not so fast. Not so fast. Plenty of appropriate parking spaces in here, give you all the room Manitoba needs to keep those pesky nicks and scratches far away. Besides, you got the extended body plan.

I sit in silence, fuming. I glance at my Apple Watch, search for my phone.

Brother, the machine continues, *just settle down. It's rare to meet another Brother in this parking lot. And I got one helluva story to tell you.*

I look in my rearview mirror. The cars are backing up behind me. What about them? I ask, pointing behind.

No problem, says the Brother in the machine.

I get out of my car and walk over to confer with the silver Volvo. When she sees my face, I can see her fumble with the controls; her window rises to close, but I can hear her screaming inside the glass. WHAT THE FUCK? DID YOU BREAK IT? A head pops out of the black Honda behind her, and he says, what's the matter? I got tickets to see the matinee. Hey, he looks at me. Let me tell you how it works. You push the call button and get some help, see? Patronizing son of a bitch. The guy in a beat-up green Subaru behind him yells to the car behind, MOVE BACK! I'm backing outta here, can't you see? The thing's busted. Him and his overpriced sports car, he waves at me. HE HAD IT COMING! The woman behind him honks and yells, HOLD YOUR HORSES. I AM BACKING OUT. CAN'T YOU SEE? Now she's yelling at me. IT SAYS IT'S FULL! FULL, YOU FOOL. I look at the signage: FULL. I point to the sign, shrug at the all the irritated drivers lined up behind me, and walk back to my car.

Microaggressions, the Brother in the machine sighs. *You have no idea. I get them all the time. Think about it. All those folks behind you, they used to be kids, cute babies and innocent children. You and me included. Now we are all in different stages of ugly.*

I get back into Manitoba. The rearview mirror frames the cars behind, backing out in various attitudes of hostility. Then, it's quiet, and the Brother in the machine begins.

If anyone knows my story, it's the short version on the headstone with my name misspelled:

Louden Nelson

Native of Tennessee

Born May 5, 1800

Died May 17, 1860

Misspelled?

What would I know? I was illiterate. Signed my last will and testament with an X. What's in a name given by a master named William Nelson? Except he named my three brothers Canterbury, Cambridge, Marlborough, and so I got to be London. Know what I'm saying?

London Nelson?

The one and only. And I might have come from Tennessee, but I was born in North Carolina. Hey, I can't complain. At least I got a headstone. Below that is a plaque dedicated in 2006. Says I was born a slave and came to the California Gold Rush in 1849, secured my freedom, came to Santa Cruz in 1856, worked as a cobbler, bought a piece of land near River and Front Streets. Before I died, I willed everything I owned, 716 acres, to the Santa Cruz School District for the purpose of education. I am buried at Evergreen, an honored pioneer. This is mostly true. Local California history for fourth graders, but wouldn't you like to hear the whole story?

I look purposefully at my watch, but the Brother is on a roll.

Like I said, I was born on a midsized rice plantation in North Carolina along the Cape Fear River in 1800, twenty-four years after the signing of the Declaration of Independence and thirteen years after that of the US Constitution. The master of the plantation, William Nelson, was a Tory loyalist for the British, but after their defeat at Moore's Creek in 1776, old man Nelson tucked away his loyalty and in the intervening years only named his slaves after places in England. You might say that my becoming London was ironic.

Wait a minute, I interrupt the Brother. Just to be clear about this, you're telling me a tall tale, right?

Brother, what I'm about to tell you is all true as best as I can pull together the facts into true fictionalization.

I shake my head. I think about ripping that box out of the cement, but it stands there solid, like London Nelson's white marble headstone itself, and it keeps on talking.

Don't you worry, what I'm about to tell you is pure poetry. Now, where was I?

Irony, I prompt.

Oh yeah. Not that there weren't others in the vicinity who supported Cornwallis, but the Nelsons were set apart, shall we say. Sometime after the last of my brothers, Marlborough, was born, old man Nelson died. The oldest son, John, had already got his inheritance and started his own plantation some parcels away. Daughter Mary married and moved to Charleston. The next son, Luke, died in a hunting accident. That left Mark, who got the land on Cape Fear, and the youngest, Matthew; he got us. Matthew got the slaves. Matthew had enough of being set apart, the Patriot vs. Tory thing, so he took himself, his widowed mama Fannie, and us—Canterbury, Cambridge, Marlborough, and me—far away to Tennessee. Some said that Matthew got the raw end of the deal, no land, just slaves. But old man Nelson had some kind of plan to keep his operation insular. He made Canterbury his blacksmith. Cambridge got trained as a carpenter and bricklayer. Marlborough took care of the horses. I became a cobbler, and I knew about planting. We all knew how to plant and raise small livestock. Matthew Nelson got us: the technology to start again. But let me be clear about this. We were still slaves, you know what I'm saying. The young Matthew Nelson put Canterbury's son and Cambridge's two daughters on the block as collateral to buy a sweet piece of land just outside of Memphis. Then the rest of us went to work, building and propagating and creating everything that makes what you know to be a plantation: white porch and Roman pillars, old oak spreading shade across deep grassy lawns, slave quarters, horse stalls with waiting carriages, cotton and tobacco as far as the eye can see.

Once Matthew Nelson set up his household with his mama Miss Fannie at the center, he got restless. He was only about twenty-something. Maybe a wife might have fixed that, but he started breeding horses, thoroughbreds to be exact. That's where my brother Marlborough came in. Turned out Marlborough was part horse himself, talked, ate, and dreamt horses, raced them to win every time. This went on for a streak, and then President Polk made it official: Gold in California. Master Matthew caught the fever, and by New Year 1849, he had a plan.

Not like we had a choice to go or not, but Marlborough and I got taken with the same fever, with the idea that we could get our freedom. Canterbury was getting along in years, but he was still blacksmithing, making everything from hoes to fancy iron gate work. This was steady income for the Nelsons. They were like subcontractors who kept all the money for themselves. Same with Cambridge, who got sent out to build houses in town. And they had wives and children and even grandkids. Marlborough and I had nothing but ourselves.

Canterbury drove us in the carriage to the port at Memphis, hauled out the luggage, boxes with picks and axes he'd made special. I remember he had a funny look deep in his eyes. He didn't linger long, didn't take to the clamor of the crowds, didn't pause to notice Negroes chained together vacating the boat's hull, didn't wait to see how a riverboat could float away on steam. Even as we boarded the plank, he was turning the horses, following a paddy wagon full of caged Black people. I stared over the deck at his hunched back, older but still powerful. In 1822, when we heard the news that Denmark Vesey had been hanged, I saw Canterbury's eyes grow wide and flood with tears, but when they dried up, I never saw him cry again, not when his wife Alyson died, not when his son Roger was sold. For him, I think life was a mean mistake. As the gigantic paddle began to churn and pull us away down the Mississippi, I thought I knew Canterbury's premonition, but I heard Marlborough whoop like he did when he raced a horse over the line. So I let the sad resignation in Canterbury's shoulders slip away from my own.

The machine goes quiet, and I think I can hear water cascading from the river-boat. I look forward and see the gate arm lifted. I say, What about the rest of the story? But the Brother says, *Please take your ticket and proceed forward.*

Days later, I'm driving to Sacramento, and Manitoba decides to start talking to me, too. The voice pops out of the cyber satellite system, and it turns out he, too, is a Brother. I think if I'm crazy, I'm crazy. Just pay attention:

You got into UC Santa Cruz on affirmative action. This was the 70s, and they wanted you. Your people came to San Francisco during wwii from Louisiana to get jobs in the war industry. Moved into emptied-out Japantown on Post Street and got to work during the day. During the night, they brought out their instruments and entertained themselves with the blues. That's where you grew up. Harlem of the West. Fillmore. That's where you got your musical education. On the streets, hanging out. Through the walls. In church. And there was the band at Galileo. Your instruments were brass with the Ts: trumpet, trombone, tuba.

Wait, I say, you are not talking about "me."

No, it says, *I'm talking about "you."* And he continues: *In those days, no one thought about what was practical. Especially affirmative-action colored kids. You were the ones with dreams. The revolution was gonna change everything, and you were gonna be there to be the change. You were not a militant Panther sort, mind you. You knew Huey hung out in Hist Con, his aides-de-camp standing around protectively, but you also knew Huey's dream wasn't exactly practical. Anyway, you were secretly in love with a white Jewish kid who played the saxophone.*

I shake my head, turn off the system, and drive to the mother lode in silence. After several miles, I call up my partner, who lives on Long Island. I'm going crazy, I tell him. You were always crazy, he responds. But this is serious, I say. I can see him over there rolling his eyes. He asks, Do you know what time it is? I don't, so I hang up.

Weeks go by. I park in the Brother's parking as per usual, have dinner a Laili's, late movie at Cinema 9. Then, I proceed to pay for the ticket at the machine, and the thing perks up like it's yesterday. *Brother*, he says, accepting my ticket, *I've been wondering what happened to you. Now let me continue my story:*

At the tail of the big Mississippi River appeared the city of New Orleans. My memory is that it was busy and colorful. And in every corner of that pretty city, in high-class hotel rotundas and public slave pens, colored people were on the block. I saw folks auctioned next to furniture and tools. I was born a slave, but I had never seen the actual commerce of it. Supposedly, Marlborough and I were going along to serve the master, but he could, in a pinch, sell one or both of us, if he fancied. Those nights in New Orleans, I rolled around on the floor at the foot of my master's bed, while Marlborough slept curled up like a kitten. In the day, he wasn't but eighteen. Freedom was a promise dangling from a long pole extended out there on the road before us. If we had known the road beforehand, would we have turned back? Turned out young master Matthew was anxious to leave too, didn't want to wait two weeks for the next ship to sail around the Cape but booked a steamer for Chagres, convinced that cutting across the isthmus to Panama would give us a head start.

On the steamer, I met two Louisiana slaves who said their master was taking them to California to set them free. Was that the case with Marlborough and me? I kept quiet. It wasn't wise to tempt fate. Night before we left Tennessee, Cambridge came to see me, gave me a small wood dog he carved himself. He rolled the carving around in his palm, probably remembering his two girls got sent away with the same carvings. It was his warning; I kept it in my pocket. Then we got waylaid an extra three days in a storm somewhere out in the Caribbean. Folks on the ship were either sick from the rolling sea or sick from cholera, we didn't know which. I figure the three of us were seasick because we didn't die. Being seasick meant we lost the stomach to eat, and not eating must have saved us from catching that plague. Every day, one or two passengers or crewmen died and found graves in the sea. I said a silent prayer for the body of one of the Louisiana slaves slipping beneath the waves. I knew it wasn't because he'd tempted fate; there was no difference between the two of us. Then the sea calmed, and as we approached Chagres, fish flew from the sea, and we managed to catch a few. Chagres turned out to be a bunch of grass huts with half-naked natives selling bananas, pineapples, coconuts, and oranges.

The isthmus from Chagres on the Atlantic to Panama on the Pacific, as the bird flies, is about forty-five miles. That's something like from here to Monterey or from here to San Jose, but with all the twists and turns by canoe, over mud trail by mules, disease, and unknown treachery—natural and human—it was maybe tripled. We might have crossed it in a week, but Master Matthew caught the fever. Before he was completely stricken, he managed to hire two dugout canoes, what they called cayucos, and two natives and gave directions to load our provisions and tools onto both, with Matthew lying under some palm leaves in one. On either side of the Chagres River it was a knitted jungle, with plumed birds in exotic colors, chattering monkeys, slithering lizards and snakes, and alligators dozing on the beaches. We rowed through this strange paradise, but it was made hell by the scalding sun always pointed directly at us. I couldn't understand a word of Spanish, but the natives hacked open green coconuts and pushed us to keep getting Matthew to drink that water. Two nights, we camped out in the canoes, roped to trees a distance from the shore, to be safe from tigers and alligators. Mosquitoes and a thousand species of bugs swarmed in thick clouds. All night I listened to the creatures, bouncing above in the foliage and flitting beneath the cayuco—hunting, procreating, eating, and playing.

In the morning, Matthew was yellow with his fever. He whispered to me about the pouch secured around his belly, and Marlborough and I secretly divided and hid the cash between us.

By noon that day, the natives docked near a particular hut on the Chagres, and we carried Matthew there. The woman in the hut was a Negro from Cuba who spoke English. She'd been a slave in Mississippi. Looking over Matthew, she shook her head. You got to rest him here. Matthew tried to rise to protest. Fever for gold is one thing, she said. But this fever will kill you. Mama Hagar? he called, his eyes glassy. What's he saying, she asked. Hagar, I said, name of my mama. Hagar is my name too, she said, and whispered into Matthew's ear, Mama Hagar says you got to rest, understand? And he calmed. So we stayed there for as long as it took for the fever to break.

The machine pauses, and I look around and check the time. It's almost midnight. What am I doing standing here? Then I hear: Please take your ticket. Do you want a receipt? Please take your receipt.

This time, I wait for my partner's call. I whimper pathetically, why are these machines talking to me? He asks, Have you tried recording what they say? Could be new material for your next book. He's right. The next day, I spend the evening at Verve, wait till closing, then drive purposefully into the Brother's parking lot. I get my iPhone ready to press "record." The machine responds, You remember that sister Edna Brodber? Like Zora Neal Hurston, she pressed record, and it just didn't. You have to listen, you hear? I put down my phone and I listen.

In that interlude on the isthmus, Hagar and I got along. If Lizzie had lived, maybe we might have been an older couple like that. My own Mama Hagar and Lizzie had their babies at the same time. Mama Hagar had Marlborough, and Lizzie had little London. But Lizzie died. Mama Hagar raised Marlborough and little London together, like brothers. You never know what it means to have kids underfoot until they are no longer there. I had to fish my boy out of the river. He was only five. I buried him next to Lizzie. We got that little bit of time together. That was my lesson.

Finally, Matthew came to, but even if he could hardly raise his arms, all he wanted was to get to the gold. Hagar went about her healing and made preparations so we could leave. One day, she stood on that rickety dock, watched us pack into the cayucos, and said good-bye. I wondered if she wouldn't ask me to stay, but all she said was, You got to take that boy, *she meant Marlborough, to California, keep him safe. Hagar knew my story. She sent me on my way. I can't help but think that's why she cured Matthew.*

To reach Gorgona, we had to help push the cayucos with poles up river. I don't know why the natives didn't just rob us blind and abandon us on some alligator beach. It must have occurred to them, but maybe they had compassion for Marlborough and me. Hagar told them: we were slaves and they were free. Put a spell on them. From Gorgona, we had to continue over land. We hired mules, one to carry Matthew and two to load our provisions. Marlborough and I went along on foot. Mules are sure-footed beasts, but this old trail was narrow and, with the rain on and off, a mud-slick trench. Loaded with their burdens, the mules sank into the muck, and not a few were rotting dead along the trail. Marlborough, half-horse as he was, cooed the mules on, adjusted their loads. On the second day, we came up on a native beating a stuck mule with a rod. There was no room to pass, so Marlborough went over to do his magic. The frustrated native moved aside, but some white man rode forward, screaming, and started flogging the native and Marlborough as well. Suddenly, a shot cracked the air, and I saw Matthew with his shotgun raised. Every day since we'd resumed our travels, I'd been cooking up a makeshift meal of bananas, dried meat, and gruel and making Matthew take Hagar's concocted medicine. I guess it worked.

Predictably, the story stops. *Please take your ticket and proceed forward.* I swing around and leave the now-empty parking lot. The exit arm swings open, sweetly. *Thank you.*

I call my partner in Long Island. I don't care what time it is. This time, he's more reassuring. He says, I googled it. It could all be true. I deep-breathe in and out.

But two days later, Manitoba wakes up and says:

You know who you are. You were that homeless Brother wrapped in three down and hooded jackets, tucked deep into a personal sleeping bag like a Black Eskimo in bubble wrap, so no matter the weather, it must have been the same weather inside. And you pushed a literal train of connected shopping carts loaded with your belongings up and down the hill from the post office to Evergreen Cemetery, up and down, every day for years. No one knew what was hidden beneath those blankets and black plastic. You could have been the next Miles Davis, the next Louis Armstrong, the next Tommy Dorsey. Then one day, you disappeared.

I think, I'm getting rid of this car. It must be the car. The car is cursed. But my partner says, You love that car, what do you mean? Why is it talking to me? It's not talking to you. It's a car. There's a homeless Brother living in my car, I scream. Do you want me to keep this car? Calm down. I take Manitoba in for fine-turning and get myself a Honda rental, but I still got to park it in the Brother's parking lot.

Panama was a dirty cobblestoned ramshackle town, crowded with men keen to get to the gold. Nobody talked about anything else. The town was surrounded by encamped men. Townsfolk exploited any opportunity to make money off these so-called Argonauts while they waited and hustled for an open berth on those ships passing around the Cape. I wonder how many of them finally got to California, didn't lose their fever to women and gambling. Matthew thought he'd cut off that long leg of travel, but now he had to compete with hundreds of other gold-seekers. Every ship arrived already full to over-crowded, the passengers on board refusing to disembark, fearing the loss of their coveted places.

In town, Matthew met a widowed lady from Louisiana with five children, the young-est a baby girl just beginning to walk. He was incredulous that she had made the same crossing over the isthmus. This was the wild idea of her husband, who, dying of cholera midway, made her promise to continue to California. Back in Louisiana, the husband had sold the cotton plantation and all the slaves; there wasn't anything to return to any-way. Before leaving New Orleans, he'd purchased two years' supply of provisions, cloth-ing, camping and mining outfits, a set of tools with all the locks, hinges, paints—even doors and windows for a house. Along the way, his widow had abandoned most of it, but even so, she arrived in Panama with eight mules' worth of baggage. The oldest girl was around ten, and every one of the five children was in some degree ill. An epidemic of measles was spreading. The widow was anxious to leave. It was Matthew who negoti-ated passage for her on an old Peruvian whaler named the Callao. The captain took pity on the woman and her sick children, and because of Matthew's attentions, she claimed him as a brother and we her slaves. In a few days, we boarded the Callao, housed in the whaler's roach-infested and windowless midsection.

As it turned out, the captain had made concessions for other families with children, but he failed to stock the ship with enough food and clean water. Rations ran low, and the children suffered the most. One child after another died, the babies first. The widow sewed her little girl in a small canvas bag, and the brothers and sisters watched their sibling tossed into the sea. When the widow became ill, Marlborough and I gathered her four remaining children and brought them up on deck into the sea air, made up small games, told them stories. Listless from hunger, they had little energy, hugged their dolls, and stared into the open sea. Tabetha, the oldest girl, watched the sun sparkle against the waves, and repeated the continuing dream: They say, when we get to California, we'll pick gold nuggets right off the ground.

At Mazatlán, the ship stopped several days to restock water and provisions. Matthew and Marlborough took a small transport and spent their time on shore. I remained behind, watching the sailors towing barrels of water back and forth. When we got out to sea again, a storm took the Callao off course. It would be another seventy-five days before we reached land again. We spent days rolling and rocking in the suffocating dark. Then the winds stalled, and once again we were low on water and food. The captain gathered the men and had us draw straws. The short straw, if need be, would sacrifice his body to feed the others. One man protested and pointed at Marlborough and me and two others who were also slaves, saying we were the ones who should be sacrificed. Matthew grabbed the man and drew a knife near his throat. You touch my boys and I will gut and truss you up for dinner now. The argument Matthew made was that, as we were not really men, we could not draw straws, but others retorted that we ate just like any other men. Later, Marlborough and I argued among ourselves over this nonsense; Marlborough defended Matthew, but only later did I understand why. In the end, the short straw got drawn by a man who, days later, died in his sleep. They saved his body somewhere, but we never got that far.

Three days later, we saw the Farallone islands, and the Callao cast anchor in the San Francisco bay on the last day of July 1849. I watched the widow, her children following single file, youngest to oldest, down the plank to port. Tabetha turned, looking back at the ship for one last time, saw me, and waved.

Manitoba comes out of fine-tuning and keeps quiet for a time. Then weeks later busts out and says, *In those days, it was a stretch to transition to woman, but you thought it might be possible. You took your chances but the drugs screwed you over. You couldn't find your balance, and you wandered away, confused. Packed your instruments, your tuba, your trombone, your trumpet in those shopping carts along with canned goods and assorted provisions, toilet paper, toothpaste, bars of soap, beers, and camping equipment. Like Sisyphus, you pushed your load up to campus every day where no one recognized you and no one cared, and nightly, you camped out and slept on London Nelson's grave. Then you rolled the whole train downtown and hung out near the post office.*

Uphill. Downhill. Every day. Every night. For an eternity. You didn't know why. You just followed the voices.

I step out and lock Manitoba. I need to walk. I walk up around the post office to the back of its parking lot, then around again, nodding to two Black homeless men propped up on the side of the building. I walk up the post office steps, pass a Black gentleman walking out on a cane. What are the chances, four Black men passing each other on the same day on a street in Santa Cruz? I need to talk to the Brother. I walk to his parking lot and pull the ticket.

As soon as we docked, the commotion of our arrival became intense. Folks charged out of the ship, thinking they were leaving behind death and disease. Except for the captain, not a single crew member remained, everyone rushing off to find gold. I could see there were ghostly boats and ships of every kind abandoned in the bay. On the docks, every sort of huckster and propositioner was selling their wares and expertise. Matthew moved discriminately and chose to speak with a man with a disinterested pose, sitting on a wagon with plain signage. Elihu Anthony, the man introduced himself. A blacksmith by trade and, he added to assert the honesty of his work, a pastor by faith. Matthew bought Anthony's pans, picks and shovels, buckets, nails. It was good quality; we could compare it with Canterbury's work. These implements were added to our baggage, and Marlborough and I got loaded up like mules. Anthony adjusted our packs but looked Matthew in the eyes, saying, Young man, you ought to know, California is free territory. Matthew chuckled, Free to get me some gold, but Anthony returned, That's not the free I mean. Matthew answered, I know the laws, sir. These boys will not be fugitives, mark my word. Anthony had nothing more to say and seemed to toss his last words indirectly but clearly: My shop and church are down the coast on the Monterey Bay in Santa Cruz. You will always be welcome there.

Matthew had a choice of taking a boat up the Sacramento or going overland. He'd had enough of boats and water, so chose land; got Marlborough to rig a horse and some mules, and we found our way to the American River, made camp, and tried to figure out how to separate the gold from the land. Eventually, I built us one of those rocker boxes with a grate and cleats to catch the gold. For seven years, we camped up and down the rivers and creeks from the American to the Sacramento, around the San Joaquin to Mokelumne, prospecting, sluicing for those gold bits. For a while we labored, heat or snow, and we could make about a hundred dollars a day. When we could sit still, I cobbled shoes. On my own, I could make some good money and got paid in gold. When you think about it, the shopkeepers who sold us provisions made off like bandits, got richer than any of the foolish miners. I realized that if I just settled somewhere and made boots, I'd be doing fine. Seven years, they say, is biblical, and at the end of it, I knew we'd more than paid off our debt to Matthew. I could have walked away I suppose, but Marlborough would have stayed on. Matthew made promises to Marlborough, promises about raising and racing horses back in Tennessee. My debt to Marlborough was over too; he was my brother but no longer my son. I'd kept my promise to both Hagars. And true enough, the unspoken secret was that William Nelson had fathered us all.

One day I had a half-dozen boots cobbled to order and Matthew sent me off on mule to finish my sales. I returned two days later and found Marlborough and Matthew, both mutilated and strung up on a tree just beyond our campsite. Canterbury's pick was tossed beneath, blood encrusted over the steel. I couldn't read the note stuck to Matthew's body, but I could imagine what it said. I cut them down, dressed them up proper, and dug their graves. I tucked Cambridge's carved dog into Marlborough's pocket and set Canterbury's pick to Matthew's side. Everything of value or use—gold, tools, and animals—was gone.

I dug up our hidden gold, followed the water downriver to a Chinese camp and hid there for a time. And then I made my way toward the Pacific, searching for a town called Santa Cruz on the Monterey Bay.

Walking Tour: Begin at the London Nelson Community Center on Center and Laurel Streets. Walk down Center Street toward downtown. Make a right at Cedar and walk down Plaza Lane (next to the Locust parking lot), past Hidden Peak Teahouse toward Pacific Avenue. Walk past Lulu's and around Verve where Pacific and Front form a fork; from there, cross over to the US post office. Walk between the post office and the Veterans Memorial Center to the parking lot back of the post office (site of London Nelson's small farm). Come through the lot to Water Street. Walk around toward the clock tower up Mission Street, just past Center to the brick steps below the former Santa Cruz City Schools Administration offices. Walk up the brick steps to the plaque dedicated to London Nelson. Walk across Mission Street to the Holy Cross Church and Mission Plaza, down High Street to the highway overpass. Walk over the overpass and make a right, following the bicycle path to the Evergreen Cemetery. Look for the Chinese arch. London Nelson is buried next to the Chinese.

Frutos Extraños

José

La foto tiene la culpa. La robé de la colección de Francisco. No fue que notara que no estaba. No era una de sus mujeres desnudas o de sus novias, de esas guardaba una pila en su bolsillo. Cuando no tenía nada que hacer, tomaba la pila y las ojeaba. Era una costumbre suya, barajarlas como naipes, como si estuviera hablándoles, una por una.

Críos aztecas. Eran personas morenas en miniatura con grandes narices puntiagudas y grandes peinados lanosos. No podía dejar de mirarlos. No llevaban ropa azteca; estaban vestidos finamente. Un día, mi abuela María vio la foto y dijo que nuestra gente había venido de España y conquistado a los aztecas. Eso hace quizás trescientos años. Estos debían ser de los últimos. Mi abuela acercó la foto hasta la punta de su nariz y la miró detenidamente con su ojo bueno. Dijo que no era de extrañar que los hubiéramos conquistado.[1]

Photographer

I came from Philadelphia to San Francisco at the end of the Civil War, discharged from the Fifth Kansas Cavalry at Fort Leavenworth. I was but eighteen years old and fortunately I did not die in that bloody war. I got a taste for the West, so

---

1. José (from Spanish): I blame the picture. I took it from Francisco's collection of photographs. It's not that he missed it. It wasn't one of his naked ladies or girlfriends. He had a stack of them in his pocket. In between doing nothing, he would take the pack out and look through them. It was a habit, flipping them like a deck of cards, as if he were talking to them one by one.

Aztec children. They were miniature brown people with large pointy noses and big woolly hairdos. I couldn't stop staring. They weren't wearing Aztec clothing; they were finely dressed. One day my grandmother María saw the picture and said that our people came from Spain and had conquered the Aztecs. That was maybe three hundred years ago. These must be the last ones. She brought the picture up to her nose and took a long look with her good eye. She said, no wonder we conquered them.

I kept going west. I also got some knowledge of the photographic business, having assisted a man with a traveling cart who made pictures of battles, Indian chiefs, and generals. Soldiers lined up to get their pictures taken and sent them home to their mothers and sweethearts.

Francisco

Esa fue mi segunda estancia en San Quentin. Mi hermano y yo estábamos ahí por matar a un pastor. Éramos vaqueros; no nos llevábamos bien con los pastorcitos esos. No debería haber muerto, pero mi hermano manejaba bien la riata y lo ahorcó. La culpa fue mía, porque el pastorcito se enteró de que me había llevado a su chica. Me tomó por asaltó, pero mi hermano era rápido, demasiado rápido. De todos modos, conocí a José en San Quentin. Estaba como yo la primera vez que entré, un niño tonto y asustado.

Descubrí que estaba ahí por robarle a la vieja señora Rodríguez. Le dije que era un idiota, que esa mujer era como una tía para mí. Mi padre cruzó los mares con su yerno Felipe para trabajar de vaqueros para el rey de Hawái. José me dijo que había sido un error. Su abuela lo mandó a trabajar para ella y no pensó que echaría de menos unas cucharas. Tampoco pensó que yo echaría de menos esa fotografía.[2]

Photographer

In San Francisco, I met E. P., Edward Payson, like me a fellow Philadelphian, a traveling photographer who also had an established business in Santa Cruz. He was a restless fellow, said he was an "artist" always looking for new opportunities. By the time he left for Nevada, I took over his gallery in McPherson's building on Pacific and Locust. E. P. advertised himself as a specialist in children. His ad in the *Sentinel* stated, "Every mother wishing pictures of those little wayfarers entrusted to their charge should make no delay in securing the shadow, before they take their flight to become angels in the sky." I continued in this tradition,

---

2. Francisco (from Spanish): It was my second time at San Quentin. My brother and I were there for killing a shepherd. We were vaqueros; we didn't get along with those sheep guys. He shouldn't have died, but my brother was good with the riata and choked him. It was my fault because the shepherd found out that I had taken his girl. He jumped me, but my brother was fast, too fast. Anyway, I met José in San Quentin. He was like me my first time in, a dumb, scared kid.

I found out that he was in for robbing old Señora Rodriguez. I said, you dumb shit. She's like my aunt. My dad crossed the ocean with her son-in-law Felipe to work as vaqueros for the king of Hawaii. José said it was a mistake. His grandmother sent him to work for her, and he didn't think she'd miss a few spoons. He didn't think I'd miss that photograph, either.

Santa Cruz Nori

selling cartes de visite for four dollars a dozen. When my own children, Purle and Willer, were born, Katie reminded me of E. P.'s ad, how it made her fear what the camera could capture.

José

Cuando vino Francisco por la casa, la abuela María no estaba contenta. Dijo que hacía solo un mes que yo había salido de la prisión, y que podía cambiar mi vida, pero no con ese rufián villano. Pero cuando Francisco me contó del circo y que quizás podríamos ver unos aztecas, le prometí a la abuela que esa sería la última vez que lo vería.

Una chica montaba a pelo un caballo al galope, daba saltos mortales y hacía volteretas. Una señora caminaba por una cuerda sobre nosotros. Una pareja colgaba de columpios y giraba y volteaba en el aire. Otra mujer doblaba su cuerpo hacia atrás hasta formar un pequeño paquete. Había payasos que hacían malabares con pelotas y hacían bromas divertidas a los espectadores. Vimos elefantes, cebras, un caballo con cuernos de África. Vimos leones y tigres y un rinoceronte de dos cuernos. Vimos pájaros extraños con plumas de colores y monos. Vimos una vaca sagrada de la India. Vimos a una mujer barbuda, un hombre musculoso que doblaba una barra de hierro, un gigante y un enano, pero no vimos aztecas. Vi todas estas cosas por primera vez en mi vida, como si fuera un sueño.[3]

Michael

My wife and I rent a house from Elihu Anthony on River Street. I'm in debt to him for three months. Things haven't been easy since I lost my job on the rails. I'm in line to get something at the powder works. Mr. Anthony understands, said he could wait. Says it's those Chinese taking our jobs.

---

3. José (from Spanish): When Francisco came around to my house, Grandma María wasn't happy. She said, you got out of prison only a month ago and you can change your life, but not with that no-good ruffian. But when Francisco told me about the circus and that maybe we could actually see some Aztecs, I promised her that this would be the last time I'd see him.
A girl rode bareback on a galloping horse, did jumps and somersaults. Some lady walked on a rope above us. A couple hung from swings and twirled and flipped in the air. Another woman folded her body backward into a small package. Clowns juggled balls and made funny pranks with the crowd. We saw elephants, zebras, a horned horse from Africa. We saw lions and tigers and a two-horned rhinoceros. We saw strange birds with colorful feathers and monkeys. We saw a sacred cow from India. We saw a lady with a beard, a muscular man who folded an iron bar, a giant and a dwarf, but no Aztecs. I saw all these things for the first time in my life, like a dream.

Sunday morning, the 29th of April, I walked out of the house and saw a man I thought was passed out drunk on the road. I ran over to my friend who heads the temperance league, but when we returned, we realized that the man had been shot. We could see the hole in my picket fence, the dried-up blood, and the way his body had been dragged across the road. The pockets of his pants were pulled out, and a swarm of flies was perched on his crotch since he'd probably defecated upon dying. As soon as people heard about it, they came out to see the sight, just like those flies.

Francisco

Encontré un folleto que explicaba la fotografía y se lo di a José. No había nada que hacer en la prisión, así que lo leyó una y otra vez, un relato de alguna expedición a una ciudad perdida llamada Iximaya, donde fueron descubiertos los aztecas Máximo y Bartola. Cuando salí de San Quentin, me olvidé de José, pero cuando vi el cartel del circo y casa de fieras californianos "Montgomery Queen", pensé en él de nuevo. Máximo y Bartola viajaban con el circo. Quizás.

Había dos tiendas grandes justo al lado de la estación de trenes de Aptos. La entrada era un dólar cada uno, pero por cincuenta centavos más se podían comprar asientos de ópera acolchados. Pensé que por qué no. Nos conseguimos entradas para el espectáculo de las ocho de la tarde, pero vi que nos vigilaba el alguacil.

Yo nací en Pescadero en un rancho propiedad de Don González. Mi padre era vaquero. Se fue a Hawái con Felipe Armas y atendía ganado para el Rey Kamehameha. Cuando regresó, se casó con mi madre, una princesa india, hija de Ponponio Lepegeyun. Ponponio era un indio miwok renegado que dirigió una insurgencia contra los mexicanos y las misiones. Se contaba que este indio era un valiente guerrero. Cuando mi padre conoció a mi madre, Ponponio ya había muerto, fusilado en Monterey por una corte marcial. Mi padre se quedó lo suficiente para engendrarnos a mi hermano y a mí, y luego se marchó de nuevo a Hawái y nunca regresó. Mi hermano y yo pensamos que está en un rancho ahí en Hawái, muy a gusto rodeado de esposas hawaianas. Así es que nos llaman mestizos a mi hermano y a mí, ¿pero qué saben? Me prometí que, como mi padre y mi abuelo, jamás iba a inclinarme ante nadie.[4]

---

4. Francisco (from Spanish): I found a pamphlet that explained the photograph and gave it to José. There was nothing to do in prison, so he read that thing over and over again, about some expedition to a lost city called Iximaya where the Aztecs Maximo and Bartola were discovered. When I got out of San Quentin, I forgot about José, but when I saw a poster for the Montgomery Queen's

Coroner

On Sunday, April 29, in the afternoon, I performed a postmortem examination of the victim. He was around sixty years of age, hands strong and callused, those of a worker. He had been shot, the ball entering his body behind his right shoulder, passing through his lungs, lodging in the left armpit. He probably did not die immediately, but finally bled to death. The slug was identified to be from an improved Russian six-shooter.

On the evening of Thursday, May 3, I performed a postmortem examination of the two Mexican half-breeds hanged at the bridge. Both died of strangulation by hanging, their necks broken. The older was about thirty-five, five foot five inches in height, dark complexion, hazel eyes, black hair, with round full features and a stout build. He had a pocked face. He had scars on the ball of his left thumb and his left and right wrists, and a thick scar on the edge of his right hand, identifying markers and none caused by his death. The younger man was in his twenties, about five foot six inches in height, similar round features, also stout build. He had dark hazel eyes, black hair, thick lips. He had black moles, one on the inside corner of his right eyebrow, and under his left eye and left nostril. He had moles on his breast and one large birthmark on his upper left arm. No evidence of bruises or open wounds.

Editor

As a newspaperman, I have a responsibility to keep the community informed. At the same time, this is a business, and I aim to sell copy.

The victim was identified as an honest man in his sixties from Maine, who migrated to California for work, a carpenter employed at California Powder Works,

---

California Menagerie and Circus, I thought about him again. Máximo and Bartola traveled with the circus. Maybe.

Two big tents were just outside the train depot in Aptos. It was a dollar each for admission, but for fifty cents extra, we could get cushioned opera seats. I thought, why not? We got in for the evening performance at eight, but then I saw the sheriff watching us.

I was born in Pescadero on a ranch owned by Don Gonzalez. My father was a vaquero. He went to Hawaii with Felipe Armas and herded cattle for King Kamehameha. When he returned, he married my mother, an Indian princess, daughter of Ponponio Lepegeyun. Ponponio was a renegade Miwok Indian who ran an insurgency against the Mexicans and the missions. Stories were that this Indian was a fearless warrior. By the time my father met my mother, Ponponio was dead, shot in Monterey by court-martial. My father stayed long enough to sire my brother and me, then left again for Hawaii and never returned. My brother and I figure he is over there on a ranch sitting pretty with some Hawaiian wives. So they call me and my brother half-breeds, but what do they know? I promised myself that, like my father and grandfather, I was never going to bow down to anyone.

taking his room and board in Felton. After his burial by the Masons on Tuesday evening, a growing number of men gathered the next day near the jail and in the nearby Mission orchard. An unusually large crowd of strangers was also in town, and the rumor spread that the Indians had confessed to their crime.

It has been suggested that the newspaper was aware of the events that would transpire on Wednesday at daybreak because of a certain letter left under our door. This was untrue. No such letter was received. We are therefore not culpable in the events that occurred. We did not suspect anything until Thursday morning, May 4, when our attention was directed to the San Lorenzo bridge. Visiting the location, we observed two ropes hanging from the crossbeams attached to the necks of two Indians or half-breeds, the bodies hanging dead beyond resurrection.

The bodies were cut down and taken to the undertakers, where a jury delivered the verdict that the deceased came to their deaths at the hands of parties unknown.

Photographer

It was the editor of the *Sentinel* who came to find me on the Thursday morning, rushing into our house on Washington Street and excitedly ordering Katie to rouse me. The editor had posed for his portrait as, conveniently, the newspaper offices are in the same building. He was particularly interested in the possibility that photographs could one day be reproduced in the newspaper. I ran with him to the gallery and gathered my equipment. E. P. had fashioned a dark room cart on wheels, a model of which I copied, and had most recently employed at the circus—portraits of clowns, bearded lady, twin trapeze artists, dwarfs. We rolled this contraption toward the bridge where a large crowd of men gathered and parted for my arrival. Swinging on ropes from the rafters over the bridge were two hanging bodies. I had, during the war, seen and assisted in the photography of dead men, my comrades, but I had never seen an execution.

Joseph

Ich kam nach Santa Cruz, weil ich von den Deutschen, Klaus Spreckels und Friedrich Hihn, gehört hatte, die in dieser Gegend erfolgreich gewesen waren. Fast sofort, so als ob Deutsche und Bier zusammen gehörten, bekam ich eine Anstellung als Bierbrauer in der Brauerei von Matt und Ruegg auf der Mission Street. In meiner Freizeit fertigte ich Körbe an. Ich hatte diese Fertigkeit in

meiner Geburtsstadt Lichtenfels gelernt. Da macht jeder Körbe. Ostern war vor-
über, und ich hatte den größten Teil meiner Waren verkauft. Es wurde Zeit,
Nachschub zu besorgen. In dieser Jahreszeit bedeutet das: Große Körbe, Kästen
zur Vorratshaltung und Korbwiegen für Kleinkinder. Also machte ich mich an
jenem Sonntag Morgen, dem 29. April, sehr früh, um halb sechs, nördlich der
Stadt auf den Weg; ich wollte dem Fluss entlang Weiden schneiden. Ich hatte
meiner Frau versprochen, zum Kirchgang zurück zu sein.

Ich sah das Opfer nie, obwohl ich um die Leiche herum gegangen sein muss,
während ich am Fluss herumsuchte und dann über die Gleise und an ihnen entlang zurückkehrte, mit einem Bündel Weiden auf der Schulter. Nahe dem nördli-
chen Ausgang des Eisenbahntunnels fand ich ein Nachthemd und eine Unterhose.
Ich dachte, hier habe es in der Nacht ein Techtelmechtel gegeben. Ein paar Meter
weiter fand ich ein Notizbuch und vierzig Dollar an Geldscheinen, die lose am
Boden verstreut waren.[5]

Henry's Pocket Diary

January 1, 1877

New Year. A cold clear brisk day. Took the train from the Felton
woods to the wharf to see the ocean, the Pacific. Not like the Atlantic
or our Maine coast, but I do not miss the snow.

January 27, 1877

When they understood my skills as a carpenter, they transferred
me to building a mansion. It's for the superintendent and his family.
When it is finished, it will be one of the finest houses in the region.

---

5. Joseph (from German): I came to Santa Cruz because I had heard about the Germans, Claus
Spreckels and Friedrich Hihn, who had made good in these parts. Almost immediately, as if
Germans and beer go together, I got a job making beer at Matt and Ruegg brewery on Mission
Street. In my free time, I make baskets. I learned this craft in my hometown, Lichtenfels. Everyone
there makes baskets. Easter had come and gone, and I had sold most of my stock. It was time to
replenish. This time of year: larger baskets, chests for storage, bassinets for babies. So that Sunday
morning, April 29th, very early, at half-past five, I set out to the north of the town, along the river,
to cut willows. I promised my wife I'd be back for church.
   I never saw the victim, though I must have circled his body, foraging along the river, then returning back across and along the rail tracks, a willow bundle hitched to my shoulders. Near the north
end of the train tunnel, I found a nightshirt and some drawers. I thought there'd been some hanky-
panky in the night. Then a rod further, I found a pocket diary and forty in greenbacks scattered
loose on the ground.

The California Powder Works, owned by J. W. Willard and the du Pont family, produces brown gunpowder for cannons, mining, and blasting, and is the most lucrative business in these parts, employing over 100 men. The forest provides the redwood fuel to turn willow, madrone, and alder into charcoal. The San Lorenzo River powers the mill to purify potassium nitrate. Then, there is the rail to the wharf, altogether an excellent location for transport to San Francisco and beyond. They say that in other company sites, mostly Chinese are employed to do this work; here they've managed to keep them out, only hire a handful to do the most dangerous work of grinding, where any spark can ignite an explosion. I've been urged to join the Workingmen's club to keep Chinese out of California.

February 3, 1877

Sarah's birthday today. I didn't forget. She would be how old? Already twenty? Time passes. Had she lived, she might be married with children by now. Addie and I would be proud grandparents.

February 12, 1877

I took a fall and had to rest today, losing a day of work. Bruised the back. I'm getting too old to climb the ladders, but there's no rest for this old body.

March 1, 1877

Monthly Calculations:

Pay: $100.00
Room/board: $20.00
Send home: $30.00
Save: $30.00
Mason dues: $1.50
Incidentals: $10.00
Remaining: $8.50

March 12, 1877

It is now a full year since I came to California. My Mason brothers have provided good support and company. The pay is good, though

it might be better in San Francisco. By my calculations, it will take
another year at least to settle accounts. Perhaps next year I can send
for Addie and the children. I have seen a nice cottage in town for
rent. Or perhaps I can build a house near the powder works or in
Felton. Especially if the company provides a school. A meadow with
sunshine. Addie can have the garden she loves in this temperate climate. Roses, sunflowers, geraniums, lilies, all kinds of bulbous plants,
not to mention berries and oranges, plums, figs, and avocados.

April 1, 1877

Easter Sunday. I attended service at the Methodist Church where
Elihu Anthony is the preacher. I talked with some of the members
about the price of land. They said about twenty-five dollars an acre
with redwood and oak timber. All the good land in California, they
complained, is covered by Mexican and Spanish grants. Of course,
no one knows about the validity of these old grants, transcribed in
Spanish, a language foreign to Americans. The Spanish-Catholic
influence is part of the local color, but surely we Americans have
improved life in these parts.

April 11, 1877

Received a letter from Addie asking that I send $10 more this month.
Billie has been taken with influenza and there are added costs for his
medicine and the doctor.

April 26, 1877

Received telegram. Billie has died. To be here on the other side of the
country. My son, my son. Sarah, now Billie. For what have I come
so far away? What should I write to Addie? She must be in deep
despair.

Photographer

It was a typically cloudy and chilly morning, the damp ocean fog only beginning
to recede. I made a quick judgment about the rising morning sunlight and moved
my equipment to the east side of the bridge, facing town. Young boys ran about,

pausing to scrutinize my equipment with curiosity and excitement. I walked back and forth, trying to reckon angle and perspective. I looked up and said, Can't you lower the bodies? That mass of men, seemingly disordered, suddenly became efficient, and with few orders, the wagon that had pulled the ropes taut, slowly rolled backward, the stepping horses obeying the commanding reins of their master. Several men climbed the bridge's tresses, controlling the slackening ropes, lower, lower, so that the feet were about a foot from the ground. Until that moment, black hoods covered the heads; these were yanked away, rolled and tucked into a pocket. The stiffening bodies turned to face my camera.

María

Yo soy de una familia de orgullosos rancheros, californios de pura raza española. Nada de este mestizaje con los indios. Hemos vivido aquí cinco generaciones, más tiempo que estos otros extranjeros y los oportunistas que llegaron más tarde. Mi abuelo llegó a Monterrey como soldado cuando todo esto era Alta California. Cuando México ganó su independencia, mi padre recibió una concesión de tierra en Branciforte, aquí al lado del río San Lorenzo. Durante la fiebre del oro, mi esposo huyó con mi padre y nunca regresó, dejándome sola para trabajar esta tierra. Entonces California se sumó a la Unión, y desde hace años hasta hoy quieren que demuestre que la tierra me pertenece. De todos modos, ¿qué vale? Cuando el río crece, la tierra se inunda, se lleva todo. Mi hijo se murió de un corazón débil. Mi hija parió a su hijo, y luego murió también. Solo quedamos José y yo, solos aquí. José era joven y tonto. Se metió en problemas. Recé a Dios por su alma, pero andaba con la cabeza en las nubes. Me dijo que ya vería, que se convertiría en un gran explorador del mundo, descubriría ciudades perdidas y regresaría a mí con riquezas. ¿Dónde está ahora? Enterrado allá en el maizal.

Mi vecina y querida amiga Antonia tiene más suerte que yo. Sus hombres se quedaron y mantuvieron su fortuna. Cuando se muera, dice que quiere entregar una parcela de su tierra a la iglesia para ser recordada para siempre. Ella puede darse el lujo de ser una santa. ¿Y yo? Desde mi casa puedo ver el puente donde se murió mi nieto. Dicen que hay una fotografía de su ahorcamiento.[6]

---

6. María (from Spanish): I come from a family of proud rancheros, Californios of pure Spanish stock. None of this mixing with Indians. We've lived here for five generations, longer than these other foreigners and opportunists who came later. My grandfather first came to Monterey as a soldier when this was Alta California. When Mexico won independence, my father received a land grant in Branciforte, here on the San Lorenzo River. During the gold rush, my husband ran off with

Photographer

I positioned my camera, carefully calculating for distance, and ordered everyone to get behind the swinging bodies. The crowd, as if primed, pressed themselves around the dead men, jostling for places. The editor then took command of the confusion, ordering short boys to the front and taller men behind to pack themselves in tight rows. I slipped under the camera hood, framing and focusing the scene, examining the hanging men who in my lens appeared eerily to float upside down. I peered around the camera and asked that the crowd step back, about a yard from the subjects; they did so obediently.

Sheriff

What were those two half-breeds doing at the circus that Saturday night, April 28, is what I wanted to know. And sitting in the special seats. Folks who come to the circus are families with children, proper people. I don't say the Indians and half-breeds can't come to these public events, especially if they are paying customers, but these were known convicts. My suspicions were aroused, and rightly so.

On Monday, April 30, I apprehended the younger of the two suspects in Watsonville, then proceeded to Green Valley to arrest the second, hiding in a hut with two women. I extracted confessions from them separately. The younger pled guilty, but the older denied any knowledge.

I identified the slug taken from the victim, which was fired from an improved Russian six-shooter. The Smith and Wesson Model 3 is a single-action, cartridge-firing, top-break revolver that was produced as a .44 caliber to supply the Russian Army. These half-breeds probably stole this gun, then abandoned it. The gun was never found.

Men from Felton, most of them workers at the powder works, came on Tuesday, May 1, to bury their friend in the Mason section at Evergreen Cemetery. The next

---

my father and never returned, both leaving me alone to work this land. Then California joined the Union, and for years until now they want me to prove this land belongs to me. What's it worth anyway? When the river rises, the land floods, carries away everything. My son died of a weak heart. My daughter had her son, then died too. It's just been José and me alone. José was young and stupid. He got into trouble. I prayed to God for his soul, but his head was in the clouds. He told me that I would see, that he would be a great explorer of the world, find lost cities and return to me with riches. Now where is he? Buried back there in the cornfield.

My neighbor and dear friend Antonia is luckier than me. Her menfolk stayed and kept their fortunes. When she dies, she says she wants to will a piece of their land to the church to remember her always. She can afford to be a saint. And me? From my house I can see the bridge where my grandson died. They say there is a photograph of his hanging.

day, they congregated around the jail, their numbers rising by the evening, then stormed it around midnight, forcing my guards to turn over the murderers.

Photographer

The hanging man to the right wore a jacket over a white shirt, but the man to the left was dressed in a dark three-piece suit and a fine pair of boots. In fact, he might have been better dressed than anyone in the crowd. He and I were perhaps around the same age. The boys below were shoeless, their feet soiled in mud and horse dung. One youngster held a coil of the hanging rope that he would later cut into pieces and sell as souvenirs.

Indian

Anochecía el sábado por *uiaks*. Un *iexo* caminaba cojeando, venía lentamente del pueblo. Una pareja más joven pasó junto a él, quizás viniendo del barrio chino, los dos *macx'en*. La *keckeima* miró hacia atrás al *iexo*, le sonrió y saludó, pero su *caaris* la apartó de un tirón, más allá del túnel hacia el bosque. *Saxei* soy *indio*, esta gente nunca se fija en mí, soy invisible. Pero entonces vinieron esos dos alborotadores, José y Francisco. Me vieron y me llamaron. —Oye, indio viejo, ¿no tienes plata para compartir? Vamos. José me empujó bruscamente, pero Francisco le dijo que me dejara en paz. Siguieron caminando. Yo bajé hasta el *rumme*, afilé un *eui* y pesqué un *uraka*. Lo levé a casa para cenar. Horas después, escuché el tren acercarse a Mora, donde entra al túnel. Para entonces la *murtei* estaba tranquila y muy oscura.[7]

Photographer

I slipped into my dark tent to begin the process of cleaning and carefully pouring sticky collodion over a prepared glass plate, then placing it into the bath of silver nitrate. I timed the process for about four minutes. Beyond my darkroom,

---

7. Indian (from Spanish/Awaswas-Costanoan): It was dusk, Saturday evening. An older man was walking with a limp, coming slowly from town. A younger couple walked passed him, probably coming from Chinatown, both tipsy with drink. The woman looked back at the old man, smiled and waved, but her man tugged her away, up past the tunnel into the woods. These people never noticed me, as I am an Indian, invisible to them. But then there were those other two troublemakers, José and Francisco. They saw me and called out. Hey, old Indio, don't you have some spare change to share? Come on. José pushed me roughly, but Francisco said, Let him be. And they walked on. I walked down to the river, sharpened a willow and speared a large fish. I took this home for dinner. Sometime later, I could hear the train approach Mora where it enters the tunnel. By then it was quiet and very dark.

I could hear the editor shouting orders and someone complaining, Wait, hold my place! I need my hat. Then everyone needed their hats, bowlers, top hats, caps. What about the murderers? Their hats fell off when they were hanged! Everyone laughed. Get them some hats, someone yelled. Finally, I placed the prepared plate in its wooden frame and emerged to find everyone, including the hanging bodies, sporting hats.

Judge Lynch

The people of Santa Cruz, finding that their lives and property were in danger from the number of murders and robberies that have been committed in this county within the past eight years—no legal execution having followed; that the nightwatchman refuses to make an arrest when the robbers are pointed out; that new trials are granted on technicalities; two Indian half-breeds were guilty of the murder of an honest carpenter beyond a doubt—resolved to hang them; that we, taxpayers and conservators of justice assembled to the number of 150; that after due deliberation, we resolved that they should pay the penalty of their crime, and that the taxpayers in this case be freed from the expense of a trial and judicial execution; that we went to the jail; that the jailor refused to let us into the jail-yard; that we broke down the gate; that we found the undersheriff on guard, and without doing him bodily injury, forced him to lead unto us the criminals; that we led said criminals across the upper San Lorenzo Bridge, where they were placed in a wagon; that they confessed their guilt; and that the older one said: 'Can't you give us a drink,' and that on whiskey being placed to his lips, he drank the bottle to its dregs; that the wagon started; that arriving at the middle of the bridge, it stopped; that ropes were passed over a beam above, and the driver told to 'Move on'; that he did so; that the murderers fell heavily, their necks being broken by the fall; that we left them alone to swing as a warning to other murderers and thieves; that their fate is but what other murderers and assassins may expect.

Photographer

I slipped the framed plate into the camera. Thankfully, it was a cool morning; the collodion would stay wet long enough. I might have another five minutes. I ran up to adjust the hat on the face of one of the hanging men, the light just capturing his dark features. I ordered the crowd. Hold your places! Eyes open. Absolutely still. Someone yelled, Still like corpses! More laughter. I returned to the camera, watching the image, and waited for the silence that would capture that moment, as they say, for posterity.

Walking Tour

Start at the corner of Mora and River Streets in front of Lloyd's Tires. Look down River Street to the San Lorenzo Lumber and Home Center where migrant workers hang out in the morning hoping to snag day jobs. Note that River Street is named for the San Lorenzo River, the view obscured now by businesses and apartment houses. Walk up Mora toward the Saint Francis Catholic Kitchen. Find the railroad tracks to the chain-link fence and the north entrance to the tunnel built by Cornish miners. Continue up Mora and take the bicycle path up the back side of Holy Cross Church to High Street. Follow High Street to the church parking lot where the old Santa Cruz jail used to be. Take Emmett Street to Mission Street and walk toward downtown and the clock tower. Continue down Water Street to the bridge. Cross the bridge toward the empty lot where a blue two-story nineteenth-century clapboard house used to stand, then take the river walk along the bank heading north. Just beyond the bridge and along the river to your right is the location of the current Santa Cruz jail and 4.938 acres originally granted to José Maria Chamala.

ACKNOWLEDGMENTS

Theo Honnef, for German translation
Sarah Arantza Amador, for Spanish translation

NOTES

The statement of "Judge Lynch" was lifted, with small changes, from the original *Santa Cruz Sentinel* article, "Murder-Arrest-Strangulation," dated May 5, 1877.

In later-half of the 1800s in California on the Monterey Bay, 25 people were lynched: 1 Chinese, 4 Native Americans, 20 Mexican/Californios (see Monroe Work Today)

Quimosabe

ABSTRACT 1

Smokeless Gunpowder Chemistry in Pyrotechnic Apparition Revisualization of Ghosts

$$2 \; {}^{\ominus}O \text{-} \overset{\overset{O}{\|}}{\underset{O \ominus \oplus K}{N^{\oplus}}} \; + \; S \; + \; 3\,C \; \longrightarrow \; K^{\nearrow S}\text{-}_K \; + \; N \equiv N \; + \; 3\,O = C = O$$

Round about 1864, California Powder Works situated itself on the San Lorenzo River, three miles upstream of the town of Santa Cruz. Here they built a dam with a tunnel, four by six feet in diameter and 1,200 feet through a granite ridge, with a sixty-foot drop-off, to power the mill's machinery. They commenced charring willow, madrone, and alder, fueling the fire with redwood, all in abundance in that dense forest. They also built a bridge over the San Lorenzo and a wharf on the Santa Cruz beach to receive shipments of saltpeter from the Atacama desert in Chile and sulfur from the Italian island of Sicily. All of this got pulverized to make black powder, by weight: 75% potassium nitrate, 15% charcoal, and 10% sulfur. In the day, west of the Rockies and the Civil War, California Powder Works was the first supplier of gunpowder.

Then, in 1867, Alfred Nobel, known to you today for the Nobel Peace Prize, invented dynamite by using diatomaceous earth, composed of siliceous diatom shells and unicellular aquatic plants of microscopic size, to absorb nitroglycerin.

53

Giant Powder in San Francisco got exclusive rights to produce Nobel's dynamite, but by 1874, Joseph W. Willard, superintendent of the California Powder Works, had basically copied Nobel's formula to produce Hercules Powder. Behind Willard was the du Pont family, long in the gunpowder business, having established a 43 percent interest in the works. Then too, William Charles Peyton, son of second superintendent Bernard Peyton, married Anna Ridgley du Pont. It was William Peyton who patented Peyton Powder, a version of a clean-burning smokeless gunpowder, employing a mixture of nitroglycerine and nitrocellulose with ammonium picrate.

Now, you need to understand that dynamite and smokeless powder using nitroglycerine was a step up from the old black powder. California Powder Works went on to produce high explosive powder for the US Army and Navy and to operate a proving ground to test rifles and cannons. In 1881, they opened a new plant in Hercules, off the San Pablo Bay, and after 1906, operated under the name DuPont. The du Ponts had worked their way west across the country from the Eleutherian Mills on Brandywine Creek in Delaware to the California Gold Rush, via the Transcontinental Railroad, and, not to forget, four wars—1812, Crimean, Civil, and Spanish-American. By 1907, DuPont had acquired some 108 competitors. Someone said that in the day, if you were in the business of explosives, you had one of three fates: dissolution by catastrophic accident, elimination by competition, or assimilation by DuPont.

Not to be owning the narrative; no, nothing like that, but this brings me to the point of this local history. On April 26, 1898, at 5:15 pm, thirteen of us workers got blown to bits: Guy Seward Fagen, 16; Charles Miller, 16, and his brother James E. Miller, 27; Luther W. Marshall, 18, and his brother Ernest Marshall, 19; Benjamin E. Joseph, 19; Ernest Jennings, 21; Henry C. Butler, 45; and Charles A. Cole, 51. These nine were buried together in the Santa Cruz Memorial Cemetery, that is, if you could retrieve the body parts. A few of us were recognizable, but they said, the rest of us *could fit into a hat*. A year later, they were still finding our body parts in the trees. Three unnamed men were buried elsewhere. Then there's me, whose name and remains just plain evaporated. Where in God's name did I go?

In about fifty years of operations, there were maybe fifty explosions. That's right, an average of one per year. The human catastrophic percentage is a bit better: some thirty-five men among us died in those explosions. It was a hazard of the business, and we were the collateral damages. In 1914, the operation was shut down, buildings dismantled; the old community—workers' houses, school, shops, Peyton family mansions—all abandoned until, a decade later, the Freemasons turned the 138-acre site into Paradise Park, a club with campsites. To be sure, if you wander the old ruins, you'll catch sight of us, bits and pieces, glimmers. Me, I'm scattered everywhere, not just into thin air, but biomolecularly into everything—air, water, soil, flora, and fauna. My cellular memory wanders this place, travels and invades everything. Hey, think about it. Not to make you feel anxious or anything, but some piece of me might be traveling inside of you, right now as we speak.

ABSTRACT 2

Lipophilic Properties of Dichlorodiphenyltrichloroethane and Bioaccumulation: Kryptonite to Mosquitoes or Toxic Colonialism?

In 1939, a Swiss chemist named Pauly Mueller, working for J. R. Geigy in Basel, figured that there were chemicals exclusively toxic to insects and discovered that the compound 1,1,1-trichloro-2,2-bis(4-chlorophenyl)ethane was effective against a wide range of anthropods: mosquito, louse, flea, sandfly. Thus, it was possible, through insects, to get to the routes of malaria, typhus, the plague, and various other tropical diseases. Now, what they meant by "exclusively toxic" I'm not sure, but this modern synthetic insecticide was used to great effect by the US Army in wwii as it advanced from Pacific island to island, taking Guam, the Philippines, Okinawa, Korea, and finally, Japan. Dusted the heck out of those tropical huts and hideouts, and virtually eliminated those bloodsuckers. Dusted the infantry too. Under the armpits, down the crotch. Said it was chemistry that would win this war. For this, Mueller got the Nobel Prize in Physiology and Medicine; the committee declared: *DDT has been used in large quantities in the evacuation of concentration camps, of prisons and deportees. Without any doubt, the material has already preserved the life and health of hundreds of thousands.*

And when the war ended, the miracles of chemical treatment were brought home to American agriculture to increase the yields of fruit, vegetables, cotton, and livestock, and to protect farm buildings, stored grain, greenhouse crops, shade trees and ornamentals. And in the day, what suburban American household didn't have one of those pump canisters to spray away aphids on roses or clear a campsite of mosquitoes, fire ants, and ticks? As advertised: *Better things for better living through chemistry.*

ABSTRACT 3

2,4-Dichlorophenoxyacetic acid: Biomonitoring Epidemiological Exposure and Evolutionary Resistance on General Populations

In 1943, Arthur Galston, a graduate student at the University of Illinois, studying plant hormones and the flowering of soybeans, discovered that low concentrations of the compound 2,3,5-triiodobenzoic acid encouraged flowering; however high levels caused abscission, that is, plant death. You never know how others will use your dissertation research, and Galston later realized that Monsanto and Dow Chemical, under the auspices of the US military, developed that compound, not for flowering but deflowering. In the next war, guys flew our planes over Vietnam and Laos ejecting Agent Orange and dousing the hell out of those dense tropical forests. Maybe we exposed the enemy, but like Galston warned, ol' Orange was a double agent.

ABSTRACT 4

Hydrophobia in Polytetrafluoroethylene

$$\left(\begin{array}{c} \overset{\displaystyle F}{\underset{\displaystyle F}{|}} \quad \overset{\displaystyle F}{\underset{\displaystyle F}{|}} \\ -C-C- \\ \end{array}\right)_n$$

In 1938, Roy Plunkett, experimenting with tetrafluoroethylene gas at the DuPont Jackson Laboratory, created by accident a waxy white stuff that turned out to be the most slippery substance known to mankind. Besides being repellent, it was also non-corrosive, chemically stable, with an extremely high melting point. Plunkett accidentally invented Teflon.

Years later, Julia Child, the French Chef, switched from cast-iron to what she called *no-stick-ums* for crepes, scrambled eggs, pancakes, and omelets. When asked about her favorite frying pan, turned out it was a ten-inch aluminum Wearever. *You get it at the hardware store*, she said. *It's perfect for omelets. I could not live without that.*

ABSTRACT 5

Mammary Carcinoma: Rogue Reactivity Strawberry Extract
Apoptosis Tumor Inhibition in Mice

As the crow flies, a mile southwest of Paradise Park, you can locate a hillside garden in the redwood forest of the university. In 1967, an English master gardener named Alan Chadwick employed what he called the biodynamic French intensive method, and with shovels and hoes, he and student volunteers terraced that hill into a garden of flowers, herbs, vegetables, and fruit trees. This experiment grew into the UCSC Center for Agroecology and Sustainable Food Systems. From this, you can find local connections to organic markets, mushroom foraging, food activism, and cuisine using locally grown ingredients.

In 1962, Rachel Carson, a marine biologist known for her writings on the ecosystems of the sea, published *Silent Spring*, warning of the misuse and dangers of synthetic chemical pesticides, provoking fierce controversy from the industry, and launching our contemporary environmental movement. Carson challenged scientists and government to see the natural world as shared living space, speaking calmly while weathering corporate threats and accusations. Two years later, at age fifty-six, Carson died from breast cancer. In 2016, the Helen and Will Webster Foundation gifted UCSC College Eight with a proper name, Rachel Carson College.

In the same year, 2016, the California Department of Pesticide Regulation reported that more than 1.54 million pounds of pesticides, principally soil fumigants and nematicides, chloropicrin and dichloropropene, were sprayed on crops in Santa Cruz County, half of which were strawberry fields. In November 2014, using an air monitoring device called a Drift Catcher, Emily Marquez and Susan Kegley collected drift samples at a Watsonville residence adjacent to two chloropicrin applications on two fields, stating: *Estimated exposure scenarios spanning a lifetime, thirty years, or various periods of childhood all resulted in cancer risks exceeding* EPA's *level of concern of one excess cancer per million people.* In plain language, this means that if residents, farm workers—seasonal and migrant, breathe in what the drift catches, they are at risk for numerous forms of cancer: lymphomas and prostate, brain, leukemia, cervix, and stomach cancers.

Meanwhile, researchers have discovered that anthocyanin and phenolic acids in strawberries inhibit the growth and spread of cancer cells.

ABSTRACT 6

Doxorubicin (Adriamycin): Red Devil Extraction from Soil Fungus Streptomyces

In the 1950s, an Italian research lab, Farmitalia, isolated *Streptomyces peucetius* from a soil sample near the thirteenth-century Castel del Monte, producing a red pigment and antibiotic effective against tumors in mice. A strain of *Streptomyces* was mutated using N-nitroso-N-methylurethane. The eventual result was doxorubicin, known to cancer patients as the Red Devil and approved for medical use in the US in 1974.

That's the Red Devil, but what happened to the headhunter's serum? In 1931, an American doctor, Wilburn Ferguson, set out for Peru and spent the next few decades studying rainforest plants, searching for new drugs for incurable diseases. While studying the Jivaro tribe and their practice of head-hunting and head shrinking, Ferguson researched, in particular, a secret and toxic herbal solution of thirty plant juices used to cook and preserve the heads. Extracting elements from this solution, he produced an anticancer formula named Amitosin with which he reported successfully treating terminally ill cancer patients. The drug never received US government approval; however, Sean Connery starred in a movie based on Ferguson, *Medicine Man*. In the movie, Connery's assistant simply injects the indigenous patient with serum, and the next day, no tumor; he's cured.

ABSTRACT 7

Toasting AC-T Cocktails: Warfare Nitrogen Mustards and Peacetime Cyclophosphamide Therapeutic Regimes

In December 1943, Germans bombed the Italian port of Bari on the Adriatic coast, destroying the US Liberty ship *John Harvey*. As it turned out, the *John Harvey* carried a secret cargo of 2,000 bombs of M47A1 mustard gas. Most of the crewmates died in the blast, but some jumped ship into a sea of mustard oil, and 628 patients, including medical staff and Italian citizens, sought treatment for mysterious symptoms linked to gas poisoning. Eighty-three of these patients died. Examination of tissue samples from autopsied victims confirmed the research of Alfred Gilman and Louis Goodman at Yale, who were studying nitrogen mustards for the treatment of lymphoma. Mustard gas suppressed cell division. Eventually they created the first intravenous chemotherapy drug: chlormethine, or mechlorethamine.

ABSTRACT 8

Taxology of the Pacific Yew: Taxus Brevifolia's Intravenous Journey

The story of the Pacific yew, or *Taxus brevifolia*, was written by Jerry Rust and Hal Hartzell in a self-published book in 1983. Rust ran for governor of Oregon on an environmental platform focused on the preservation of the yew. Everything you want to know about the yew—its biology, its relationship to forest ecology, and its human contact history—was written in this book. Since only 500 copies were printed, at least 500 readers learned this version of the Pacific yew, but that deeply reverent tree biography reflects the resonating story driving the conservation movement to save old-growth forests in the Pacific Northwest. The Pacific yew, along with the spotted owl, were losing their habitats and in danger of becoming extinct.

The Pacific yew is an evergreen conifer found along the Pacific coast from southern Alaska to Central California. Its needles are short and flat, dark green on top, light green beneath. The seeds develop into small red berries, and the bark is a patchwork of peeling brown and gray scales over a smoother inner layer of purple and red-brown. In nature, color attracts but also might be a warning. The yew is poisonous. In the old days, it was known as the "graveside tree."

In 1964, Monroe Wall and Mansukh Wani at Research Triangle Institute in North Carolina discovered that extracts from the bark contained cytotoxic activity. For the next three decades, thousands of pounds of bark were harvested from the Pacific yew for cancer research. The problem was that the Pacific yew was slow-growing and hidden in the understory of old-growth forests. Considered a weed tree, it was usually trashed and burned in the process of clearcutting, but when the Pacific yew became valuable in the search to cure cancer, everything changed. The calculated estimate was six yew trees per cancer patient. Do we destroy the forest to cure cancer?

On August 7, 1992, the yew got its own congressional act: The Pacific Yew Act, with the purpose of ensuring the conservation and sustainable harvest of Pacific yew trees, located on lands of the National Forest System and on public lands administered by the Bureau of Land Management, for the successful treatment of cancer. But by this time, researchers at Bristol Myers Squibb developed a way to semi-synthesize the chemical paclitaxel from the common Canadian yew, *Taxus baccata*, which could be cultivated commercially, thus saving the endangered Pacific yew.

ADDENDUM

War on Drugs/War on Cancer: Designer Receptors Exclusively Activated by Designer Drugs (DREADD) Suppression of Intuitive Toxicological Binary Contradictions

The National Cancer Act was signed into law in 1971. President Richard Nixon described this commitment to establish the National Cancer Institute as a "war on cancer."

Common chemotherapy drug side effects: pain at site of infusion, eyes watering, red to pink urine, darkening of nail beds, darkening of skin, problems with fertility, low blood counts, blood cancer, tumor lysis syndrome, poor appetite, bladder irritation and bleeding, hair loss, arthralgias and myalgias, peripheral neuropathy, nausea and vomiting, diarrhea, mouth sores, hypersensitivity reactions—fever, facial flushing, chills, shortness of breath, or hives.

AUTHOR NOTE

In January 2020, I consulted oncologist Dr. Amy McMullen about my breast cancer. Flanked by my husband and sister, we had a silent agreement. Depending, we were going to spend my pension wad traveling, wherever, didn't matter. But then Dr. McMullen said confidently, *We can cure this.* I thought, okay, why not, a new experience being cured. I know my sister had privately studied it, but I had no interest in the science. I just thought they should prove it by doing it. I had other things to do, like write. I joined the program and followed it obediently. Started chemo treatments, lost my hair and appetite, got sick, then rallied for the next chemo.

By the third chemo, the entire world had shut down in pandemic, joining me in isolation, quarantine mode. My eight chemo-room buddies on La-Z-Boys in various stages of intravenous pumping were suddenly gone, banned in social distancing. For the rest of these procedures, I sat alone for hours watching the intravenous drip dripping of antinausea meds, then Red Devil or AC-T or Taxol. I missed the commotion of my cancer companions, especially since I had started writing a sitcom called *The Chemo Room*. What happened to Nurse Rachel, to Fred, Sophia, and Gilbert?

I watched Nurse Mia or Nurse Hillary pump me with the red stuff. Then there was Taxol, which required ice packs on my feet and hands to prevent neuropathy. Finally, I asked, *What is this stuff anyway?* Mia gave me the lounge copy of a book about the story of Taxol. Honestly, I didn't understand most of it, but I did understand that whatever a research lab had invented to kill, it was also involved in research of the same stuff to save. Maybe the labs were different, but they were really all the same, in cahoots, and that is how I drifted off to sleep on the La-Z-Boy, dreaming into my complicity, the contradiction of my living and possible dying.

PS: Infinite gratitude to: Dr. Thanh Vu; Dr. Kenneth Averill; Dr. Amy McMullen; Alice McCurdy, Physician's Assistant; Nurse Rachel; Nurse Mia; Nurse Hillary; Dr. Jessica Santillano; Tea Taylor, Lymphedema Therapist; Lilinoe Manischalchi, Hand Therapist; Dr. Charlotte Kim; your staffs and support teams.

ACKNOWLEDGMENT

Chemical structures by Rachel Snelling, PhD

This Is Someone's Paradise

Here comes the buzzing
of the bullet
which bears my name.
It's a bee looking
for the hive of my neck
and I must lay still
for its sweet entrance.

"TOBERA," JEFF TAGAMI

Wednesday, January 8, 1930

On this evening, the Northern Monterey Chamber
of Commerce adopts a resolution charging that
Filipinos are undesirable, possess unhealthy habits,
and are destructive of the living wage of whites and
Mexicans in agriculture and industry, resolving,
therefore, to exclude Filipino labor from the State
of California. This resolution is sent to Governor
C. C. Young and Senator Hiram Johnson.

We do not advocate violence but we do feel that the
United States should give the Filipinos their liberty
and send those unwelcome inhabitants from our
shores, that the white people have inherited this
country for themselves and their offspring . . .

My son Fermin was born to me, Valentina Ibarra, and
my husband, Mariano Tuvera, on the fifth of July in 1908,
in the town of Sinait, Ilocos Sur, on the island of Luzon.

Friday, January 10, 1930

Evening Pajaronian: "Resolution Flaying Filipinos
Drawn by Judge D. W. Rohrback,"

Judge Rohrback: *Filipinos . . . little brown men, but
ten years removed from a bolo and a breechclout . . .
will soon be well clothed, and strutting about like a
peacock and endeavoring to attract the eyes of the
young American and Mexican girls . . . there will
soon be 40,000 halfbreeds . . . before ten years have
passed . . . a brown horde that will finally eliminate
the white laborer in the State of California.*

By 1930, the U.S. Census counted 30,470
Filipinos in California.

My son Fermin left our home in Sinait in 1927, headed
for Hawaii. Fermin was not even twenty years old. Then
Claro, two years older, followed Fermin to California in
1928. Maybe you could call them men by then, but I only
saw my boys, smooth faces and bright eyes. When Claro
followed Fermin, I said, *Look after your brother.*

Saturday, January 11, 1930

Filipino Club leases hall at Palm Beach, hiring nine
white girls to set up a dance hall for Filipinos.

A local white protests: *Taxi dance halls where
white girls dance with Orientals may be all right*

in San Francisco or Los Angeles but not in our
community. . . We won't stand for anything of the kind.

My boys were not alone. When the recruiters came,
many others from our region, Ilocos Sur, also caught
the fever to make money in America. *Get your papers*
in order, they said. *Filipinos are us nationals. Not like*
Chinese or Japanese. You have a right to enter America to
work. It's all legal.

Thursday, January 16, 1930

10,000 copies of *The Torch*, a local pamphlet, are
distributed in which David P. de Tagle responds to
the insults of Judge Rohrback.

We Filipinos were brought up under the Christian
principle that God created men equal, and so we
do not believe in "racial-superiority." We welcome
Americans and other nationalities in our family
circles, and Americans, more than any other
foreigner in the Philippines take more Filipino
women to the altar. We feel that as human beings we
have the same inalienable rights in this country to
take those who love us as our legitimate wife.

Before my sons left for America, we went to San
Nicolas de Tolentino to pray before Apo Lakay. I
prayed that their journey would be safe, that they
would prosper, and that, one day, they would return.
What did Claro and Fermin pray for, their hearts so
filled with the call of adventure?

Congressman Richard Welch of California
reintroduces his exclusion bill seeking to reclassify
Filipinos as "aliens ineligible to citizenship."

Sunday, January 19, 1930

In a mass meeting, chaired by A. Antenor Cruz, in the
Hall of the Monterey Bay Filipino Club in Palm Beach,
three hundred Filipinos of Watsonville and Pajaro
Valley unanimously approve a resolution protesting
the resolution adopted by the Northern Monterey
Chamber of Commerce, and, in a demonstration of
self-respect and human attributes, request that *our
home government through the Philippine Legislature
including the Resident Commissioners at Washington,
D.C., . . . use all just and honorable means by
appropriate legislative measures for the preservation
of mutual trust and confidence of the peoples
concerned . . . for a just and equitable remedy.*

You asked, was Fermin at the Filipino meetings? Was
he even allowed to be there, a poor migrant worker?
Did he speak? He did not speak English, but he
understood. What did he hear?

In the afternoon and evening, sporadic fights break
out across the county. In a Chinatown gambling
establishment, Chinese and Filipinos battle each
other with chairs, wrecking furniture, and sending
two wounded to the hospital.

On Front Street, whites drive Filipinos into a house
in retaliation for a thrown rock. Inside the house,
Filipinos arm themselves with knives.

On Van Ness, outside a Filipino boarding house, a
group of whites and Filipinos clash in fisticuffs.

At 11 pm, one hundred men emerge from pool halls
along Main Street and commence fighting on the
bridge, throwing Filipinos into the Pajaro River.

In America you say drink was prohibited. I thought this
was good. It would keep my boys out of trouble. Fermin
was always a gentle child, courteous to the elderly, always
ready to obey. He would not break the laws.

Monday, January 20, 1930

On the streets, two hundred whites form Filipino
hunting parties, but police foil the mob, smuggling
little brown brothers from a pool hall on Main Street
into the dark night.

In Chinatown, whites and Filipinos square off,
when a group of twenty-five Mexicans arrive, align
themselves with the whites while paring their nails
with eight-inch knives.

My sons were strong. They could defend themselves, but
they would not go after trouble. Maybe Claro could be a
boxer. Fermin could be feisty too. Our people from Ilocos
have a history. We do not run from a fight.

Tuesday, January 21, 1930

At 1:30 am, a man yells into a bunkhouse at Matt
McGowen Ranch: *Any Filipinos in the joint?*

The six Japanese within answer, *No!*

A carload of whites empties a fusillade of shots into
the bunkhouse walls, then drives away.

Miraculously, no one is shot.

My son Fermin worked on the John Murphy Ranch
and lived with eleven other Filipinos in a bunkhouse
on San Juan Road. I believe they lived like brothers,
feeding and looking after each other.

At 11 pm, thirty carloads of white men gather around
the Filipino Club in Palm Beach, tapping gasoline
from their cars, intending to burn the hall down and
drive the Filipinos into the sea. The owners of the
property, E. L. Paddon and William Lock-Paddon,
hold the mob, grown to some four hundred men, at
bay with shotguns until the arrival of the police. Two
boys are shot, one in the cheek and the other in the
hand; as it turns out, the shotguns are filled with rice.

The mob leaves, yelling epithets. *Goo-goo lovers!*

Wednesday, January 22, 1930

A brick is thrown into the front window of a Filipino
residence on East Walker Street. *You black sons
of a bitches, let our white girls alone!* A Filipino
emerges with a shotgun.

Two hundred and fifty whites gather in front of a
Filipino residence on Walker and Ford. Filipinos fire
into a car while others hide under beds.

Forty-six Filipinos, beaten and bruised, hide in the City
Hall council room, rescued from a mob of five hundred
men and boys, who, robbed of their prey, shatter windows
and wreck the interior of the brown men's dwellings.

At the Pajaro bridge, eight Filipinos and six whites
fight with knives and rocks.

Ranches along the San Juan Road where Filipinos live
are invaded. A party of whites invades Matt McGowen
Ranch searching for stray brown men. Five hundred
whites, armed with clubs and firearms, drag out twenty-
two Filipinos from Frank Riberal's labor camp. Near
midnight a carload of vigilantes drives to Murphy
Ranch and fires into a Filipino bunkhouse, killing one
worker, Fermin Tobera, and wounding another.

On Wednesday night, Fermin returned to the
bunkhouse from a long day in the fields harvesting
lettuce. He worked even though men rioted in town.
He lay down on his cot, on his right side, facing the wall,
and closed his eyes. He would not open them again.

Sixty whites invade the Andrew Storm Ranch. When
police arrive, one man flees, leaving behind his car
and a left shoe in the mud.

Seven white boys are arrested: George Barnes, 18;
Ramon Davis (Melvin McVickers), 18; Fred
Majors, 25; Charles Morrison, 28; George Sias, 23;
Raymond Smith, 18; Ted Spangler, 27.

Nine white girls residing at the Filipino Club are
ordered to return to Guadalupe by Sheriff Nick Sinnott.

Thursday, Jan 23, 1930

Seventy-five members of the police, American Legion,
Spanish War Veterans of America, County Deputy
Sheriffs, constables, and private citizens patrol the streets
and finally bring peace to a community in turmoil.

In the morning, Mariano Liana, who had befriended
my son, rose from his cot next to Fermin's. You said

he taunted Fermin. *Hey, get up! How could you sleep through that? They were shooting through the walls! We crowded into that closet like a bunch of naked sardines.* But my son could not answer.

Friday, January 24, 1930

A warrant is issued for A. Antenor Cruz, president of the Filipino Club, for conducting a dance without a license.

Salinas District Attorney Alfred E. Warth charges Ted Spangler, Raymond Smith, and George Sias, in addition to rioting, with assault with intent to rob, having pointed a gun at Filipinos.

Edward Fry, 18, is arrested, his shoe found in the mud, tracing him to the attack on Storm Ranch.

A contingent from the Los Angeles Filipino Citizens League arrives to promote peace and tranquility.

You said Dr. O. C. Marshall performed the autopsy and found a .35-caliber bullet in Fermin's heart. Then they transferred his body to the morgue and finally to Mehl's Funeral Home on 222 East Lake Avenue. Was it really possible Mariano and the others ran to save themselves and did not hear Fermin's cry? Did not see his blood pooling beneath his bed? I have felt my son's dying anguish. His horrible pain. You told this story as if Fermin died alone in his sleep.

Governor General of the Philippines Dwight Davis cables the Bureau of Insular Affairs *urging protection for the Filipino Laborers.*

In San Jose, a mass meeting of Filipinos assembles
to prevent Filipinos from resorting to violence.
Filipinos will be asked to rely on the police for
protection if necessary, rather than taking the law
into their own hands.

Saturday, January 25, 1930

Labor leader Pablo Manlapit, writing for *Ang Bantay,*
a Filipino-American weekly based in Los Angeles,
describes the riots as *wholesale murder* and blames
Judge Rohrback for the violence of the riots.

The Young Communist League distributes circulars
condemning local elites for fomenting anti-Filipino
violence and accuses Judge Rohrback of advocating
white supremacy.

Fermin was only in California for one year, one cycle
of harvest. What did he learn besides hard labor, what
a body can be forced to do? Maybe if he had lived, he
would have joined the union, fought for his rights. He
did not live to answer your question.

In Washington, DC, Resident Commissioner of the
Philippines Pedro Guevara testifies in Congress that
had a Filipino mob attacked Americans in Philippines,
the United States would have sent the army or a
battleship to quell the riot. Further, as Filipinos *under*
the American Flag, we feel entitled to come here and
engage in the same kind of work as Americans, and we
will expect the full protection of the law.

Paul Scharrenberg, leader of the California State
Federation of Labor states: *The race riots . . . and their*
bloody issue are inevitable as the result of the third

invasion of California by Oriental labor. I predicted them
and I predict that they will increase if this new swarming
of "cheap labor" from across the Pacific is not stopped.

Sunday, January 26, 1930

Carrie Victorini, daughter of local rancher Manuel
Victorini, is reported missing after being remonstrated
by parents for *consorting with Filipinos;* she is rumored
to have been kidnapped by Filipino laborers.

Raymond Smith, arrested in the riots, reports that he
hit a Filipino in the mouth for insulting his female
companion, Elsie Trevison of Reno. He then met up
with nine other men to search for the Filipino culprit.

Every day I've wept for my son, who was my strength
and my promise. Why did he have to die in an ugly
manner not sanctioned by God?

Congressman Arthur Monroe Free of San Jose
declares: *The Filipinos of Watsonville are of the very*
lowest type . . . I am going to show that the so-called
rioters were sorely tried by the vicious practices of the
Filipinos in luring young white girls into degradation.

Resident Commissioner Pedro Guevara is applauded for
his speech in Congress in favor of independence: *If the*
United States cannot make the Filipinos safe and if it
cannot give them the protection it promised them, then the
only alternative is to separate and sever our relations.

Monday, January 27, 1930

Eight Watsonville youth, charged with rioting and
beating at the Dethlefsen Ranch, appear before
Judge Rohrback this afternoon.

Fearing a riot, Gilroy officers clean up the Oriental
section, giving unemployed whites and Filipinos five
minutes to vacate the city.

In San Francisco, Jose Francisco and Reseguno
Peralto are severely beaten by a gang of men who
saw them escorting white women on the corner of
Turk and Larkin. Judge George Steiger gives them
thirty-day sentences for *provoking the attacks
because of their aggressive pursuit of white girls.*

Did Fermin have a girlfriend? My boys didn't share
that with me. Perhaps Claro was bold, but Fermin was
shy. Maybe he changed in America. Perhaps he found
someone to love.

Manila Chief of Police Columbus E. Piatt asserts
that the riots in Watsonville are *purely local* and
will not extend to retaliation against Americans
in the Philippines.

The *Manila Daily Bulletin* editorial argues:
*Many of the Filipino laborers in California are
of a low class . . . they come into contact with a
correspondingly low class of American laborers . . .
riff-raff on both sides. The class of woman to be
found as dance hall girls catering to that class
of laborer is well known . . . He who for political
reasons promotes the spirit of ill feeling which
prolongs or spreads the rioting is doing nothing
more than trying to have the Philippine question
settled in the California lettuce fields and the
dance halls of the vegetable gardening districts
by floater laborers.*

Tuesday, January 28, 1930

Beecher Stowe, attorney for the Filipino Citizens League
of Los Angeles, arrives in Watsonville and announces his
intention to sue the county sheriff and DA for damages
and humiliation suffered by Filipinos during riots.

In San Jose, Alfred Johnson is stabbed and four
Filipinos severely beaten in the melee.

Leonard Brasette of San Jose is arrested for
planning to use dynamite to blast Filipino homes
and gathering places.

In Stockton, at midnight, an explosion wrecks the
Filipino Federation of America clubhouse.

Fermin sent money to me every month. He and Claro
never failed to send something, even when their pay
was very low. You said their labor was cheap, but
I valued every penny.

Governor of Hawaii Lawrence M. Judd opposes the bill
proposed by Congressman Richard Welch, which would
prevent immigration of Filipinos to the Hawaiian Islands.

Wednesday, January 29, 1930

Guards are increased at the Monterey Presidio after
a report by a Filipino houseboy that Filipinos plan to
seize arms and munitions to start an uprising.

In Los Angeles, riot-squad cars patrol Main Street where
three thousand white women are employed by Filipino
dancing clubs, fearful of retaliatory attacks by white men.

I did not send my sons halfway around the world to
work, never to see them again. Fermin said that one
day he wanted to bring me to America too. Of course
I'd go. Anything to be with my sons again.

Senator Millard Tydings of Maryland suggests
Filipino immigration restrictions.

In Congress, Resident Commissioner Camilo
Osias claims: *The anomaly is that we are under the
American flag and we are not eligible to American
citizenship, which is the greatest benefit the flag
confers,* to which Congressman Henry Barbour of
California queried: *If you put up your own flag over
there, will you keep your people at home?*

Thursday, January 30, 1930

The Paddon brothers, property owners of the Filipino
Club hall in Palm Beach, publish in the *Evening
Pajaronian* their statement in response to the riots. They
prefer to rent their premises to Filipinos for use as a
private club rather than to those who would operate a
speakeasy. Within the Filipino Club, all the women, with
the exception of one, accompanied by her mother, were
married to Filipinos or to hired musicians. *It is a rank
injustice to refer to their club as a vice den . . . they are
conducting their club in a most exemplary manner, the
men at the head of it are highly educated men . . .*

About the taxi dance, what's that? You said Filipinos
were splendid dancers. Worked in the fields by day,
then, like magic, turned into fancy dancers at night.
They knew all the latest American steps. Maybe
Fermin learned to dance. He loved music. He had a
beautiful voice and liked to sing.

Senator Hiram Johnson argues that the Filipinos have *brought the antagonism upon themselves,* having a *peculiar propensity* to cross the color line.

Chairman of the California Athletic Commission announces a *ban on Filipino boxers in programs in the state.*

Friday, January 31, 1930

Governor C. C. Young intends to appoint a commission to investigate the riots.

In Los Angeles, lawyer and labor organizer Pablo Manlapit chairs a meeting of one thousand Filipinos, drafting a protest resolution to Governor C. C. Young to ask for an investigation of the riots and to bring vigilantes to justice.

Fermin wrote to me. I took his letters to Padre Zamora, who read them to me. I made him read them several times so I could memorize the words. They were not long letters, but they were always happy. If he suffered, he did not say. Instead he wrote about how he missed my cooking. I have a small garden with okra, tomato, eggplant. I went home and made his favorite pinakbet.

Harry Carr, columnist for the *Los Angeles Times* writes: *Mobbing Filipinos is becoming an entertaining form of popular amusement. The reason for this is that they are mostly scared little boys who can't fight back. It was a great mistake that the police of Watsonville did not deal adequately with the first mob who started this merry ruffianism. That would have ended it right there.*

Students at the University of the Philippines protest with signs: *We Protest Against the Watsonville Outrage! Can't the Flag to Which We Have Sworn Give Us Protection?*

United Press in Manila writes that *the California riots had done much toward increasing agitation for independence.*

Saturday, February 1, 1930

Fred Hart, Salinas farmer, states: *The Filipinos will not leave our white girls alone. . . . Frequently they intermarry.*

You asked about the Great Depression. When has life not been difficult? Poor people like me, we have to go to where the work is. With my sons, I dreamt of America.

Sunday, February 2, 1930

Poet José Corazón de Jesús makes an impassioned speech to take possession of the islands. *Americans were welcomed in the Philippines with open arms, but Filipinos are welcome in California with coffins.*

Dean of the University of Philippines School of Law Jorge Bocobo petitions for independence. *Would we be worthy of our sacred past and of any glorious future if we did not protest against humiliating events in America? . . . Despised as an inferior race and deprived of equal economic opportunities, how can we Filipinos accept our present status under the American flag?*

You said fifteen thousand people gathered in Luneta Park before the monument of our national hero José Rizal. Others said it was only one thousand who gathered at the University of the Philippines to

protest. This was a Day of National Humiliation to
mourn my son Fermin. You said people wore black
armbands and placed wreaths in his memory.

> While no California community programs
> are organized for the Day of Humiliation, Filipino
> dance halls are closed today.

Monday, Feb 3, 1930

> In Manila, ten thousand veterans of the Philippine
> Revolution meet and urge support of a resolution
> introduced by Senator William H. King of Utah to
> grant immediate independence to the Philippines.
> They also pass a resolution asking President Hoover
> to protect Filipinos in the US.

> Revolutionary leader Emilio Aguinaldo criticizes
> Manuel Quezon, president of the Philippine Senate,
> for leadership *more personal than national in interest*
> and suggests dissolution of the Democrata and
> Nacionalista political parties, to enable the Philippine
> people to represent a united front.

They held a funeral in Watsonville for Fermin at
Mehl's Mortuary. Did they dress him in a nice suit?
He would not have had money to buy a fancy suit or
even shoes. Perhaps his Filipino brothers shared their
clothes to make Fermin look respectable. At least they
should have washed his body of the blood, closed the
incisions on his chest.

> Sheriff N. P. Sinnott files with Judge Donald Younger
> misdemeanor charges for Theodore Splanger, Charles R.
> Morrison, and Raymond A. Smith, having shot through
> a cabin of Filipinos on Dethlefsen Ranch.

In San Francisco, Augustine Vallego, busboy,
is struck over the head by inebriated whites and sent
for emergency treatment.

Wednesday, February 5, 1930

The trial of the eight men arrested for rioting began
today, Judge D. W. Rohrback presiding, with District
Attorney Alfred E. Warth representing Monterey County
and A. Q. Lomba of Oakland representing the defense.

Four of the accused are common laborers; two are
painters; one is a high school student. Fred Majors
runs his father's trailer park. George Barnes is on
probation for a previous conviction. Edward Fry is
already suspected for burglary.

What did they say at the funeral? Who was the priest
who prayed and blessed my son? Who spoke about
Fermin and the young man he was? What did his
brother Claro say? What did he remember about his
brother? Why couldn't you tell me?

W. M. Schneiderman pens in the *Daily Worker: The
funeral of Tobera was turned into a priest-chanting
affair, led by a Filipino priest who had turned police
informer during the riots, and who was instrumental
in the arrest of Communists in the valley.*

Thursday, February 6, 1930

In San Francisco, the Filipino Emergency Association
is formed *to prevent participation by Filipinos in any
further California race rioting with whites.*

Gabriel Arellano of the Philippine Civic League of San
Francisco states: *The people making the attacks don't
represent the American people, but the hoodlum class.
We put our faith in the better class of American people.*

Apolinar Velasco, Philippine official investigating
the riots, states that events were provoked by
migratory laborers *who don't represent the best type
of American citizen. Not only the American Legion,
but the good citizens of Watsonville . . . are doing
everything possible to protect Filipinos.*

The crowd in support of the eight vigilante defendants
is so disruptive that Judge D. W. Rohrback halts the
proceedings to be continued at a later date.

When asked, Claro declared that no one was
authorized to seek contributions to pay to sue for
Fermin's death. We are simple folks with small means.
How could we seek justice?

Friday, February 7, 1930

José Roldan and José Tintanuavo testify that
Raymond Smith held them at gunpoint while George
Sias and Ted Spangler searched their pockets.
However, Constable Cano testifies that, on arrival, he
did not find any weapons.

Charles Morrison, witness for the defense, testifies
that the boys went to the ranch to save Filipinos.

A. Q. Lomba, attorney for the defense, raises a motion
to dismiss case; Judge Rohrback denies the motion.

How would we pay to bring Fermin's body home? He
was already in debt for the trip to America.

In Portland, Oregon, Vincent Catoda is assaulted and
beaten, left bloody and unconscious on the sidewalk,
by a gang of eight whites.

Saturday, February 8, 1930

Twenty-five percent of all the lettuce, "green gold,"
shipped from California comes from Watsonville.
Filipino labor is essential to this production.

Local farmers respond to the riots: *What makes us
sore is the fact that the principal ringleaders in those
mobs were youths whom any able-bodied policeman
could have handled with a stout rattan rod.*

*We lettuce growers have thousands of dollars
invested in that industry. We pay heavy taxes on
the same. Why should we be advised to stand by
our property and shoot—shoot to kill—as mobs of
our own people were coming out to set fire to, and
burn down our property?*

Maybe Fermin gambled. How should I know?
Gambled what he didn't send home. If he lost, he lost.
If he made a little more, he could eat or dress better.

San Francisco municipal court judge George Steiger
describes the typical Filipino who walks *our streets
clad in the extreme loud pearl-buttoned suits,
wearing spats, light hats, brightly colored ties, who
follow our high school girls . . .*

Monday, February 10, 1930

Judge Rohrback moves the case to the Superior Court
in Salinas as a fair trial in Watsonville is unlikely. He
places a $1,000 bail on each defendant.

I heard you say that we Filipinos and Americans live
under the same flag. What did you mean by that?

Wednesday, February 12, 1930

Dr. H. G. Marquez, president of the Filipino
Emergency Association, petitions Mayor of
Watsonville C. H. Baker and District Attorney
Alfred E. Warth for *executive leniency on the eight
American youth accused for the murder of the late
Fermin Tovera. The Filipino Emergency Association,
in the name of Filipinos in San Francisco and the
surrounding cities, hopes that you would transmit to
your people our message of goodwill.*

My son Fermin was a smart boy. He taught himself to
read and write. He should have gone to school, but that
life was not possible for us.

Thursday, February 13, 1930

In Stockton, Filipino Felisberto Suarez Tapia marries
a Japanese girl Alice Chiyoko Saiki; since her father
has intervened to separate them, Japanese and
Filipino are boycotting each other.

I dreamt about Fermin last night. He came to me and
held my hand. I saw the sadness in his dark eyes. I
wept and could not speak.

Saturday, February 15, 1930

> Congressman Adolf Joaquim Sabath of Illinois
> introduces a measure to grant $5,000 to the heirs
> of Fermin Tobera and to observe the Jones Act or
> Philippine Autonomy Act of 1916.

You said Fermin's body was placed in a coffin and put on
train from Watsonville. His body traveled north up the
Pacific coast, passing all the farms where he had picked
apples, plums, peaches, and grapes, cut asparagus and
lettuce. Finally, he crossed the border of Canada to the
port city of Vancouver. There they transferred him to
the cargo section of a great ocean liner, the *Empress of
Canada*. He began his journey home.

Sunday, February 16, 1930

I appealed to the government of my country, if it had
any power at all, to demand that the murderers of my
son be made to pay damages; for, because of them, I,
a poor woman, was deprived of the help of my son.

Monday, February 17, 1930

> In the Superior Court in Salinas, before Judge
> Jorgensen, six of the eight accused plead guilty:
> Ramon Davis, Edward Fry, Charles Morrison,
> George Sias, Raymond Smith, and Ted Spangler. Two
> others plead not guilty, requesting a jury trial: Fred
> Majors and George Barnes. All are identified as part
> of the mob at Andrew Storm Ranch.

On the *Empress of Canada*, Fermin was not the only
Filipino. There was the newspaper editor, David P. de
Tagle, and my other son Claro, and there must have
been Filipino busboys and cooks and mariners. And you

said there was one Filipino couple, Mr. and Mrs. Isidro
Paradas. Their names were inscribed in the passenger
list, traveling second class. Who were they? Perhaps
newly married, meeting in America as pensionados. Or
perhaps a middle-aged couple on tour. Did they know
that Fermin's body lay in the hold beneath them?

Friday, February 21, 1930

Empress of Canada
Cold Luncheon on Deck
Herrings in Tomato * Chilled Consommé
Halibut Mayonnaise * Prague Ham * Roast Lamb,
Mint Sauce * Galantine of Chicken
Salads: Endive * Spiced Beetroots * Potato *
Kohl Slaw * Tarragon French Dressing
Raisin Pie * Fruit Salad * Vanilla Ice Cream
Cheese: Canadian * Craft * Biscuits
Ice Tea * Ice Coffee

After ten days, Fermin's body arrived with the *Empress
of Canada* as it docked in Honolulu. On this day, you
said that Filipinos in Hawaii met to honor his death.

Tuesday, February 25, 1930

Judge H. G. Jorgensen sentences eight accused to serve
two years in the state penitentiary at San Quentin.
However, probation is granted to four. Four others are
sent to county jail for thirty days, then put on probation
for two years, *during which time they must keep away
from pool halls, abstain from intoxicating liquors . . .
must never molest Filipinos, and on the other hand, they
are to lead sober, industrious lives.*

At the inquest over Fermin's body, they decided that
the person who fired the fatal shot was unknown. But

who put the .35 bullet in the gun that shot my son in
his heart? Who pulled the trigger? The person who
did that knew and kept that secret lodged in his heart
for the rest of his life.

In Los Angeles, Superior Judge J. A. Smith rules that
marriage between whites and Filipinos is unlawful
in California, denying Ruby Robinson, 22, and
Tony Moreno, 24, a marriage license.

Saturday, March 1, 1930

The commander of the *Empress of Canada* is Samuel
Robinson, decorated Most Excellent Order of the
British Empire and Officer of the Royal Navy Reserve.
Commander Robinson, as captain of the *Empress of
Australia*, is known to have aided in the evacuation of
Tokyo during the 1923 Great Kanto Earthquake.

The *Empress of Canada* docked in Yokohama. Here,
too, an obituary meeting was held in Fermin's honor.
Even General Artemio Ricarte, living in exile in Japan,
came to receive and honor my son's remains. At every
place the ship docked, Filipinos lived and worked.
You said that cherry blossoms in Tokyo were almost
awakening, a sign that greeted the return of my son.

Sunday, March 2, 1930

The *Empress of Canada* is equipped to carry 453
persons in first class, 94 persons in tourist class,
and 934 in third class. First-class fares between
Vancouver and Manila are between $420 and $1,424
per person, depending on the cabin.

The *Empress of Canada* docked in Kobe. What did it
cost to transport Fermin's body?

Wednesday, March 5, 1930

In Manila, six thousand high school students strike to
protest derogatory comments made by an American
teacher. The strike closes all four of Manila's high
schools and the Philippine School of Commerce for
the rest of the school year.

Fermin's body arrived in Shanghai. This was his
nineteenth day at sea. You said there was a cool
breeze. The sea was calm.

Saturday, March 8, 1930

William Howard Taft, twenty-seventh president
of the United States and former civilian governor
of the Philippines, dies.

Fermin's body arrived in Hong Kong. This was his
twenty-second day at sea. Every day at sea, in my
mind, I rocked with Fermin in his coffin. I held his
head and sang songs to bring him home to me.

Tuesday, March 11, 1930

Hermenegildo Cruz, Philippine labor commissioner,
enacts a new order to permit enlistment of Filipino labor
for Hawaii sugar plantations. In signing the recruiting
license for the Hawaii Sugar Planters Association, he
suggests they offer a bonus to laborers to prevent them
from moving on to California.

Now I wondered, if Fermin had lived, would he have
returned to me? I saw his brother Claro in another
dream, dressed in the uniform of the US Army. I did
not know the meaning of this dream, but I saw my
other son disappear into war.

Wednesday, March 12, 1930

After twenty-six days at sea and 8,477 miles, Fermin's
body arrived in Manila. You told me that they carried his
coffin down the ramp from the *Empress of Canada* and
onto the pier where he lay in state. Students from Ilocos
Sur and members of labor unions stood on guard around
his coffin. For two days, thousands of people lined up and
passed by his body in solemnity to honor him.

On the dock at Pier 7, David de Tagle delivers the death
certificate in the name of the Filipino Association in
California to Representative Francisco Varona.

Representative Varona declares that *Tobera's return
to his native land to find his resting place shows
the world that he has a country and a people.* He
also states that the student strike provoked by *the
insulting remarks* of an American teacher, Miss
Brummitt, is connected to the *abuses and insults*
endured by California Filipinos.

There were speeches and a band to play a dirge. Then
there was a parade to escort his body in a funeral
procession, as if he were a revolutionary war hero. I
was grateful for their ceremony, but if only he could
have come home alive.

The casket is lifted and placed in the cortege and
escorted to the Funeraria Quiogue on Rizal Avenue,
where two hours later, labor leader Isabelo Tejada of the
Congreso Obrero de Filipinas advises his fellowmen *not
to leave the country since there are many opportunities
in their own,* and Joaquin Balmori declares that Tobera
*did not go to the United States to dance and gamble but
to earn money for an honest livelihood.*

Eugene A. Gilmore announces his resignation as Vice Governor General of the Philippines, causing political agitation for a Filipino governor. In Washington, DC, Representative Manuel Roxas confers with President Hoover and urges him to appoint Senator Sergio Osmeña.

Four months later in July, Carlos Bulosan arrives in Seattle at the age of seventeen.

Thursday, March 13, 1930

On the front page of the *Philippines Herald* is a photograph of labor leaders carrying Fermin Tobera's casket. Among them are Councillor Herrera, Director Cruz, Mr. Bayani, Representative Confessor, Councillor Yuseco, R. Cristobal, and others.

Monday, March 24, 1930

Today, four years later in 1934, the Tydings-McDuffie Act, officially the Philippine Commonwealth and Independence Act, is signed by President Franklin D. Roosevelt, providing for Philippine independence to take effect on July 4, 1946.

Tuesday, March 25, 1930

In Manila, Tomás Confesor, representative of the Philippine Legislature, says the bullet that killed Fermin Tobera *was not aimed at him particularly; its principal target was the heart of our race.*

You said my son Fermin had become a martyr.

Santa Cruz Chinatown

Walking Tour: Start near the pond with water lilies in San Lorenzo Park off Dakota Street. Walk over the San Lorenzo River by way of the Chinatown walking bridge. Cross River Street, and walk down China Lane, stopping just behind Mobo Sushi. Find the commemoration plaque for old Chinatown. Continue walking toward Front Street, turning toward the clock tower on Water. Near the clock tower, find the Mission steps and walk up. From the top of the steps, walk down School Street past the old Santa Cruz Mission, crossing the plaza, down High Street, and over the highway overpass. Make a right after the overpass and walk on the bike path along Cabrillo Highway until you reach Evergreen Cemetery. Find the Chinese arch.

> *"Forget it, Jake. It's Chinatown."*
> CHINATOWN BY ROBERT TOWNE

Chinatowns have bad reputations. Poor people. Illegal folks. Gambling dens. Opium. Prostitutes. Secret societies. Underground tunnels with trap doors. Kung fu killers. Some of this is true because *why not?* It makes good storytelling. And it's part of true history: the coolie trade, Chinese Exclusion Act, Great San Francisco Earthquake, paper names, Boxer Rebellion. But I'm not here to repeat history. Just saying that Chinatowns are microcosmic worlds justified by the past. Outsiders visit like tourists, pretend no one can see them eating cheap chop suey while partaking in so-called illicit activities. They go there to hide. So when they say there were gambling houses in Chinatown or that a Chinese pimp named Den Kee or a white lady named Madame Pauline once ran brothels down the street, all frequented mostly by white men—the common and the prominent—it's probably true as well. But when I was a kid growing up, scooting on a bicycle past old clap-board houses over dirt roads, free to hide in the tules to fish in the San Lorenzo, there behind my ma's vegetable garden of mustard greens and winter melon, and to hang out on creaky wooden porches with old Chinamen who made sure I had a piece of candy, or let me lick out of an open can of sweetened condensed milk, or showed me how to set off firecrackers in the street, what did I care about the place's reputation? I was at home in the present. Now I know what the old Chinamen knew. I was the future. They were the past.

One day I saved up to get myself a camera, and after that I was never without it. It was an old used German Rolleicord, with a flip-up top and window you peered into from above. I learned how to adjust the apertures, develop film, print my own work. I used to get copies of *US Camera* and study everything in it, wearing out the pages. That's where I saw photos by Edward Steichen, Walker Evans, Dorothea Lange, and Arnold Genthe. It was Genthe's photos of San Francisco Chinatown that got to me. I could do that, and, to be honest, I could do it better. I walked from my Chinatown to school to my job at the camera shop, back to home on China Lane, and saw my world framed and focused through the Rolleicord. I spent every spare moment hanging around the Chee Kong Tong, what outsiders called the joss temple. It was where the old bachelors conspired for the Chinese nation, got loans and charity, celebrated, prayed, lived, and died. It was an all-purpose benevolent association. At the end of a long life setting rail ties, doing laundry, cooking, pick-ing plums, fishing sardines, drying seaweed, abalone, and squid, they hung their hats at the Tong house. They had no families except each other and us. I followed them around, watching them gamble, make tofu, dry fish, dig gardens, kill chick-ens, smoke cigars, putter about, talk shit, and lose their memories. When they died off, one by one, they got buried at Evergreen. Who would have thought? Now, the only thing we got left of them are my photos: Lee Lam Bok, Ah Fook, Yee Hen Bok, Mook Lai Bok, Moon Lai Bok, Ah Chin Bok.

They had a party for Ah Chin Bok when he turned ninety. Of course, no one knew his real birth date. Ah Chin probably made it up, something auspicious. I did the calculations, and it was possible. He said he came with his dad just before the Civil War. His dad was recruited to cook for the army, and he went along as the water boy. What army? we asked. The Yanks! He got insulted, but that's why we asked every time. Who do you think? By the end of the war, he was wearing the blue uniform and carrying a rifle. How old was he? Fifteen? His dad was killed in the crossfire. Buried him at Gettysburg. I was there, he said, when President

Lincoln gave his four-score speech. Even in his old age, his eyes filled with tears. We freed the slaves. Ah Chin shook his head. He was not a black man nor a slave, but he knew irony. Even though he fought for the Union, they never made him a citizen. What did Ah Chin do from after the Civil War up to his birthday at ninety? It was a long seventy-five-year trek from Gettysburg to California, but it always began with the Civil War. Dynamiting tunnels for the railroad, cooking out of covered wagons, panning for gold, cattle driving, working the harvest south to north. All that labor with nothing to show for it but the memory. One day he settled into the Tong house. Enough. We toasted Ah Chin again and again, and when he was drunk enough, he would sing: *Mine eyes have seen the glory of the coming of the Lord. His truth is marching on! Glory! Glory! Hallelujah! As He died to make men holy, let us die to make men free! His truth is marching on!*

When Ah Chin died, the Tong put up money for his funeral. Used to be they got two horse-driven wagons, but by Ah Chin's time, they got two open trucks. First truck was filled with his leftover clothing and food, fruit like oranges and bananas, and cakes and chicken. They put together a band and played from the truck, you guessed it, the "Battle Hymn of the Republic." In the second truck was Ah Chin in his coffin. We followed the trucks through town, winding around past the places Ah Chin knew, giving him a last look. At Evergreen, they burned his effects in the stove up there. He didn't have much, but burning it meant it went with him, plus paper money for the road home. Then they finished roasting the chicken in the oven. The town kids and the hobos all followed our processions but waited at the cemetery gate, like they were being proper mourners at a distance. The crisp burnt barbecue smell of chicken skin wafting over the graves must have reached their noses. The offerings were placed around the grave with prayers and incense. Then the procession marched away, past the poor kids and hobos, who removed their hats and bowed, waiting patiently for the last Chinese to disappear down the hill. I don't know what they thought, thought Chinese were dumb, leaving all that food, baskets of fruit and that roasted chicken there for the ghosts, but it was Ah Chin's spirit that would be fed because they were fed.

Finally, the war came for us too. I got into the navy and took photos for the military. I got to travel, take more photos, and then it was time to come home, finish school, and do what I always wanted to do: marry my girlfriend, start a photography business, and make a life of it. In 1955, Steichen published the photographic book, *The Family of Man*. One day, I was going to be one of those photographers. But that was the same year that the rain fell like crazy and torrential waters rose from the San Lorenzo. I slogged home from work, my camera slung around my neck. I thought I could document the storm. It was Christmas, but when I saw a tree with its glass ball trimmings floating through the streets, that's when I started to run, camera thumping hard with my heart against my chest. Just beyond my house, I could see an old Chevy trundling like a big boat through the backyard, busting the wall of the chicken coop. The chickens who could escape were squawking on the roof when the whole thing just floated away. I saw a wall of water with great chunks of Ma's garden rising over China Lane, and there was Ma wading with the grandkids, little George in her arms, and clutching Linda behind, her dress afloat like a yellow lotus. I grabbed Linda, and we struggled for higher ground. That was the end of my Chinatown. The end of China Lane, the gambling and boarding houses, and the Chee Kong Tong joss temple. Since my people arrived for the Gold Rush as early as 1849, there had been many renditions of China Camps and Chinatowns, all finally destroyed by fire and flood. Stubbornly, folks got back on their feet, went to work again— cooking, washing, fishing, harvesting, building. But even if we did the work, no one really wanted the heathen Chinese. Superstitious Chinese say the number four is unlucky, means death. Maybe the fourth rendition of Chinatown was anyway doomed. So my home drowned and disappeared forever. If you look for traces, the watermarks might still be there.

∞　∞　∞

My daughter was born just as Chairman Mao was dying, September 9, 1976. Depending on your point of view, to make such a claim can be subversive or, well, I don't know. For me personally, something ended and began. The others before her all died, failed. How many were there? I lost count. She was the first and only who survived, but I was sure when she opened her eyes and we first met that I would not let them take her from me. I examined her tiny palm; he would have hidden the truth there. I studied the tiny lines in her delicate hands, memorizing every trace, not knowing how to read her mystery, but I knew I would find a way to her freedom and to her future.

How we left and where we went is complicated. Perhaps we crossed the border into the Soviet Union or into Hong Kong or into North Korea or Japan. At those crucial crossings, he was still there with us, worried himself about the transition that must inevitably occur and unsure about which side would prevail in power. His credentials were impeccable. When things cooled over, he was sure that his expertise, his science would be required, or, if necessary, that he could sell his knowledge to the enemy. She was his ticket. As long as my breasts were full and she was fed and content, he was pleased. Therefore, in those days, he made sure I was well nourished. Perhaps that is why I nursed her for so many years, even after she and I made ourselves disappear. One night, we left him in a stupor, crept away, and ran and ran.

We moved from Chinatown to Chinatown across the earth. You would be surprised to know how many Chinatowns exist. Even if there is no Chinatown, there is always a Chinese restaurant. In every country in the world, Chinese live. It was like Chinese closed their eyes, spun the globe, and stopped it with their index finger pointing somewhere, and that's where they settled. There we hid pretending to be like every other Chinese. Chinese, of course, are not all the same, but the pretense was useful. I made a life for us in any way possible, cleaning houses, washing dishes, collecting trash, but eventually, I found that I could sketch portraits or paint famous landmarks and sell them to tourists. The Eiffel Tower. Ponte di Rialto. Pão de Açúcar. Big Ben. Taj Mahal. Statue of Liberty. Pyramids of Giza. I pretended modestly that my talent was recently acquired, that I had not dedicated years of study to create the social realist posters to promote the cultural revolution, Chairman Mao at the radiant center surrounded by the farmers and industrial workers and the People's Liberation Army. We moved from place to place. If I sensed that we had become in any way comfortable, it was time to leave. He was never far away. My daughter came to understand this feeling, an anxious tugging of the heart, a whiff of something in the air, and her look also said that it was time.

But finally, I landed a good job in San Francisco in advertising, and after so many years of fleeing what had become his shadow, tentatively, we tried to stay. Even so, we never remained in any apartment or house very long; we had become used to our discomforts. Language and learning came easily to her. But of course. She had his scientific mind, the one he had crafted with cunning. What of me did she possess? I remember sleepless nights staring at her, wondering, feeling her again moving inside me. Would there be nothing in her of me? She was beautiful. I was plain. She was brilliant. I was trained. How many times had I examined the palm of her hand? It had not changed but become more defined. She moved through school quickly, almost as if she knew we could not afford to lose any time. She finished high school and college with honors in anthropology and genetic biology. This worried me, but I said nothing to dissuade her. Then she chose the field of forensic anthropology.

One day, she came home with a worried face. Despite her intuitive know-ing about our constant wandering to hide, I sensed a difference in her concern and feared her questions as always. Our lives, I had tried to pretend, were part of an adventure that others would never know. She had volunteered to work the midnight shift at the university laboratory, and, always anxious for her safety, I remained awake, waiting for her return at dawn. Ma, she said, always seeing me arise from the sofa, the television a snowy buzz, why haven't you gone to bed? This time, she sat next to me and leaned her head into my shoulder. How are the speci-men? I asked innocently. I knew her dedication, that the tests had to be conducted around the clock, and she was the only student who agreed to come at that hour. She answered, I spoke to the janitor, Mr. Nelson, tonight. He always comes in late to clean. He said he noticed my devotion to this work, that he did not meet many students like me. I nodded sleepily, but she continued. Ma, he wanted to warn me. I sat up awake, suddenly afraid. Warn? Yes, he said that he worried that science might take away my soul. He said that Dr. Q had approached him one day to ask if he would offer his daughter to participate in her experiment. His daughter, Ma, is mentally disabled. Tears filled my daughter's eyes. I took her hands in my own, and as I had done time and time again, I traced her lines softly with my fingertips. It had become our way of consoling each other. She did not go back to the lab. I knew then that, even if we were separated forever, he had failed.

∞   ∞   ∞

I first saw her at the restaurant. She was with a group of professors who usu-ally came to dine there. These professors, as usual, joked casually with me, as if Chinese restaurants should of course have Chinese waitresses, even if the owners were white and the cooks in the back were all Mexican. I learned it was just a game we played, but maybe it made the food taste authentic. Later I discovered that they were testing her with their questions, trying to demonstrate a friendly scru-tiny, showing her that there was Chinese food, Sichuan Chinese to be exact, in our not-so-provincial town, that the chili dumplings were exquisite. She laughed with them. Took sips of wine and said smart things. By dessert, they were very satis-fied, very impressed. But I must have been a great distraction and almost thwarted her chances for the position for which she was vying. I knew she knew that I, this waitress who came to host the table, felt her shock of recognition. I might have dropped my tray, trembling, a great blushing wave searing my face and neck. If we were not twins, what could we be? I watched her leave, her eyes fixed away while her forced composure cast anxiety in her wake. Not one of the professors seemed to have noticed anything awry. It's a cliché of course to say that we all look alike. It would be a long while before I saw her again.

I knew later that she was given a position in the department of anthropology, and very soon after she became involved in a local project at the Evergreen Cemetery behind the Harvey West Ballpark and the Portuguese Hall. The cemetery was exhuming the bones of the old Chinese buried there. It was a forty-by-eighty-foot plot against the hill, the stones worn and fallen, the Chinese characters now unreadable. But perhaps she could read the bones after all these years. That was her job. I knew she loved this work. Later, she told me that it might be possible to understand diseases in the past by examining and taking samples from the old bones. She could learn about their labor, what they ate, how they aged. I understood that stories were in those bones.

One day, she came to the restaurant alone. We sat at a table and stared at each other over tea. She admitted that she had been afraid to return. We compared stories. We were both born in Canton, but I had been adopted by a Kuomintang family who fled to Taiwan. Our birthdates were different. I was older by two years. Adopted? Do you think? She pondered. There is only one person who can answer that. Can you come with me to San Francisco?

She chose to drive up Highway 1 along the coast, starting early to enjoy the scenic ride but also to take our time, stopping in Pescadero for lunch or parking at the lighthouse to look out for whales moving south in herds. We were tentative in our conversation, trying out one story or another. She was not married, had no boyfriend. I had one daughter who lived with her grandparents in Taipei. My daughter's father had left for Macao, and we never saw him again. I sent money to my daughter every month. I had not seen her in three years. The twists and turns, however, of her life with her mother, always moving, left me dizzy. I could not imagine such a road. My life had not been easy, but much simpler by comparison. I feel, she said, that I am always being followed. She looked at me significantly. Maybe you will help me change that.

In San Francisco, I walked with her into the large rooms with high ceilings of an industrial warehouse remodeled into an art gallery. On the walls were hung enormous paintings, portraits of Chinese families posed before world-famous tourist spots. I perused the catalog titled *Intellectual Property*. The style remembered the Chinese posters I knew as a child, propaganda of the People's Republic, but surreally reenvisioned, happy camera faces slightly grotesque, weary. I moved from painting to painting and felt an uncanny twinge, feeling the eyes of a center personage always following the viewer. Waiters came with trays of canapés and thin glasses of champagne, tiny bubbles festive and sparkling. Fancy people moved languidly with their glasses, making eye contact and smart comments.

She had left me to find her mother, the artist of these paintings. I turned to see her leading an elegant woman, hair coifed perfectly, dressed in blue silk and pearls. As she approached, her face drained of color, consumed in panic. Her glass crashed, and she crumpled to her knees. I dropped to catch her, and she stared into my face in horror. No, she cried. He promised. He lied. The crowd spread around us, and we picked her mother up. Ma, she asked. Are we twins? No, she cried. Sisters? Yes. No, no, no. She pleaded, Ma I thought you'd be happy. A good surprise. I found her. No, no, no. She grabbed me, pulling at my hands and staring into my open palms. Her fingers traced the lines as if scripted characters. She seemed to understand something there, nodded, then curled my fingers into a fist, and grasping that fist, pulled it to her heart. Words rasping, tears washed her powdered face. Girls, he told me, disposable. Experiments. She commanded me. You must not let him. The eyes in the paintings followed us around and around.

At that moment, I saw a Chinese man walk through the crowd toward us. I recognized his face, the same face staring from the paintings. He raised his gun. Three shots. The third shot missed me, and I ran after him, down the dark and empty industrial streets. I realized that I could run, and run fast, overtake him easily. I was surprised. I knew I was strong, but not that strong. I knew I was fast, but not that fast. He stared in a kind of amazed terror at me. I opened my fist to show him my bare palm, and he, too, read its character. He asked in Mandarin: Have you ever been sick? My shock must have revealed the answer. My adopted mother was so proud of my perfect health. Not even a cold or sniffle, ever. He continued: Do you have children? What happened next was intuitive, the prophecy embedded in the palm of my hand. I cracked his neck and heard it lose its breath. I put his body in her car and returned down the coast.

The excavations of the Chinese plot at Evergreen and her reading of the bones were still in process. It was a deep forty-by-eighty-foot archaeological dig, cordoned by yellow tape, but when it was known that she had died tragically, they quickly replaced the bones, finishing the foundations for the memorial arch and commemorative stones for Lee Lam, Chong Lee, Chin Lai, Lou Sing, and "all those Chinese buried at Evergreen and in unmarked graves throughout Santa Cruz County."

Indian Summer

On 9/11, I flew out of JFK on a 6:00 am flight headed for SFO, ignorant of danger and spared the consequences of the disaster in my wake. Though later preoccupied for months by my narrow escape and devastated by any news of friends and old acquaintances, I had long resolved to leave New York for a new start in the central coastal town of Santa Cruz on the northern peninsula of the Monterey Bay. Upon arrival, I turned selfishly to unpacking and situating myself in a comfortably clean and furnished rental, bathed in warm dry winds and swirling heat, hot days interspersed with cool, the fall season intervening in fits and starts. We call these days Indian summer, supposing that the Indians had long ago marked our calendar with their climate wisdom. By contrast, having just traveled in Europe from August to September, I was surprised to note, while in Fiesole, the autumn coolness trade away the summer heat, as if on schedule, from August 31 to September 1, which made me think that the parsing of seasons is a European expectation of time passing.

I had been offered a lectureship in art history on the subject of American architecture and the Arts and Crafts movement. My particular focus was the design of Frank Lloyd Wright and the architects of his Taliesin Fellowship, and the turn toward and uses of a Japanese aesthetic. On arrival in California, I thought I knew little of this coastal town, but this assumption of ignorance was eventually reversed. My previous forays to California had been brief and directed: for example, a tour of works by Julia Morgan including Hearst Castle in San Simeon, Asilomar in Pacific Grove, and various YWCA centers and gracious homes in San Francisco and on the East Bay—Oakland and Berkeley. While quaint Victorians, trolleys running beneath bay windows of pastel painted ladies, were charming, I focused on the modern—the use of concrete and natural stone, exposed beams of giant redwood and extended garden landscapes; seaside cypress, crooked and windswept, reaching beyond glass open to natural light, wavering through sunset and fog. I was thus pleased to discover in Santa Cruz examples of the architecture of Aaron G. Green, protégé of Frank Lloyd Wright. Aaron Green had in the 1950s established himself independently in San Francisco and was the West Coast representative of Wright himself. I happened upon a building by Green somewhat by accident, a combination of fortune and misfortune, fortunate for my research and misfortunate in view of my health.

Soon after arriving in Santa Cruz I was plagued by dizzy spells, and while walking to class across the wooden bridges spanning long gullies that cut through the redwood campus, I experienced a curious sense of vertigo. I would stumble into my lectures, grip the podium for several moments to regain my balance, trying with difficulty to assure myself and any students who bothered to notice my distress that I had control of the situation. I learned that if I directed my concerns quickly to technology, in those years the use of a Kodak carousel projector, I would soon forget my dis-ease and turn to the subject of my lecture that day, whether interior design and Craftsman furniture or perhaps the use of water as natural falls, pools, and flowing sound. So it was: I sought medical advice and was directed to a laboratory for a series of blood tests. The laboratory was located in a medical plaza of low-roofed structures. As I walked into the waiting room, I immediately recognized the architectural style, the latticed windows just above waiting-room seats—built-in couches facing a brick fireplace. While the narrow windows stained amber afforded very low light, light tumbled into the waiting room through a central Japanese garden atrium enclosed in glass. Such a waiting room for a medical laboratory seemed entirely out of character, but it was, as I knew, the architectural design of Aaron Green influenced by Frank Lloyd Wright, and built in 1964. I would come to frequent this waiting room numerous times and would note over the years subtle changes that remade and distorted the original intensions of design and aesthetic, but these were changes of time and age and inevitable forgetting.

You walk around the architectural model placed at the center of the large conference table and smile. You note the location of your future office with the insertion of a Japanese garden atrium. From above, you can see an open square in the low roof encasing a miniature maple, stones, and a pond embedded in moss. At the plaza center, a pharmacy is placed strategically in a pagoda, buildings graced with low eaves and convenient circling parking. You've driven up to San Francisco with your colleagues in your maroon Rolls-Royce, enjoying the day and the pleasant ride along the coast up Highway 1. You exude a sweet confidence, your dress casual however smart, a red-and-gold silk scarf tied jauntily around your neck— your signature stylishness. Perhaps you, your doctor colleagues, the builder contractor, and the architect will dine in nearby Chinatown. You order for the group: Chinese chicken salad, roast duck, pork tofu, gai lan, bowls of steamed rice, beer for your companions, tea for you. Red lacquer and circling dragons swirl through the dining hall. You see yourself reflected infinitely in the surrounding mirrors, seated next to the architect as you discreetly suggest that you may be acquiring a mountainside acreage; would he be interested in visiting the site?

Initially I was put off by the laboratory phlebotomist in charge, a commanding woman who seemed to bark out orders from the desk ensconced behind a half-door that served as a check-in station. *Insurance card? Medicare? No doctor's orders; who is your doctor? Are you fasting? Drink some water before you leave. What, no urine sample? Can't pee today? Take this home, and bring me back some pee.* Passing through the half-door, I realized she was a one-phlebotomist show—intake, paperwork, and phlebotomy all in one draw. That she managed this operation with efficiency and accuracy was a tribute to the job. She could slap my arm, tighten the rubber strap above the elbow, locate the vein, stick in the needle, and suck out my blood into five tubes in a matter of minutes. And despite all this, she remembered all her victims by name and likely our blood types and disorders, and when in her infrequent absences, I truly missed her, those replacing her would commiserate with me. *Ah yes, the general is on vacation.*

Yet despite the general's efficiency, I found myself on that first day sitting for perhaps forty-five minutes in the waiting room with a pile of student papers, which I intended to grade in spare moments. Losing interest in student responses, I drew out the parameters of the space. The fireplace had ceased use, a potted plant in its altar, dark traces of smoke and ashes clearly smearing the brick within and above. The cubby designed to hold firewood was empty. I walked to the tall slabs of glass panes that served as the transparent wall to the garden and peered in. There was a pond with a small fall of flowing water and goldfish surrounded by grass and moss and flowering azaleas. A small maple shaded the area. And to one side was a bronze plaque set over a cement block imprinted with five names. Presumably the garden was a memorial to these names. Studying these names, I felt an uncanny awakening, a sudden sense of familiarity. I returned to my seat, pressing a nervous palm into a slippery stack of papers, and waited for the general to bark out my name.

You hike up an uneven path, the architect behind you. You point out trees and markers that designate the perimeters of the ten-acre hillside you've recently purchased. At some point in your trek, you turn around and look out toward the town below and the bay beyond. The view is spectacular that day, sunlight glinting off blue waves, the outline of the bay sweeping with lush clarity across the horizon. The architect nods with sympathetic pleasure, notes the southern-facing direction, and agrees that this is the perfect open vista; no trees need to be cut or removed from this clearing. You will require a survey and structural engineering evaluations, but the architect imagines that retaining walls and foundation pylons to secure the structure to bedrock will pose no problems. The architect understands your intentions to create a home in concert with the living site, low to the ground and unobtrusive, bringing the natural outside into the gracious space of the home. You trade thoughts about your admiration for Frank Lloyd Wright. While living near Chicago, you'd admired examples of Wright's homes; you admit your fascination for his architecture, bicycling through Oak Park and viewing the houses from the street, one by one. But you were a medical student and an intern in those days, and practical matters set you on a course away from your artistic pursuits. Your hobby has been furniture, following a Craftsman aesthetic. Included in the plans, you'd like a carpenter's studio separate from the house, a place to which you can retreat. You and the architect trade thoughts about the work of Isamu Noguchi and George Nakashima, but you demure, of course; yours is a hobby, something to pass the time away from your busy practice, your boisterous family.

I jumped to the general's command, passed into the general's quarters, and sat obediently at my designated seat. She peered, skewering her head toward my hanging face, staring into my eyes, and surprised me with her sharp query: *Are you going to faint on me?* I shook my head and woke to attention. I could not succumb to a dizzy spell at that moment if I were to discover the source of my malady. I thought that she must first draw my blood, and then I could faint. *Look that way,* she ordered and pointed away from her needle, rubber hose, and tubes. I was offended; I had no problem with the sight of blood. I purposely showed my strength and determination in this matter and caught her every movement with a purposeful fascination.

I watched my blood siphon away into the general's rubber hose, filling glass vials, one by one. By the last bloody vial, I knew the source of my discomforting remembering. The face of the young woman rose in my vision, someone I had not thought of in more than twenty years.

Over time, you and the architect form a close relationship. He wants to see your furniture design ideas, incorporate them into the interior, and you've read about Frank Lloyd Wright's Taliesin Fellowship, prompting the architect to talk about his tutelage with the great master. The architect studied with Wright during the prewar years, became a conscientious objector contending that his work with Wright was an important effort for democracy. He explains his keen enthusiasm for Wright's philosophy of organic architecture, an architecture tied to natural space and the education of the individual. He spreads his initial draft plans over your dining table. Architecture with Wright was a calling, but when the war really began in 1941, the architect volunteered for the Air Corps. You bond over the Air Corps; both you and your brother volunteered to fly as well; your brother was a paratrooper in the war. You say your brother survived, came home, got his degree, then got back into training, but died only a year later, a jet pilot over Bavaria in '51. You guess the war isn't ever over. Democracy is a hard mistress. Your last stint was in Dayton, Ohio, at Wright-Patterson, in ophthalmology. When that was over, you piled the family, the wife and four kids and three cats, and some of your furniture into a Volkswagen van and drove across country to Santa Cruz. Camped out for a while at your sister's place, then started your practice. Despite everything— the war, prejudice—you believe that America has done right by its people, given you the opportunities your parents dreamed for. You peruse the ground plans surrounding the house—landscaping, swimming pool, garden with a pond and small fall. The architect asks if you know of any Japanese landscaper or gardener friend with whom you'd like to work.

I remembered her exquisite beauty, perfect Eurasian features. It was 1976, the year I began my graduate studies in architecture at Columbia. I was in the elevator scaling the Solomon R. Guggenheim Museum to the top. Through the faces and bodies in that rising box, I spied her in the corner, shy but with a certain nonchalance and happy innocence. I followed her through the elevator doors and wandered after her at a careful distance. I lost track of time and purpose and spent an entire and long afternoon in the museum as if smitten. I had originally intended to view a particular Léger and perhaps a matching Picasso, carefully attempt to memorize the structural design of the building itself, and then to rush off to my afternoon class. Instead I wandered and lingered in rooms, leaned from various viewpoints to view the hanging Calder—a cloud platter of red blood cells turning silently, ponderously—and followed her slow snail descent to the bottom. She wore the jeans of the day, bell-bottoms over boots, covered by a heavy oversized pink Irish fisherman's sweater, hand-knitted I assumed. On her head she wore a worn brown leather cap, which at some point she pulled away. I remember gasping at the glorious motion of her thick hair falling in graceful rivers across her face and shoulders. I was at the time studying architecture at Columbia with an emphasis on historic preservation. That moment in the elevator followed by my circling decline through the museum was the beginning of a tumultuous and torturous year for me, in which I seemed to have lost all sense of direction.

You follow the execution of architectural plans with the extreme precision of a surgeon. In your line of work, perfection is a requirement. From the structural integrity of the foundation to the application of a subtle shade of paint, you meticulously manage every detail. The architect and contractor are conciliatory, as you are kind but assertive, even forming your commands as gentle requests followed by astute observations and independent research. That is to say, before you make your recommendations, you hit the books, study the matter, prepare with knowing. Your assumption of authority was learned in the military, but gentleness was trained at the hospital bedside. But there is another veneer not so easily interpreted. You were born into one of the few Japanese families in a small rural town in Montana. Your father came at the turn of the century, labored as a foreman to complete the Northern Pacific—Minnesota to Spokane—and one day made enough to pay for your mother's passage, a picture bride. As you come of age, you and your family represent an enemy from a place you have never known. To compare the small tight-knit fishing villages of your parents to the rugged, mountainous cowboy town of your upbringing is to imagine a folktale about two distant and exotic lands. If only it were a folktale and not a navigation through territories of hatred. Within months after the bombing of Pearl Harbor, you are aware that less than two hundred miles away, across the border in Wyoming, ten thousand Japanese Americans evicted from the West Coast have been incarcerated in the same spectacular but desolate landscape in which you continue to be free. But it is a perilous freedom, especially for your immigrant parents designated enemy aliens. Thus every movement, every action, every facial expression must avoid trouble, anticipate a precarious future. Like any other kid from Montana, your older brother volunteers for the military. Your mother embroiders a thousand knots into a woven cotton belt that he obediently wears under his uniform, a protective talisman; so he returns, only to be killed in peacetime. You follow your brother's path as if to complete what can never be completed, but you are driven to succeed. You skip lunch and drive from your medical practice at midday to see the rising stone escarpment, 650 tons of quarried Arizona sandstone, flashing a toothy grin toward the Pacific, a gesture of grandeur and place against a precarious future.

I followed her out the museum's glass doors down Fifth Avenue to 86th, where she disappeared underground and caught a train downtown. Impetuously and mindlessly, I hopped on and emerged at Astor Place, following her to Cooper Union and into a classroom that I immediately surmised as a drawing course. Conveniently, I removed a drawing tablet from my satchel, sat unobtrusively in the rear, and leafed past my architectural renderings, mimicking other students with pencil or charcoal in hand. To my thrill and distress, I saw the object of my pursuit, now robed, walk barefoot to a middle dais. The white silk kimono slipped from her body, and there she stood, sans pink fishermen sweater, sans jeans and boots and leather cap—my Eurasian Aphrodite rising. I drew frantic, lousy drawings, one after the other, a cubist montage of breast, nipple, waist, shoulder, buttocks, nose, pubis, and eyes; my heart racing, my mind a bubble about to burst, and all my sensations a loaded gun.

You host an open house. The architect calls a few days before, delighted about the invitation. He asks if a writer for *Architectural Digest* might also be invited. The writer would come with a photographer. You generously agree. The day is perfect, though somewhat chilly, but this is Santa Cruz. Guests who arrive early are greeted with the full expanse of the Bay and sit in the stone veranda watching the fading sunlight cast a quiet orange glow. Your wife has ordered catering for the event—large platters of sushi, barbecued teriyaki on skewers, elegant pastel petit fours, saké cocktails, and champagne. You've gathered your entire family. Your mother from Montana and mother-in-law from Illinois have both flown in to visit. Your two young sons run in and out of the house with their friends with abandon. Your two daughters, teenagers now, appear and disappear with their cadre of friends, nodding politely when asked about their individual bedrooms, choice of colors and décor. You watch your wife as she becomes visible through the interior light beyond glass doors. The bubble of her blonde coif shines in a halo. You fondle the stem of a champagne glass and nod at the comments of the writer, but your mind wanders to the day you first met your wife, your initial insecurity; could you hope to win the heart of such a beautiful girl? It hasn't been easy, the loss of your first son, but she has weathered every difficulty, growing more beautiful as the years pass. You have become the perfect couple, the perfect family, and this house itself is confirmation. The photographer weaves about, surreptitiously it would seem, pointing a Nikon, capturing the house and décor from every angle, backdrop for beautiful people. Transmitted over pool waters, you catch the waves of a distant argument, something about bombing in Vietnam, and you wander in that direction with a wide smile, wanting nothing to spoil this perfect evening. Your very presence dissipates disagreement, a change of subject, compliments about the house, and *you Japanese really understand nature.* You glance again toward the lighted fireplace where your relatives seem huddled apart with your mother. In another room, your wife is showing off her current project on the loom; she's weaving natural fibers, dyed naturally, for throw pillows. You feel your heart might burst. Meanwhile, the architect is telling the story of his mentor Frank Lloyd Wright to a group of rapt listeners. Wright built for Mamah, his second companion and lover, the house he named Taliesin on family farmland in Wisconsin. Tragically, while Wright was in Chicago, Mamah and her children and four of his apprentices were murdered by the housekeeper, a man from Barbados, who also set the house on fire.

At the break, twenty minutes later, I rushed from the classroom to the toilet, stood inside a stall, trying to calm the shaking in my knees. I threw cold water on my face and stared at myself in the mirror, unsure of my own reflection. During the course of three hours, I did the same at every break, but I could not tear myself away. At the end of class I lingered, waiting for her to emerge from the dressing room. A young man entered the room, and sure enough, to my sinking heart, he greeted her clothed body, and together they left the building. By this time it was evening, and a slight drizzle had wet the dark streets. I watched the couple under an umbrella merge and disappear into the crossing crowd in a blur of car lights and neon. Reflecting back on this day, this was the moment at which I should have simply returned to my apartment in Harlem and continued my studies at Columbia, but I was ensnared in a design with a destiny I felt sure I must pursue to know. To be brief about the ensuing year, foolishly, I all but abandoned my coursework and research and was placed on probation. I forgot and lost contact with my friends and colleagues; if they showed concern, I shrugged away their questions and kept my secret counsel. I cannot precisely or chronologically relate with any detail what I did or how I lived during this time. All I remember is that my full-time occupation was that of a detective, self-hired and certainly unpaid, to know the daily life and moment-to-moment whereabouts of that young woman. I admit that my curiosity was made of infatuation, but it was an infatuation without any idea of finality, that is of meeting or consummating a relationship. Late into the early mornings, I pulled sheet after sheet of architectural drafting paper over my drawing table and feverishly designed structures of every sort, engineered houses in lilied valleys or on craggy promontories, next to astounding waterfalls, under snowpack, among bamboo groves, in tropical and desert climates. As much time as I spent as a detective, I was also enmeshed in geographical, climate, and environmental studies, always concerned with aspects of natural space and local materials. I was astounded by the beauty of my designs, the organic interwoven nature of place and structure, and always, she hovered ghostly above myriad drafts, rising perfectly from a white silk kimono.

The last time you speak with the architect is over the phone. The architect's voice tremors, then retrieves his confidence with an edge of anger. He wonders what Frank Lloyd Wright would say if he were alive? The Marin County Civic Center was one of Wright's last projects; he died in 1959 and never lived to see the final inauguration of the building. It was the architect who had completed the work. Every aspect of the center—its spacious elegance, skylight roof over interior gardens, arched windows framing the soft rise of distant hills, innovative jail design, the carefully studied configuration of the courtrooms themselves—honored Wright's desire for democratic space. But this: first, the hostage-taking in the center's courtroom and the shootout, the deaths of the prisoners and the judge and now, bombing the courtroom. You've read in the papers that some group called Weathermen say they are responsible. You commiserate with the architect's sense of confoundedness and outrage. Everything the architect and you believe in is being contested and turned upside down.

At first I thought she led a charmed life, prancing around the city from art to dance class to photo shoot. For example, I managed to follow her into the New York art scene—art receptions and openings where the likes of Yoko Ono, Isamu Noguchi,

Nam June Paik, or the young up and coming, such as Theresa Hak Kyung Cha, might be the featured artists or emerge among the invitees. Despite her youth, she moved with an easy grace among celebrity. Always fashionably attired, she wore designs both chic and elaborate with a casual body language that said, *of course*. Modeling for art classes turned out to be a side job she did occasionally as a favor to her former teachers at Cooper Union. Professionally, she worked with a prominent agency, and I was able to catch glimpses of her strut the runway for Ralph Lauren, Yves Saint-Laurent, Hanae Mori, and Stephen Burrows, to name a few. Despite her success, I followed her weekly to the office of a psychiatric therapist. I waited patiently for the hour to end and tried to discern the results of each session; I comprehended nothing. I clipped her photographs from *Vogue* and *Elle*, taping them to every inch of my small one-room studio. In the night, sleeping on an old futon, I could hear the tape peeling away with the bad paint job, the magazine photos fluttering to the floor like autumn leaves. One particularly snowy night, I entered my cold apartment, banging on the old lever of the radiator, and finally noticed gashes of blood-orange paint beneath the powder blue, scarring the walls, her colorful images scattered. I saw my breath in the cold air of that horrid old apartment and wept.

You stare at the man with the gun who can't be much older than your eldest daughter, thankfully safely far away, studying art in New York. He accuses you of crimes against the environment. You think you recognize him, a long-haired fellow, but they are all long-haired these days; even you are letting your hair grow out stylishly. Perhaps he came to the office for a case of pink eye. He told you how much he liked the garden in the middle of the office, never seen an office with a garden. His eyes were so infected they were almost glued together in gunk, but he could see the garden. But, he said, you can't live in a little garden like that; maybe the Japanese could, but anyway he lived in the forest up there in the mountains, lots of room and close to God, he said. Nothing artificial. You nodded in agreement. Japanese gardens are artificially natural, miniature vistas to create the sensation of distance and expanse. Gardening is an art. You were thinking about your father's garden in Montana. He thought about this and said he liked his art original, wild. No stunted bonsai for him, but of course he'd never been to Japan. Neither had you, except for a short R&R at a base in Okinawa before returning to the states. Looking at your watch and into the crowded reception room, you knew you didn't care to reply. He had no insurance, no money to pay. You waved him off, told the receptionist to make an exception. She looked up, and her eyes said, *another exception*. As the fellow left, the mail arrived, and your receptionist handed you a box with a small card. You opened the card: *Doc, a small token of thanks for your handiwork on my cataract. Sure is great to see clear again.* You handed back the box of See's Candies and pointed to the reception room, gesturing, *pass it around.* Perhaps it is not the same long-haired fellow, but you, your wife, your two sons, and the receptionist will die today.

One day late in October, I scanned the Halloween paraphernalia decorating shop windows, the proliferation of jack-o'-lanterns, witch hats, black cats, and skeletons along my route. I had affected a disinterested manner, gazing with feigned interest in odd directions, at window treatments or sidewalk displays. At this particular shop, I pretended interest in a skeleton mask, knowing she was passing on the sidewalk behind me. In all the time I followed her, our eyes never met, and I supposed she never knew or felt my presence. But this time, for some reason, she turned back to look my way, and our eyes met through that mask. I saw her disgust and terror. She stumbled away, walking hurriedly, if not running, into the underground. I abandoned the mask and followed with trepidation, chasing my sight line for her white trench coat, the slip of red-and-gold silk scarf trailing in the overheated draft of our descent. Surfacing at 86th Street, she walked quickly toward Fifth Avenue, fall colors of Central Park sparkling beyond. I slowed my pace, knowing her frequent destination. It was her habit to visit Magritte's *The False Mirror*, staring into that surreal sky eye. I should have anticipated this day, but I was obsessed with my own arrogance, my manic certainty of my own artistic genius, poet and prophet. Mulling about in the crowd below, only I looked upward from the rotunda into the last rays of October light streaming through the glass dome and saw her body tossed from the top of Wright's magnificent nautilus, her white trench coat flapping, windswept black hair separating in silky strands, red-and-gold scarf fluttering along, passing the silent Calder, imposing an unusual commotion on those glorious clouds of vermillion.

Even though you were buried Catholic, you wander the past as a Buddhist. There is no extinguishing your anguish. The beauty of this place has betrayed you. After the murders and the fires, they rebuilt it all completely new again, but unlike your wife and your children, it returns no love, a temple of permanent and radiant beauty. A real Japanese has been hired to keep the gardens in a state of eternal beauty, constantly trimming and replanting, leaves and fading blossoms flutter onto rock and still water to form exquisite traces, never rotting. Koi flap about, red and gold and white, turning their bodies in chaos or moving gracefully in liquid silence. The bodies of you, your wife and children and associate lie beneath in the dark shoals where your blood pools like lead. One night in Indian summer, I climb the hill to your house and meet you there. In the tepid night, I see you shape-shift between father and lover, doctor and architect, artist and prophet. I guide you to the Rolls-Royce, and together we siphon gasoline, spread it gallon-by-gallon at the most vulnerable corners of your beloved architecture.

NOTE

This is a work of fiction, however based on true events.

With gracious thanks to Frank Gravier, bibliographer for Humanities at UCSC McHenry Library; Paul Shea, director of the Yellowstone Gateway Museum in Livingston, Montana; and Lucy Asako Boltz, research assistant.

Midsummer Night's Dream

The lunatic, the lover and the poet are of imagination all compact.
THESEUS, *A MIDSUMMER NIGHT'S DREAM*, SHAKESPEARE

Because you hate fantasy, you stand in reality at the corner of Soquel and Seabright Avenues, at the entrance to Lillian's Italian Kitchen, previously the old site of the Harley Davidson Museum and dealership. That's right, motorcycles traded for meatballs. Walk the crosswalk and dance with a gangly girl in glasses and headphones, pumping signage to inaudible music. Twirl and jitter. She's Zumba on steroids. Breathless and panting, you look across Soquel Avenue and note the old but refurbished Rio Theater. No longer a movie theater, it's the Santa Cruz venue for live shows, concerts, and lectures. The original Rio Theater was inaugurated on June 12, 1949, with a state-of-the-art cycloramic screen, cruise liner décor, and double feature of the movies *Song of India* and *Law of the Barbary Coast*.

Song of India starred the Indian actor Sabu. Sabu was born near Mysore, the orphaned son of an elephant driver, discovered by director Robert Flaherty to play the title role in the film *Elephant Boy* in 1937. An overnight hit, Sabu went on to play a variation of the same role in *The Drum* (Prince Azim), *The Thief of Bagdad* (the thief Abu), and *Jungle Book* (Mowgli). By 1949, at the age of twenty-five, though he had served with distinction in the US Armed Forces during WWII, in his *Song of India* role as Ramdar, the savior of animals, he continued to be festooned in a turban, his smooth, hairless brown body exposed but for his ubiquitous short dhoti wrap. In these films, it's impossible not to follow Sabu's handsome, boyish features, his natural charisma, and the only body not in brownface pretending to be Indian. Sabu's appearance at the Rio is a trivial fact in the theater's long history of live, internationally famous performers. Even so, the flickering shadows of film after film waver and vacillate as ghostly traces; Sabu is the theater's first ghost.

Sixty-five years later, on the evening of May 8, 2014, the Rio was packed to its last seat with UC Santa Cruz students, faculty, locals, and reading fans of the science fiction/fantasy author Ursula K. Le Guin. After her keynote talk, Le Guin shared the stage in conversation with scholars James Clifford and Donna Haraway. Clifford and Haraway are philosophers of their respective fields, anthropology and biology, emeriti professors of the History of Consciousness. While they are internationally famous in their fields, Le Guin fans present that evening were unimpressed and grumbled that the academics had spoiled the evening. Well, you can judge for yourself; a video of the event is archived online. You would think that the meeting of three great minds would create a great conversation.

One summer night long after Ursula Le Guin has died and James Clifford and Donna Haraway have published their books with sections and chapters dedicated to Le Guin, you slip into the dark theater, sit in the front row, and ask Sabu what really happened. Sabu smiles his boyish smile. *Memsahib, do you really want to know?*

Cut that out, you snap. *Do I look like some white imperialist?*

Just joking. He pauses, then says, *I will need some help.* He flies away on his magic carpet and returns with two unlikely friends who transform the stage before you.

Scene: the dense forest (or jungle)

Characters:
    Storytellers:
        Mowgli, changeling boy
        Puck, forest imp (Camille)
        Ishi, last Indian
    Playwrights:
        Pandora
        Stoneteller
        Chthulu
    Players:
        Oberonzo, fairy king (Alfred and Abe)
        Titanica, fairy queen (Theodora and Willow)
        Bottomsup, companion species (Ursula and Owl)

Chorus/Extras:
    Blue Fairies

In addition: costumes, makeup, lights, special effects, orchestra, maestro.

And that is how this story finally begins.

Prologue

(Mowgli hoisted on a great elephant is poised at center stage. Ishi shoots an arrow. Puck flits about like Tinkerbell, and everything lights up like Disneyland.)

MOWGLI

Sahibs and Memsahibs, do you remember me? Perhaps not. I am the Indian changeling boy, Mowgli. Check your Cliffs Notes. If it hadn't been for me, there would be no story. The fairy king and queen fight over possession of me, but then, I am forgotten.

PUCK

Of course, you are forgotten. What are you doing here anyway? This is my play. Robin Goodfellow's play. Who cares about a pretty changeling darkie? Who can forget my iconic line: *Lord, what fools these mortals be.*

MOWGLI

And what about him?

(Ishi stands still in the spotlight)

PUCK

He's the last Indian.

MOWGLI

Hey, I'm Indian too.

ISHI

I am the last Yahi.

PUCK

He's the last of his kind. Extinct. Like the dodo. Like Lonesome George, the last tortoise of the Galapagos. Like dinosaurs. Kaput.
Be careful. They took his brains. They'll take yours too.

ISHI

(extends cupped hands)
Take a look.

MOWGLI

Oh, there you see? The frontal lobe. And here, the temporal and parietal. And down here, the cerebellum.

PUCK

How do you know this stuff?

MOWGLI

I'm South Asian.

ISHI

Actually, this is your brain.

MOWGLI

Mine?

ISHI

Yes, it was removed to study a human cub raised by wolves. Your brain and my brain side-by-side, like two little savage pillows in the Smithsonian.

MOWGLI

What about theirs? (points to Puck, then draws a dagger; Ishi draws an arrow)
How about it, Robin? A small contribution to science?

PUCK

Science fiction. Can't we start this play?

MOWGLI

It's not just a play. Parts of it are opera. An opera within a play.

ISHI

There are three playwrights trying to write an opera. They should be collaborating, but each has written a different libretto.

(playwrights Pandora, Stoneteller, and Chthulu appear)

PUCK

Their narratives are based on an original play: *a tedious brief scene of young love; very tragical mirth.*

MOWGLI

In the original narrative, Oberonzo, a virile vampire squid sea god,

PUCK

and Titanica, a luscious, sexy winged sky goddess, passionately join their genitals

ISHI

and produce Bottomsup, a hybrid of wings and tentacles. If things had only turned out like that, life on earth might have been very different.

(players Oberanzo, Titanica, and Bottomsup appear, reenact original play)

SONG

It was the midsummer solstice,
the longest day of the year,
the shortest night,
but it would only take
one short night of folly.
Folly, folly, folly!

My body might be fantasy
My body might be fiction.
I might be a faggot on fire
of your imagination,
but I am here for real.
Real, real, real!

PUCK

But hark, who goes there?

(*Enter Pandora, Stoneteller, and Chthulu*)

MOWGLI

The playwrights, thick in their conundrums.

ISHI

Should we hide?

MOWGLI

Are you daft? They only see us when they want to.

STONETELLER

May there not come that even bolder adventurer—the first geolinguist, who, ignoring the delicate, transient lyrics of the lichen, will read beneath it the still less communicative, still more passive, wholly atemporal, cold, volcanic poetry of the rocks: each one a word spoken, how long ago, by the earth itself, in the immense solitude, the immenser community, of space.

PANDORA

It raises the inescapable question, if it's a work of utopia, utopian fiction, what kind of utopia is this? Or more profoundly, is it even possible to conceive of the future?

CHTHULU

Bioengineers and biomolecular engineering folks who study the living world and its connectedness very much as a question of evolutionary engineering . . . are really deeply interested in the design dimension, in the bio design, how it works . . . which I find beautiful and ties me to the world . . . is also very much part of the robo-bee drone to replace the honeybees, is very much part of the biomimetic military engineering world.

PUCK

What are they talking about?

MOWGLI

Beats me. Rocks? The future? Honeybees?

ISHI

What sort of opera is this?

PUCK

Oh, they need help. What if we sent them dancing?

MOWGLI

Wandering. Singing.

ISHI

Dreaming. Make them dream.

(Playwrights scatter into forest.)

Act/Opera I

(note on music: Classical operatic Euro-American; however may be also performed on contemporary, electronic, international, and indigenous instruments)

PANDORA

The story begins here:
A man emerges from the forest
Giving himself over to civilization.
But what is civilization?

ISHI

I am that man who
Leaves my forest home
I am alone, the last of my people.
I shed my old skin
Leave it behind to die
I will enter a new world
To understand.

MOWGLI

I am the human cub birthed
From a cave of wolves

PUCK

I am the fairy imp
Exiled

PANDORA

Different dreams of first encounters.
Two men meet, first nation to first world,
This man Ishi and this man Alfred Kroeber.
Who do they see through the mirror of their dreams?

ISHI

I make the choice to live or to die
At the hands of my enemy

OBERANZO (AS ALFRED)

I meet my other, until now a shadow on this landscape

ISHI

They send this man who tries to speak my words

OBERANZO (AS ALFRED)

Salvaged tongue in the voice its story

PANDORA

Two men bound to each other
In knowledge and curiosity
An exchange of mind and spirit
And yet, their roles predetermined
Researcher and researched
Teacher and guide

ISHI

Big Chiep

OBERANZO (AS ALFRED)

Ishi

PANDORA

In the museum of anthropology
In a glass case archived, implements
Basketry, pestle, shells, flint stones

ISHI

I know this very basket.
I know this flint stone.

OBERANZO (AS ALFRED)

Salvaged tools in the hands of their purpose

PANDORA

Authentic man untainted
Save what is lost forever
Five years, a small window of life in a new world
And then, it is over

ISHI

(to Oberanzo) I go. You stay.

OBERANZO (AS ALFRED)

(to Titanica & Bottomsup) I go. You stay.

PANDORA

And when they go, who is left to tell the story?

BOTTOMSUP (AS URSULA)

My mother Theodora Kroeber will write the book.

TITANICA (AS THEODORA)

I write to save their memory.

TITANICA (AS THEODORA) & BOTTOMSUP (AS URSULA)

Women write what men cannot see
Take care

BOTTOMSUP (AS URSULA)

Take care
Always coming home, never to arrive

MOWGLI, PUCK, ISHI, AND BLUE FAIRIES

SONG

Your utopia, your perfect world
May be someone's genocide
Your nostalgia, a dangerous fantasy
We are noble savages
We stay. You go.

Act/Opera II

STONETELLER

Two centuries later, the story opens
No virgin people left
In the Valley of the Na, where the world is
In the City of the Con, where the world was

TITANICA (AS WILLOW)

I am Willow, a weaver in the Valley of the Na

OBERANZO (AS ABE)

I was Abe, warrior son from the City of Con

TITANICA (AS WILLOW)

He comes on a motorcycle, under a helmet cherry red
Sealed in a coat of black leather

OBERANZO (AS ABE)

She wove me a cloak of soft lambs' wool
And so I stayed

TITANICA (AS WILLOW)

He comes to war, but what we make
Are days of peace

STONETELLER

How many times is this story told?
A love story across opposing tribes

PUCK

Crossing tracks

MOWGLI

Crossing species

ISHI

Crossing time

OBERANZO (AS ABE)

One day, called back to war, I left

TITANICA (AS WILLOW)

He leaves behind his leather coat and little Owl
I empty myself of love

BOTTOMSUP (AS OWL)

I am Owl, daughter of the valley
And daughter of the city
This is my story

STONETELLER

A child of two peoples must find her way

PUCK

Neither of one, nor of the other

MOWGLI

Belonging nowhere

ISHI

One door closing on the other

BOTTOMSUP (AS OWL)

My body holds valley and city, a bowl of sapped desire
Yet, my story learns the arrogance of machines
The endless storage of human history and for what?
My story learns to listen: living silence between earth and sky
Woven life and sacred dead

MOWGLI, PUCK, ISHI, AND BLUE FAIRIES

SONG

Myths of origins
You arrive as wreckage at the shore
Coyote tosses stones
Go away. Leave. Go back!
But you persist
Coyote trots away

Myths of endings
You drive your motorcycle
To the edge, unmapped
Get off. Get lost. Awwooow!
Yet you persist
Live gently. Leave quietly.

Act/Opera III

CHTHULU

Passing five generations into the future
This is a marriage comedy of three

OBERANZO

What you call a ménage à trois

TITANICA

We practice playful triangulation

BOTTOMSUP

No to binaries in constant skirmish
Struggling to be the one

CHTHULU

This story begins with a kinship dream

OBERANZO

We dream the dream of royalty

TITANICA

From its chrysalis, threaded delicately, to milkweed

BOTTOMSUP

Emerges a golden monarch

OBERANZO

And in this dreaming moment
We generate a human child

TITANICA

A child of our compost

BOTTOMSUP

Her destiny in symbiosis with our dream
Joined to that golden butterfly

PUCK (AS CAMILLE)

I am Camille, that human child
My mother's milk is mixed with bitter weed
I grow a soft beard, probing with antennae
I sprout the monarch's gilded wings
My skin translucent pulsing light
See my vanished sisters here in me

MOWGLI, PUCK, ISHI, AND BLUE FAIRIES

SONG

I'd rather be a butterfly
Flitting in the breeze

I'd rather be a caterpillar
Mooching in the soil

I'd rather be a pupa
Hanging by a thread

Epilogue

PUCK

Oh, my my my, we've offended you.

MOWGLI

Living as we do, thinking below our navels, we're not supposed to speak.

ISHI

Yet, waking from this dream, we shall have the last word.

Neverneverland

Walking tour: Start at the end of the Santa Cruz pier. Peruse live crab dozing and lobsters straitjacketed in bubbling tanks; slabs of salmon, cod, and rockfish; steaks of halibut and shark; piles of clams, oysters, squid, and shrimp. Taste-test smoked salmon; get a cup of shrimp cocktail. Above the fish market is Stagnaro's restaurant and bar.

From the pier, look back toward the shore and see the Boardwalk Amusement Park, Giant Dipper roller coaster, and the length of Venetian-style buildings that house a dance hall and game galleries. It's a preserved throwback to a vintage time before Disneyland. Walk down the pier, noting the curio shops, Marini's candy shop, Italian and Mexican restaurants, whale watching and kayak rentals.

At the beginning of the pier, find the Ideal Bar and Grill and walk around and into the Boardwalk. Lose yourself in the park. Buy a T-shirt that says san-ta cu-ru-zu in Japanese. Munch on cotton candy. Have a corn dog slathered in catsup and mustard. Drink Corona beer. Ride the merry-go-round. Look for the Lost Boys, coifed long hair or punk-spiked blonde, looking nastily pretty on motorcycles. Wander into fun houses. Look for underground passages and two identical little Black girls, one in a Hands Across America T-shirt and the other in a *Thriller* T-shirt, both licking giant lollipops.

Walk back toward the pier to the roundabout, and turn right on Pacific Avenue. Stay right onto Front Street. Cross Second Street and continue up the hill to Third. At the corner of Front and Third, notice an elegant Victorian house painted in pink and white and the sign, Sunshine Villa, originally the site of Hotel McCray, but also the site chosen by Alfred Hitchcock for the Bates Motel.

From the villa hill, look north into the Santa Cruz hills toward the UCSC campus, and search for the head and supplicating hands of an enormous unblinking doll with a ponytail, in a striped blue and white sundress, peeking over the redwoods.

My grandma Lily Chan, in her day, was a hotshot computer programmer, one of the few women in the business. She said the rest were geeky guys who basically lived in caves filled with trash—stacks of greasy pizza boxes, Chinese takeout, empty cans of Mountain Dew, Cheetos, Cup Noodles. Disgusting. They ignored her Chinese face, flat chest, and skinny butt, even jerked off right there in the next cubicle—until she solved some code; then they hated her guts. She called them the Lost Boys. Losers. Wet dreamers humping Hello Kitty. Fake avatars suited up like wormy dicks slithering around the Matrix. She took no guff. Her work area was pristine, antiseptic. She ate her lunch with silver chopsticks. She drew a line and raised her chopsticks. *You cross that line; I put your eyes out.* Lily was one cool bitch. Within earshot, they called her "Tiger Lily"; beyond earshot, I can only imagine.

Years later, Lily was a young ninety, and we were at Stagnaro's at the end of the pier, dipping fish and chips into tartar sauce. She leaned over the table, sipping her mai tai, and pointed the end of a pink paper umbrella at me. "You break me out tonight. We drive off this pier and never come back. I feel like visiting Napa. Check into a winery for a change. I make it up to you. When did you ever hang out in Napa?"

"Grandma."

"Don't Grandma me. This is your daddy's fault."

"He's remodeling your bathroom. New tile. Top-of-the-line fixtures. Ask him for a Jacuzzi."

My dad had checked Lily into an eldercare home for a few months to wait out the mess of construction. She hated it.

"Try to trick me."

"It's for real. I saw the plans. Chrome handlebars. A Toto toilet!"

"What I need a bidet for? What sex I get these days?"

"*I* want a Toto toilet."

"You having good sex lately?"

"Hey, just for the pooping part. Don't you poop?"

People at the table across glanced sideways at us. Not dinner talk. Lily couldn't care less. She continued her rant, "Then *you* move into that sunshine prison, and I move to your place."

"Sunshine Villa," I corrected her. "California sunshine."

"You got to be kidding. Gloom. Fog. Shadow. Darkness. End of life. Death. The place is an approaching eclipse."

"Good grief, Grandma."

"You know what's inside there? Bunch of old white people drying on the vine. Shriveled raisins. What I got to do with those wrinkled old farts? Gives me the creeps."

It was true. Old Asians don't shrivel; they blossom into golden Buddhas. At least my dad could have placed her somewhere with other Asians, not to mention Chinese food. But he figured since I lived and worked up at the university, I could drive down and visit her every day, keep her company on the weekends. Basically, it was like a hotel, plus they chased her down for her meds, assisted with her bath, washed her clothing, fed her nutritious meals. The unspeakable words rolled around in the back of my brain: assisted living.

I drove her back up the hill to the villa. "Look, Grandma, I've got classes. I can't just pick up and leave work. It's only been a week. Can't you give it a chance?"

We were at a standoff staring through the glass doors, the saccharine smile of the night receptionist with her manicured hand hovering over the automatic door opener. Lily smirked. "You remember that nurse in *One Flew Over the Cuckoo's Nest*? That's her."

A voice behind us stated, "Nurse Ratched."

Another voice asked, "Is she bothering you?"

A third said, "We can kill her for you, if you like."

They all laughed. In the glass reflection, I could see a woman in a wheelchair, pushed by a man, sandwiched between two other women. The women were all what Lily called "villa inmates," aging old crows. And to complete the tableau, there was a gigantic old panting, drooling dog.

I turned, and the man exclaimed, "Amaya Chan!"

"Oh," I said, "J. Michael?"

Lily glared. "You know him?"

"Grandma, this is J. Michael Darling. He teaches poetry."

"Wendy Mother," he said to one of the women. "We just hired Amaya to teach fiction."

So that was how Lily met her crew at the Villa. There was nonbinary Norma Bates in the wheelchair; J. Michael's mother Wendy, professor emerita of cultural studies with her companion species, a Newfoundland named Nana; and Adelaide Wilson, African American choreographer.

Norma said, "We've just returned from a funeral."

Wendy said, "My partner Petra died." She pointed at a box in Norma's lap. "That's Petra."

I said, "I'm so sorry."

Adelaide said, "When you get to be our age, all your friends die."

Wendy patted the box and said, "Petra and I need a drink." She smiled at Lily. "Will you join us?"

I watched Lily march over the threshold, never turning to look back. J. Michael smiled. "Don't worry. They'll take care of her."

"You don't know my grandma. No one takes care of her."

J. Michael and I returned to Stagnaro's and sat in the bar gazing over the dark bay, neon of the Giant Dipper on the Boardwalk undulating over waves. I decided to try the mai tai; it was syrupy and kinda awful, but the rum did the work, while J. Michael explained his life. He was the son of four parents, two gay fathers and two lesbian mothers. If I wanted the details, I could read his new memoir. "You know, being the only son of four parents, I was really spoiled." He teared up, then laughed. "If I didn't get what I wanted, I could try three more times." His fathers had both died a decade ago, and now Petra. He hadn't prepared himself to be left behind. Wendy was his biological mother, and she was the last. She and Petra moved into the villa about five years ago. They made friends with Norma and Adelaide. Norma periodically slipped into schizoid dementia, at which time she'd become Norman. For some reason, the women disliked Norman and usually taunted Norma back.

"Taunted?"

"Yeah, slap them around so to speak. Don't ask me." J. Michael nursed a bourbon over rocks. "It seems to work."

"What about the old Black lady?"

"Adelaide? She integrated the villa, but she's still the only one. I bet she hates the place more than your grandma. She's got issues. Your grandma seems badass. She'll fit right in."

We toasted. "L'chaim!"

After that, Lily became occupied with her new life at the villa and didn't talk again about escaping. I had to dig up her old mahjong set; apparently, she was busy recreating her version of the Joy Luck Club. For sure, this was an alternative motherhood. Take Norma, for example, who occasionally slipped into the personality of her son Norman. Then, there was Wendy's gay/lesbian family and the spoiled J. Michael. As for Adelaide, who didn't mind being called the "Black widow," here was someone who never withheld the dark side of her perceptions. Lily explained, "Some people wait to get old to say what's on their mind," then shrugged, "Why wait?" Truth is, my dad was not really Lily's son; down the line, he was one of the programmer Lost Boys who happened also to be Chinese. He'd gotten a scholarship to study in America, effectively defected, and Lily adopted him. I never knew my mom, who died just after I was born. It was Lily who brought me up, if what happened to me was what you call bringing up a kid.

One day, Lily sent me home with a big box. "What's this?"

"Gifts from Norma."

Inside was a stuffed rabbit and a stuffed rat, each mounted on polished boards. "Eww!" I jumped.

"Norma made them. Used to work for the natural history museum. She's got them all over her apartment." Lily shook her head and did the circular thing with her finger near her ear. "Talks to them."

"Taxidermy?"

"Yeah, take them away. Bad luck."

I stared at their shiny glass eyes. "Why?"

"I told her you were year of the rabbit."

"And you're the year of the rat?"

Lily nodded. "Cultural exchange."

"What if I were the year of the tiger?"

"Actually, you are tiger year. Just be grateful."

This should have been a sign, but when we thought about it later, we were both in denial.

One night after finals, J. Michael announced that he was inviting everyone over to his place for dinner. Everyone meant the neo–Joy Luck Club, plus Adelaide's son Jason, who happened to be visiting, and me.

We got there early because Lily insisted on cooking. That meant that she was executive chef, and J. Michael and I did all the work. We had a long list of groceries, a couple of days of prep, driving back and forth to San Jose for condiments, steamer, wok, chopping block, cleaver. In the end, we achieved a Chinese banquet. J. Michael was ecstatic. I was exhausted. But Lily was pissed off. The ladies picked at their food, eating only the rice. Only Jason scarfed up everything like he hadn't eaten for months. "Damn, this is delicious!"

"Lily honey, is there garlic in this dish?"

"Garlic in everything."

"Oh my."

J. Michael asked, "What's the matter with garlic?"

"It seems we're all allergic. It's what connects us, we guess."

"When did this happen?"

"Something we discovered recently."

"It was that nutritionist. What's his name, Adelaide?"

"Vlad." Adelaide sneered.

Wendy glanced over at Nana, her bearlike form napping, copious drool damp in a towel pillow. "No scraps for Nana. She's allergic too."

"Nana?"

Norma piped in, "Where's Petra. Petra can eat garlic."

"Norma dear, Petra died."

Norma seemed to think about this, then spoke in a masculine voice, "No problem, Mother, I'll eat that for you. Lily's gone to a lot of trouble to make an authentic Chinese meal."

But before Norman could partake, Wendy grabbed his chopsticks, and Adelaide slapped him repeatedly across the cheeks. "Norma! Come back, Norma. That's an order."

I looked at Jason and J. Michael, but they were happily eating and drinking. J. Michael asked Jason, "How's that documentary of yours coming along?"

Between bites, Jason said, "Looking for funding. Have you seen my crowd-sourcing page?"

"Now remind me. What's it about?"

"It's based on the little-known history in the 1860s about an ex-slave London Nelson—"

Adelaide slapped a three-ring binder on the table and pushed aside Jason's plate. "Here's the script," she announced. "I finished it. I told you I would."

Norma, who'd returned to being Norma, said, "I've read it. It's sensational. Bound to be a blockbuster."

Adelaide said, "You need to stop making those tedious PBS shows. Nobody cares about reality these days. What people want is this."

I leaned over to see the title. "Dopplegängsters."

Jason patted his mouth with a napkin. "Okay, Mom." He looked at J. Michael for support, but Wendy had left the table to retrieve her own manuscript.

Wendy placed it between her son's nose and his approaching chopsticks. "Here's mine. This time, it's a novella, short and sweet. You can publish under your name or an alias. I don't care. This"—she tapped the ream of paper—"will make you money. You can start a series."

Norma said, "It will go viral."

J. Michael asked, "What's it about this time?"

"Vampires, of course."

"What happened to feminist Marxism? The contradiction of neoliberalism and late-stage capitalism?"

"Have you ever read Anne Rice?" asked Norma. "That woman makes a ton of capital. Ask Petra."

"Norma, Petra is dead."

"The critique of capitalism is embedded in this narrative." Wendy waved her hands around like she was molding the air with her argument. "There is no reason why the fictive narrative cannot express critical theory."

Adelaide growled, "Cut the bullshit. We've done all the work. Just find an agent and insist on six figures."

Jason sighed heavily, then looked at Lily, who was eating stonily. "Lily, do you like music? Hey, Mikey, how about some music?"

J. Michael jumped up, and Jason followed me into the kitchen with dirty plates. "Amaya, sorry about our mothers, but you know, dementia. They get crazier and crazier as the years pass. Thing is, those women are why J. Michael is an experimental word poet with about a hundred readers and I'm an impoverished documentary filmmaker. Then suddenly in the last few years, they're obsessed with our making money, literally getting fame and fortune. Anyway, let your grandma know her dinner was amazing." He thumbed the pages of Adelaide's script. "Every time I visit, she has another script for me." He tossed it into the recycle.

We left the kitchen to find the mood changed in the living room. J. Michael was deejaying Michael Jackson's *Thriller*. Adelaide moonwalked across the floor, but more bizarrely, so did Wendy and Lily. Norma's body, from within her wheelchair, had achieved the agility of a worm. Even Nana could have been pressing her furry paws into the moon. Okay, Adelaide could moonwalk; she was a dancer, but the others? Their combined ages were about three-and-a-half centuries. It was a surreal form of butoh. For a moment, I felt folded into their metamorphosis, saw faces go ashen, eyes go bloody. But then everyone was laughing. So we all danced together into the night, and I thought Lily had forgotten the oriental garlic fiasco.

Over the next months, I got busy teaching summer school and working on my graphic novel. I assumed Lily got up at the crack of dawn to do tai chi in the villa courtyard, simultaneously with an imagined one billion Chinese. And at night, she played mahjong with the neo–Joy Luck Clubbers, whom Lily began to refer to as the night bats. "Sleep all day. Drink all night." She scoffed at their bad habits.

I'd go over faithfully for my daily visit, take Lily for walks along West Cliff or Natural Bridges. She was never leisurely but walked at a quick pace, with purpose. "What's the hurry?"

"What's a matter with you?" she jeered. "You getting flabby." She made a fist. "See this? Muscle tone."

"You training for something?"

"Old age." Then she busted out in some kung fu kicks.

"Shit."

We stopped to look at the surfer statue, bloody rose petals kissing his bronze toes.

"You bring what I asked for?"

I had to make a special trip up to her old apartment. She'd been very specific. Other than the crochet hooks and yarn, the rest of it was her entire collection of silverware, carving knives and forks, goblets, her infamous silver chopsticks, letter opener, fine jewelry, chains. All of it together weighed a ton. I had to get a dolly to wheel out the boxes.

"What do you need all that stuff for? Don't you want to know how the remodel is coming along?"

Grandma pivoted away from the surfer and crossed the street. "One more thing." She headed across the lawn toward the Catholic church. I followed her in. She pointed at the altar. "That."

"The painting?"

"No, that Jesus thing."

"Crucifix?

"Get me one of those. You got Costco card?"

"Grandma, they don't sell that at Costco."

"Not that. You get me garlic, three-pound bags, colossal."

So by now, you'd think I should have figured it out. But living with Lily was one of those apprenticeships where I had to interpret koans on a need-to-know basis. If I had to ask, what kind of dummy was I? As it turned out, she had retrieved Adelaide's script and Wendy's novella from the trash. She pushed them on me. "This is your homework. You gotta pass the test." I felt sorry for Jason and J. Michael. As a teacher, bad writing from students was a given, but from your mother? Still, I wouldn't have had a problem inviting the old bats to my fiction workshops. They were mimicking the horror genres, but they showed potential. That's what I told Grandma.

"You some kind of dummy?" she exploded. She was furiously crocheting these necklace things with curly flowers and little leaf pouches at intervals. In the pouches, she inserted cloves of garlic. "Put this on. Don't take it off." Then she said, conspiratorially, "Tonight you take me to a nice dinner. You wear only black."

"Like black tie?"

"No, like black hoodie."

That night, we shared medium-rare steaks and fries at the Ideal Bar and Grill, then headed with the crowds into the Boardwalk. Lily pulled a black beanie over her white head and moved through the amusement park like a ninja tracker who knew the terrain intimately. We waited in the shadows, and then they appeared, escapees from assisted living: Wendy pushing Norma, and Adelaide with Nana on a leash. They disappeared into the pirate ship. Lily motioned to follow. Some blonde guy dressed as Captain Hook came forward and said in accented English, "Madame, dogs are not allowed."

"But she is a service dog. Can't you see? My friend is blind." Sure enough, there was Adelaide in dark glasses smiling like Stevie Wonder.

After that, everything went pretty fast, well, fast for old ladies. Norma pulled out a butcher knife and stabbed the kid in the stomach. Too bad the hook on his hand was only plastic. He fell over Norma, and Wendy and Adelaide struggled to wheel Norma out, clutching Captain Hook beneath her blanket. Bumping over the cold sand, they hid under the pier. After the deed was done, their voices wafted in the fog. "Was he East German?"

"Romanian, definitely Romanian. That's how they taste."

"They all taste like beer."

"You'd think they'd give these jobs to Americans."

"What American kid wants this summer job?"

"Underprivileged minority youth from the inner city?" Adelaide snarled.

I thought about this. This was her script idea.

"They advertise it to Eastern European students: an exotic summer in Surf City. Irresistible."

"Anyway, good for us. America is a dangerous place. Things happen. No one will miss him."

Back at the bar at Stagnaro's, Lily ordered a glass of sauvignon blanc. "From now on," she said seriously, "no red wine."

I nodded over a gin and tonic.

"Did they kill Petra?"

"No, Petra died regular. Wine got passed around, but she didn't drink the Kool-Aid. In the end, she just wanted to return to Neverland."

"Are you kidding?"

"No, that's what they say. Bad joke. Think about it. If I were your age, maybe. But, never say die to these old boobs?" Lily clutched her nonexistent breasts dramatically. "In perpetuity? No fun. Petra got lucky, and they know it."

"Did Nana eat the Romanian, too?"

"Pet abuse."

"So they're going to outlive their sons?"

"Except for Norma."

"She'll always have Norman." We clinked glasses.

"That's why they need their sons to make the big bucks. Leave a fortune so they can continue immortal life at the villa. You know what your dad is paying for that prison?"

I shook my head and thought about the manuscripts in recycle. "It might be easier to rob a bank."

"I'm going to kill them."

"Can't we just call the police?"

"That's not how it works. Nobody insults my cooking."

I had to admit there is some kind of justice to die by your own writing. It wasn't that Lily had a plan exactly; she read those mothers' stories like programmer manuals. Proof of the mirror. Crucifix to ward off. Holy water to burn. Garlic to defend. Silver to penetrate. Stake through the heart. Sunlight to burn.

Wendy and Adelaide lived in the villa's top-floor cushy penthouse apartments, but Norma was exiled to the Alzheimer's unit housed in the old Victorian house attached by a bridge to the main villa. The main villa was a remodeled, dressed-up vestige of the Barbary Coast. I began to dream about aging saloon girl bats, their vengeful slave Adelaide, and Chinagirl Lily. My nightmare could have been one of Adelaide's scripts.

After nighttime mahjong, Norma got wheeled back to the dementia house and tucked into bed. One night, Lily disabled the alarm system and snuck into Norma's zoological apartment, winding her way around the dead animalia.

"Norman," she nudged the sleeping body. "Get up."

Norman woke groggily and said, "What?"

"Your mother wants to talk to you."

Norman rolled over. "Go away."

"Norman, she says it's important."

"What does she want now?"

Lily got Norman up and into the wheelchair and rolled him out to the front porch.

"Where is she?"

Lily looked at her watch. "She'll be here in a moment." She steered Norman to face east. They gazed over the town toward the hills. It was a vision that Norman hadn't seen in years. What was it? "There she is!" Lily exclaimed and scampered from the porch into the bushes. It was one of those rare seaside mornings, not a speck of fog.

Norman stared at the cold golden corona shivering into sunrise. His eyes filled and burst. "Mother!"

The fire on the porch at the villa caused the evacuation of the dementia unit. When all the muddled-headed patients were rolled back in, Norma was unaccounted for.

She'd vanished. The police came around to investigate. "Those police are stupid," said Lily.

"What do Wendy and Adelaide say?"

Lily imitated Adelaide's growling undertone. "What the hell are we going to do with all her dead animals?"

"A compassionate response." How many Romanians had they eaten? Still, I imagined the old bats had their suspicions. Lily had to move fast. But then, there was the matter of Halloween.

You could have predicted it, Wendy dressed as Dracula, and Adelaide as a Michael Jackson *Thriller* zombie. Nana got demon horns. Equally predictable, Lily was a Shaolin kung fu monk, and I was a hooded ninja. The difference between kung fu and ninja was pretty much lost between us, but we were there for business. Lily had melted down her silverware into weapons: swords, daggers, and nunchucks.

Parading through the tight crowd, someone yelled, "Look," pointing at Adelaide, "he's back from the dead!" It was true, she could have been a ninety-year-old version of the King of Pop.

We followed closely behind. Lily pulled a perfume spritzer from her backpack and nodded at me.

"What's that?"

"Holy water. Special Chinese recipe. I bless it myself."

She sprayed my wrist. "Ouch."

"Tien Tsin chili, Szechuan peppercorn, garlic; one pound each, concentrate and distill."

Adelaide, distracted by all the attention, every kind of zombie pressing against her, didn't know when the back of her red leather jacket got graffitied with invisible holy water.

"Michael!" they yelled. "Let's break out and do it!" We were gang-pressed into the House of Mirrors, the place throbbing with *Thriller*. I searched for Adelaide in the humping mass, but as Lily knew, she could not be reflected. Instead, I followed Lily's dancing graffiti. In broken flashes, when I could connect Adelaide to the blood-splashed Chinese character, slipping and jerking among her doubles, I could see her terrified anger. She could not see herself dancing, and yet she was surrounded by poor imitations, incompetent dancers, distorted and multiple versions in Blackface. I was truly horrified.

Lily slapped me out of my trance. "You lost your mind?"

"I'm gonna kill all of these racists." I felt resolute in my outrage and pulled out my silver dagger.

"They gonna die anyway. Stick to the plan. Follow the ghost."

"Ghost?"

"Can't you read?" she pointed at the looming Chinese character.

I turned to find Adelaide hurtling forward, smashing me into looking glass, icicles splintering into her toothy fangs. I plunged in my dagger, pushing her backward. Then, I watched Lily, in slow-motion, slice off Adelaide's growling head. Maybe it was my imagination, but I saw that golden head rocket through the ceiling, a burning meteor soaring into the night sky.

The final coup de grace was performed behind the lighthouse surfer museum on the teetering cliff edge of the dark bay. Monstrous waves thundered; night birds screeched. The moon disappeared and reappeared seductively between cloud lace and ocean spume. Wendy's cape whipped and rippled like liquid black-and-blood satin. Panther fangs busted from her bloody mouth. She towered against the night, a great Medusa sporting a writhing wig of snakes. At her side, Nana was posted stoically, drooling from her fangs. Lily poised herself, kung fu master with her glinting sword, and I was swinging silver nunchucks like Michelangelo. If my life hadn't been on the line, I'd have said it was a pretty cool scene.

It's probably an exaggeration to say we fought for hours. But being two ninety-year-old ladies and one incompetent ninja wannabe, you can imagine us running around in slow-motion, stumbling, missing targets. It seemed endless. At least Adelaide could choreograph her thrilling death. We were a bunch of amateurs. Wendy had some monster tricks, but then Lily was wise to all that CGI. I imagined Michelle Yeoh at ninety. Daily tai chi and fast walking on West Cliff had paid off. My nunchuck actually knocked off one of Wendy's fangs, ka-chunk, and Lily sliced away a bunch of snake extenders. Wendy managed to sprout bat wings and grab me by my feet; she groaned upward into tortured flight. I tried tossing the silver nunchucks, only singeing her flapping wings, but then Lily slung her dagger into the night. I ducked away and saw it swivel and churn and burn into bat flesh. We tumbled earthbound, but Wendy was not spent. She pounced forward, grabbing my neck, bore down upon me with her remaining fang. Beyond her writhing head, I saw Lily come from behind, silver chopsticks glinting, their binary curse puncturing each ear. Wendy flailed backward over the cliff, spewing blood. There at the edge was Nana, one giant inscrutable Sphinx, her ubiquitous leather leash dangling like a question mark.

I peered over into crashing sea and vertigo. Wendy dangled there, hanging onto Nana's leash. The silver chopsticks sizzled in her brains, but Wendy still pleaded to Nana. "Pull me up," she commanded. Nana seemed to think about this, then with ethical resolve, opened her great mouth and closed her fangs over the leash, severing her tether to her mistress. Wendy screamed, "You always liked Petra better!" I watched her body twirl downward, massive cape ballooning and cascading, chopsticks spinning their silver DNA, to the final plummet into relentless and endless sea.

Not long after, my dad arrived to move Lily out of the villa and back into her remodeled apartment. We carted boxes and bags back and forth. When it was all done, I snoozed in bubbles in her new Jacuzzi. Nearby, Nana observed me from her pillow throne. Lily came in with treats for Nana. I opened one eye. "Hey, how about me?"

True story: The story above is not based on a true story, but you already know those horror stories set in our guileless town. Truth is that my mother, a Japanese American nisei checked into the Sunshine Villa for the same reasons; our bathroom and kitchen were being remodeled. Every day during those months, I came to visit her at the villa. I thought she'd love it; it really was a hotel in the sense they changed the sheets daily, had a restaurant and room service, a nail and hair salon, plus exercise and art classes, book clubs, movie nights, field trips, and birthday parties. She hated it. Refused to participate in healthy eldercare and sulked in her room with her books. When I arrived in the morning, she complained about not getting her copy of the *New York Times*. When I arrived in the evening, she'd dragged in large cardboard boxes she found in the corridor; needed, she said, to pack up her stuff. She was leaving tomorrow. When was I picking her up?

True, my mother was probably the first nisei to ever live in the villa. "Hey, you're making history integrating this place." She was not impressed. This was not Little Rock. She wanted out. When my sister and I checked her in, we were asked where in Japan she was born. My sister responded with outrage, "She was born in San Francisco! She's an American!" She might also have said that Asako graduated Cal Berkeley in 1941 and taught grammar school for nineteen years. The administrators blanched, and I wondered if my mom, hard of hearing, had heard that crazy exchange. In the end, her only favorite person at the villa was the chef and cook, who, likely primed by the director, came out to greet my mom exclaiming, "We have something in common. I was born in San Francisco too!"

Eventually the remodeling was done, and my mom moved back home. Years passed and one day at age ninety-nine, Mom died. I can still see my sister coming through the door of our house, a paper bag loaded with the box carrying Mom's ashes in one hand and a piece of paper in the other. My sister shook the paper at me angrily. "Mom would be so mad!"

I woke up from the couch where I was covered with student papers.

"Look at this!" She rattled the document at me.

I perused what turned out to be Mom's death certificate.

"Do you see that?" She pointed.

I tried to look more carefully. Bureaucratic forms are meant to be skimmed. I sat up.

"Look! There!"

In the box designated "race" was typed: Caucasian. I busted up laughing.

"I knew you'd laugh!" My sister was furious, then appeased.

We both knew the terrible truth. People come to Santa Cruz to die white.

Acknowledgments

Early in this project, friends joined, often unwittingly, my walks and wandering around Santa Cruz, and in so doing, contributed in large and small ways to these stories. And because some of these stories were written throughout the COVID-19 pandemic and our evacuation during the fires in the Santa Cruz hills, other friends contributed from a distance on email and Zoom—reading, critiquing, and sharing research. My sincere thanks to all of you. I list below by story my memory of those of you who came along for those first speculative jaunts and the inquiry that ended literally, or in our imaginations, with a Spam musubi picnic next to London Nelson's grave, under the Chinese memorial arch in the Evergreen Cemetery.

"Mystery Spot: 95065"
Anjali Arondekar
Kate Bernheimer

"The Missing Testicles of Padre Q" /
    "Los Compañeros Ausentes del Padre Q"
Kat Bailey and the Santa Cruz Mission State Historic Park
Micah Perks
Juan Poblete
Hisaji Quintus Sakai

"The Brother's Parking Lot"
Ronaldo V. Wilson

"Frutos Extraños"
Wanda Alarcón
Sarah Arantza Amador for translations to Spanish
Cindy Cruz
Binh Danh
Theo Honnef for translations to German
Sally Iverson and the Santa Cruz Museum of Natural History
Lourdes Martínez-Echazábal
Marla Novo and the Santa Cruz Museum of Art & History
Milton Torres Oliveira
Arturo Villaseñor and the Santa Cruz Public Library

"Quimosabe"
  Amy McMullen and Central Coast Oncology & Hematology
  Rachel Snelling for molecular drawings

"This is Someone's Paradise"
  Howard Pat Boltz
  Lucy Mae San Pablo Burns
  Dorothy Fujita-Rony
  Theodore Gonzales

"Santa Cruz Chinatown"
  Bonnie Rhee Andryeyev
  Boreth Ly
  George Ow Jr.
  Carrie Xiao

"Indian Summer"
  Lucy Asako Boltz
  Ronaldo Lopes de Oliveira

"Midsummer Night's Dream"
  Anjali Arondekar

"Neverneverland"
  Jane Tomi Boltz

Special thanks to Lucy Asako Boltz, Jonathan Van Harmelen, Howard Pat Boltz, Noah Baum, and Russell Wei Shen Soh for extensive and meticulous research into the archives and history behind the fiction of these stories. Humble thanks to Ruth Hsu and Sima Rabinowitz, who generously read and commented on every story as they were drafted to completion. And to Khushal Gujadhur, who, after one walk, became inspired to continue these walks for another generation.

And most of all, grateful kudos to Angie Sijun Lou, for taking on the big task of the other half of this book, for curating and imagining its more expansive planet and speculative coordinates under the pen of eight gifted mythographers, including herself. With sincere gratitude to Angie, Sesshu Foster, Saretta Morgan, Thirii Myo Kyaw Myint, Craig Santos Perez, Brandon Shimoda, Juliana Spahr, and Ronaldo V. Wilson. Finally, and as always, thanks to the staff at Coffee House Press and our special editor, Erika Stevens.

Bibliography

The Missing Testicles of Padre Q/Los Compañeros Ausentes del Padre Q

Castillo, Edward D., ed./trans. "The Assassination of Padre Andrés Quintana by the Indian of Mission Santa Cruz in 1812: The Narrative of Lorenzo Asisara," *California History* 68, no. 3 (Fall 1989): 116-125. https://doi.org/10.2307/25462397.

The Brother's Parking Lot

Bingham, Tabetha F. "New Orleans to San Francisco in '49," *Overland Monthly*, 1892, transcribed by Russell Towle, February 1995. http://explore.museumca.org/goldrush/tales-new1.html.

Yetman, Norman, ed. *Voices from Slavery: 100 Authentic Slave Narratives*. 1970. Mineola: Dover Publications, 1999.

Frutos Extraños

Duncan, McPherson, ed. "Murder-Arrest-Strangulation," *The Santa Cruz Sentinel*, May 1877, 22:2.

Dunn, Geoffrey. "Hanging on the Water Street Bridge: A Santa Cruz Lynching," *Santa Cruz is in the Heart: Selected Writings on Local History, Culture, Politics & Ghosts*. Capitola: Capitola Book Company, 1980.

Work, Monroe Nathan, www.monroeworktoday.org

Quimosabe

Brown, Barry. "The California Powder Works and San Lorenzo Paper Mill: Self-Guided Tour," Santa Cruz, CA: Paradise Park Masonic Club, Santa Cruz Public Library Local History, 2008.

Goodman, Jordan, and Vivien Walsh. *The Story of Taxol: Nature and Politics in the Pursuit of an Anti-Cancer Drug*. Cambridge: Cambridge University Press, 2001.

Google (this and that; it's endless)

Hartzell, Hal and Jerry Rust. *Yew*. Self-published, H. Hartzell and J. Rust, 1983.

Marquez, Emily and Susan Kegley. "Air Monitoring for Chloropicrin in Watsonville, California: November 3-12, 2014," *Pesticide Action Network*, April 2015.

Santa Cruz Sentinel, April 1898.

This Is Someone's Paradise

Baldoz, Rick. *Third Asiatic Invasion: Empire and Migration in Filipino America, 1898-1946*. New York: New York University Press, 2011.

Burn, Lucy San Pablo. "'Splendid Dancing': Filipino 'Exceptionalism' in Taxi Dancehalls," *Dance Research Journal* 40, no. 2 (Winter 2008).

The Daily Worker, 1930.

De Witt, Howard A. "The Watsonville Anti-Filipino Riot of 1930: A Case Study of the Great Depression and Ethnic Conflict in California," *Southern California Quarterly* 61, no. 3 (Fall 1979): 291-302. https://doi.org/10.2307/41170831

Bogardus, Emory S. *Anti-Filipino Race Riots: A Report to the Ingram Institute of Social Science of San Diego*, Ingram Institute, 1930.

Empress of Canada Passenger List, 15 February 1930, Canadian Pacific Railway, Chung Collection, University of British Columbia.

Evening Pajaronian, 1930.

Fujita-Rony, Dorothy B. "Fermin Tobera, Military California, and Rural Space," *Making the Empire Work: Labor and United States Imperialism*. Edited by Daniel E. Bender and Jana K. Lipman. New York: NYU Press, 2015.

Habal, Estella. "Radical Violence in the Fields: Anti-Filipino Riot in Watsonville," *Honolulu Star-Bulletin*, 1930.

Kramer, Paul A. "Empire and Exclusion: Ending the Philippine Invasion of the United States," *The Blood of Government: Race, Empire, the United States, and the Philippines*. Chapel Hill: University of North Carolina Press, 2006.

Kurashige, Lon. "Silver Lining: New Deals for Asian Americans, 1924-1941," *Two Faces of Exclusion: The Untold History of Anti-Asian Racism in the United States*. Chapel Hill: University of North Carolina Press, 2016.

Los Angeles Times, 1930.

Okada, Taihei. "Underside of Independence Politics: Filipino Reactions to Anti-Filipino Riots in the United States," *Philippine Studies: Historical & Ethnographic Viewpoints* 60 no. 3, Transnational Migration: Part 2: Imperial and Personal Histories (Sept 2012): 307-335. http://www.jstor.org/stable/42634724

Philippine News-Tribune, 1930.

San Juan Jr., E. "Reading the Stigmata: Filipino Bodies Performing for the U.S. Empire," Countercurrents.org, 2015.

Showalter, Michael P. "The Watsonville Anti-Filipino Riot of 1930: A Reconsideration of Fermin Tobera's Murder," *Southern California Quarterly* 71, no. 4 (Winter 1989): 341-348.

Tagami, Jeff. *October Light*. San Francisco: Kearny Street Workshop Press, 1987.

The Torch, January 1930

The Washington Post, 1930.

Santa Cruz Chinatown

Dunn, Geoffrey, ed. *Chinatown Dreams: The Life and Photography of George Lee.* Capitola: Capitola Book Company, 2002.

Lydon, Sandy. *Chinese Gold: The Chinese in the Monterey Bay Region*. Capitola: Capitola Book Company, 1985.

Midsummer Night's Dream

Clifford, James. *Returns: Becoming Indigenous in the 21st Century*. Cambridge, MA: Harvard University Press, 2013.

Curry, Arwen. *The Worlds of Ursula K. Le Guin*. PBS, 2018.

Flaherty, Robert J., dir. *Elephant Boy*. United Artists, 1937.

Haraway, Donna J. *Staying with the Trouble: Making Kin in the Chthulucene.* Durham: Duke University, 2016.

Haraway, Donna J. "A Cyborg Manifesto: Science Technology, and Socialist-Feminism in the Late Twentieth Century." In *Simians, Cyborgs and Women: The Reinvention of Nature*, 149-181. London: Routledge, 1991.

Kipling, Rudyard. *The Jungle Book*. Sahara Publisher Books, 1894.

Le Guin, Ursula K. *Always Coming Home: Author's Expanded Edition*. Edited by Brian Attebery. New York; The Library of America, 2019.

Le Guin, Ursula K. "The Author of the Acacia Seeds." In *The Ascent of Wonder: The Evolution of Hard SF*, edited by David G. Hartwell & Kathryn Cramer, 547-552. New York: Orb Books, 1997.

Rogell, Albert S., dir. *Song of India*. Columbia Pictures, 1949.

Shakespeare, William. *A Midsummer Night's Dream*. London, 1600.

Le Guin, Ursula K., with Donna Haraway and James Clifford. Filmed May 8, 2014 at the University of Southern California, Santa Cruz, CA. Video, 1:14:50. https://vimeo.com/98270808

Neverneverland

Hitchcock, Alfred, dir. *Psycho.* Paramount Pictures, 1960.

Garland, Alex, dir. *Devs.* Disney, 2020.

Schumacher, Joel, dir. *The Lost Boys.* Warner Bros. Pictures, 1987.

Peele, Jordan, dir. *Us.* Universal Pictures, 2019.

Previously Published Stories

"Mystery Spot: 95065." In *Xo Orpheus: Fifty New Myths*, edited by Kate
Bernheimer, 359-363. New York: Penguin Books, 2013.

"Indian Summer," *Sansei and Sensibility*. Minneapolis: Coffee House Press, 2020.
Originally published in *Boom California*, May 2, 2017, University of California
Press, Jason Sexton, ed.

"Frutos Extraños." In *Georgia Review*, edited by Gerald Maa. Spring 2020.

"Santa Cruz Chinatown." *The Harvard Advocate: The Migration Issue*, 2021.

"Midsummer Night's Dream." In *Zyzzyva: Arts & Letters: The Inter/Transnational
Issue* 37, no. 12, edited by Oscar Villalon, (Winter 2021): 81-93.

"The Brother's Parking Lot." In *Interim: Black The[or]y* 38, no. 4, guest edited by
Ronaldo V. Wilson.

"Quimosabe." In *Mantissa*, edited by Mark Axelrod (forthcoming).

Santa Cruz Nori Coordinates

Mystery Spot: 95065
37.0172695°, -122.0041811°
The Mystery Spot
465 Mystery Spot Road
Santa Cruz, CA 95065

The Missing Testicles of Padre Q
36.9776996°, -122.027901°
Santa Cruz Mission State Historic Park
144 School Street
Santa Cruz, CA 95065

The Brother's Parking Lot
36.9762113°, -122.0262003°
United States Postal Service
850 Front Street
Santa Cruz, CA 95060

Frutos Extraños
36.9782921°, -122.0245522°
Water Street Bridge
Water & River Streets
Santa Cruz, CA 95061

Quimosabe
37.0075413°, -122.0428777°
Paradise Park Masonic Club
211 Paradise Park
Santa Cruz, CA 95060

This Is Someone's Paradise
36.854754°, -121.639174°
San Juan & Murphy Roads
Watsonville, CA 95076

Santa Cruz Chinatown
36.9782228°, -122.0257558°
149 River Street
Santa Cruz, CA 95060

Indian Summer
36.9803925°, -122.0191616°
550 Water Street
Santa Cruz, CA 95060

Midsummer Night's Dream
36.9800104°, -122.0104498°
Rio Theater
1205 Soquel Avenue
Santa Cruz, CA 95062

Neverneverland
36.9646282°, -122.0248846°
Sunshine Villa
80 Front Street
Santa Cruz, CA 95060

801 Silver Avenue *after Hom Wong Shee*

Brandon Shimoda

On August 12, 1940, the immigration station at Angel Island, in San Francisco Bay, burned down. The cause was an electrical fire, but could it have been the angels? The immigration station was on a hill tucked into a cove, China Cove, named for the country from which a majority of the immigrants were arriving. Angel Island was named by Juan Manuel de Ayala y Aranza, Spanish explorer, and one of the first white men to invade San Francisco Bay. When Ayala anchored his ship off the island, he must have felt something, maybe even the touch of what he described, romantically—sinisterly—as an *angel*. The island is just over one mile square and shaped like a stingray. For thousands of years, the Coast Miwok rowed small boats from the mainland, set up camp in the coves. They built houses of branches and bulrushes, hunted and fished, gathered acorns and greens, then dismantled their houses and erased their footprints. They were there when Ayala arrived. Ayala referred to them as *tender lambs*. Those who were not enslaved were forced off the island. Those who were enslaved got sick from the white man's food, were infected by their diseases, and/or died.

The immigration station was built to enforce the Chinese Exclusion Act, signed in 1882, which greatly restricted immigration from China. The ban, however, did not prevent people from arriving, as bans—like walls—do not, paradoxically, have the ability to do, but instead made the process more convoluted and harrowing (its actual power), with immigrants forced to balance their lives, their luck, and their bodies on a knife edge. The immigration station was also a deportation facility, which contrived the keystone misunderstanding of what immigration continues to mean, especially in the white imagination, especially of those farthest removed from the realities of immigration: to arrive and to be summarily expelled, days, weeks, months later, or immediately.

Actually, only the administration building burned down, which is where the women were detained, and where, awaiting the adjudication of their histories and their futures, they carved poems into the walls. Unlike the hundreds of poems carved by the men into the walls of their barracks—poems that have been translated, published, enshrined as memorials—the poems carved by the women exist only in the memory of the dead. One, an immigrant named Mrs. Loo, remembered seeing *plenty of poems on the wall.* Another, an immigrant named Lee Puey You, remembered seeing *the bathroom filled with sad and bitter poems.*[1] The building was already falling apart. It was only a matter of time before it fell apart completely, taking lives with it. The authorities seemed satisfied to let that time pass. It embodied the peculiar contradiction of being both the frontline fortification of the nation's war on Asian immigration and completely neglected. Electrical fire? I think it was the angels. And even though that was the end of the immigration station's thirty-year reign on Angel Island, the immigration station itself was lifted out of the embers and off the island and set down on a hill across the bay in San Francisco, at 801 Silver Avenue.

801 Silver Avenue is a large brick building that houses the Cornerstone Academy, a private school, pre-K through eighth grade, run by the Cornerstone Evangelical Baptist Church. The church was founded in 1975 by Chanson Lau, a Chinese American pastor. His bio on the church's website begins: *After accepting Jesus Christ as his personal Lord and Savior in high school, God took Chanson on the ride of a lifetime.*[2]

The building bears the hallmarks of being fearsome and imposing—tall doorways like teeth, dark, glowering windows like eye sockets, the haunted look of an asylum—but seemed, the day I visited, innocuous, almost sunny. There were no shadows on its façade, unlike in black-and-white photographs, in which the building, occupied by Immigration and Naturalization Service, looks like it can be entered but not exited. Its sunny quality must have had something to do with it being filled with children, and the idea, even, of the busyness of their classrooms.

---

1. Erika Lee and Judy Yung, *Angel Island: Immigrant Gateway to America* (New York: Oxford University Press, 2010), 104.
2. "Meet the Staff," Cornerstone Evangelical Baptist Church (website), copyright 2020: https://www.cebc.net/meet-the-staff

And yet, the building was quiet. Was it nap time? Do eighth graders take naps? Were the windows closed? Was everyone out on a field trip? The thing that made it sunny was also what made it fearsome and imposing: its skull-like anonymity. I did not know, when I visited, that it was a school. I visited not knowing what it was, only what it had been. It was completely illegible from the street what kind of building it was or what was going on inside of it.

Before INS, 801 Silver Avenue was home to the Training College of the Salvation Army, but the college went bankrupt. After the war, it was home to Simpson Bible College, a Christian missionary school. Cornerstone Academy bought the property in 1989. The purchase was made, according to their website, *by a miracle of God.*

The architectural requirements of a school—in these instances, watched over by God—are apparently the same as that of a detention facility. Within three days of Pearl Harbor, nearly one hundred issei men from Northern California and the Bay Area were detained at 801 Silver Avenue. A month later, forty more issei were detained. A month after that, nearly 180 issei were detained, adding to a population that included German and Italian men, and Chinese immigrants, including women and children. The issei were removed from their families and homes, their communities and places of work, and detained with the Germans, Italians, and Chinese. The issei were detained, with the Germans, Italians, and Chinese, in the gymnasium. They slept on bunk beds three beds high. There was nothing to do but think or not think, talk or not talk, await interrogation and eventual transfer to another detention facility: Sharp Park in Pacifica, Fort Lincoln in North Dakota, Fort Missoula in Montana.

I went to 801 Silver Avenue to visit with the memory of the issei, and to get a sense, however speculative and atmospheric, of their first view of the war. It was a school day, but the parking lot was empty. The lobby was small, not as grand as the building suggested. Carpeted, with potted plants and a small table with brochures. It felt like the foyer of a church, which I guess it was. An Asian American woman was sitting at a front desk that looked like a reception area at the dentist's. She was friendly, asked how she could help.

I'm visiting places where Japanese Americans were detained during World War II, I said. I felt, saying it, and so straight, like a schoolchild.

The woman froze. The walls were decorated with drawings by children, their names scrawled at the bottom. All of their names were Chinese.

Chinese immigrants too, I said, which was true, but I was recalculating, thinking that the woman might be more interested in Chinese immigrants than in Japanese Americans.

This used to be a detention center, I said. But as soon as I said it, I felt embarrassed, then ashamed, like I, a stranger, was pushing at the woman some terribly negative energy, which I wanted desperately to take back.

I don't know, she said. *I don't think so.*

I guess what I said sounded like a question, like I was lost and was asking for directions to the nearest detention center. (Later that day, while looking for the site of the Sharp Park detention center, I got lost and asked a woman in a bright pink golf outfit, who also happened to be Asian American, for directions.)

I am not sure what I was expecting. I suppose I thought that the woman, or whomever I might encounter, would let me wander the building or, more absurdly, offer to give me a tour. Then I would have been peeking into classrooms full of children, and how would I explain myself then? Would I have interrupted each class to tell the students that their classroom was once used to detain Asian people?

For the past few years, I have been visiting sites where Japanese immigrants and Japanese Americans were incarcerated during World War II. Although my visits have been intentional, they have not been programmatic. I rarely know what I am looking for, and when I find what I do not know I am looking for, I often turn away and look at something else, something that has nothing, or nothing obvious, to do with the past, but that becomes its emissary, at least that is how it feels. I am drawn especially to sites in which no trace of the past remains, or in which the past is propagated, at most, by traces, which have to be manifestations of missing—but missing what? Broken slabs of concrete beneath a bush, a staircase floating away from a broken foundation, crimson-colored trees on a hill above a wash, white roses outside a shopping mall.

Whenever I am getting close to these sites, I carry with me the delusion that everyone who is there—who I see and meet—is not only aware of the site and its history, but carries a piece of it with them, if they are not a piece of it themselves. The delusion is based on a simple desire: that we know where we are, which means knowing what happened there. The desire is based, in turn, on the feeling that I do not know where I am, which means that everyone who is there, even if they arrived only moments before, knows at least a little more than I do. I have met many people in the ruins of incarceration who did not know that is what had happened there, and though I used to be surprised, I am increasingly confirmed in my understanding of the United States, in particular, as a megalithic antimemorial to everyone and everything it has disappeared and/or destroyed, and of its citizens as the stewards of that disappearance and destruction.

On November 19, 1941, a Chinese woman named Hom Wong Shee committed suicide at 801 Silver Avenue. Wong Shee, 46, had been in detention with—yet separated from—her two youngest sons for twenty-five days when she drove chopsticks into her ears and cut her throat with a pocketknife. It was after midnight. Everyone was asleep. The matron on duty said that Wong Shee had, in the days before, been *acting queerly*, that she had been *getting up out of bed and making noise*, that she kept saying that she was *crazy*.[3]

What Wong Shee said was: *I'm at my wit's end.*[4]

Wong Shee spoke Taishanese, a Cantonese dialect from Guangdong Province, the Pearl River Delta. She immigrated to the US in 1922. She married a Chinese American businessman named Hom Hen Shew, who served with the American Expeditionary Forces in WWI. They lived in Pittsburgh for ten years and had seven children. In 1932, they returned to China, had two more children, sons, Hom Lee Min and Hom King Min. Hen Shew returned to the US, to New York, with all of the children except for the youngest sons. It could be imagined that Wong Shee wanted to stay longer with her family in China, but when Japan began bombing Guangdong, Wong Shee, Lee Min, and King Min moved to Hong Kong, then returned to the US to rejoin the rest of the family. They arrived in San Francisco on October 23, 1941, and were immediately detained and separated—Shee to the women's quarters, her sons to the gymnasium. Wong Shee made repeated requests for her and her sons to be detained together, then, when those requests were denied, to at least be able to see them. Those requests were also denied, for the reason that her sons were *old enough to take care of themselves*. They were eight and nine. Wong Shee was eventually allowed to see Lee Min, but only briefly. He got sick and had to be taken to the building's hospital. Wong Shee was invited to the lobby to see him only after his sickness, as he was being taken back to the gymnasium.

---

3. "41369/11-29 Wong Shee," "Separate Lives, Broken Dreams: Saga of Chinese Immigration," Center for Asian American Media, 13: caamedia.org/separatelivesbrokendreams/chop13.html
4. Jenny F. Lew, "41369/11-29 Wong Shee," "Separate Lives, Broken Dreams: Saga of Chinese Immigration," Center for Asian American Media: caamedia.org/separatelivesbrokendreams/chop.html

In the days that followed, Wong Shee became increasingly desperate. The head matron, Helen Louise Nelson, heard high-pitched screams coming from her room, which the nurse told her was typical of Chinese women. *They sometimes act that way when disappointed*, she said.[5] Wong Shee watched as other women failed their hearings and were deported, and feared the same thing happening to her and her sons. She had no money, owed debts on her return to the US from Hong Kong, her family had not been informed about their detention, she was suffering high blood pressure, and had a hearing disorder. Less than two weeks after seeing her son in the lobby, Wong Shee committed suicide in the bathroom.

Wong Shee's oldest son, Hom You Yee, a soldier in the US Army, stationed at Fort Benning in Georgia, wrote a letter to INS asking about his mother's death—which neither he nor anyone in the family received information about. A letter came back that began, *Inasmuch as you are a member of the same family . . .* The language was inscrutable, senseless. It offered no condolences, but mentioned You Yee's young brothers, who were still in detention. *Hearings . . . will proceed as soon as conditions permit*, the letter concluded, making clear that despite their mother's death, they would receive no special attention.[6]

An investigation conducted internally by the San Francisco division of INS confirmed Wong Shee's mistreatment: her being separated from her sons, her requests to be reunited with them neglected or denied, not receiving medical or mental health attention, the fact, more generally, that the staff at 801 Silver Avenue neither spoke nor understood Chinese, not to mention her dialect. It was also revealed that her mistreatment was not exceptional, that she had been treated no different than any of the Chinese immigrants at 801 Silver Avenue or any of the thousands on Angel Island, which included the fact that not only her mistreatment but the results of the investigation into her mistreatment were lost, buried in bureaucratic language, in the archives, out of reach and out of consciousness.

I did not know about Hom Wong Shee when I visited 801 Silver Avenue. My interest in her grew out of an acute and insistent disquiet that grew out of a more general disquiet that surrounded my memory of visiting 801 Silver Avenue, and which sent me back into the fogged-over archive. I was disturbed by the school, by how

---

5. "41369/11-29 Wong Shee," "Separate Lives, Broken Dreams: Saga of Chinese Immigration," Center for Asian American Media, 13: caamedia.org/separatelivesbrokendreams/chop13.html
6. "41369/11-29 Wong Shee," "Separate Lives, Broken Dreams: Saga of Chinese Immigration," Center for Asian American Media, 10: caamedia.org/separatelivesbrokendreams/chop10.html

easily it seemed to have consumed the history with which it shared a building. Most of the incarceration sites I have visited have been converted into memorials, ruins, or some uneasy combination of the two, or have been replaced by some form of American decadence or oblivion—a shopping mall, a campground, an archery range—but 801 Silver Avenue was, and is, still there on the hill, more or less unchanged. The Cornerstone Academy's mission, based on Christian principles, includes preparing students for *productive lives as responsible citizens in a free and competitive society.*[7]

What do these words, individually and together, mean, and in relation to children? I hear in them the language of an institution that wants to rebrand its image, if never its function, less in the spirit of preparing individuals for life and more in the business of reforming them for an illusory release.

Wong Shee wanted to go home. She wanted her sons, she wanted the three of them to go home. Even though she had lived in, and even though she and her sons had already entered, the US, she was being held at its border, which the war was making stronger and more obtuse. The border was wherever she was.

If I had known about Hom Wong Shee, would I have approached the building differently, or at all? An immigration station, a detention facility, an interrogation room, a gymnasium filled with beds stacked *Squid Game*–style, where hundreds of men and two young boys keep or lose track of time; a room where women are kept awake by the distress of a woman kept awake by the thought of her sons on the far side of several impenetrable walls; is already a funereal space, but death changes it, deepens it, makes it irrecoverable. Would I have oriented myself and my questions to the memory of Hom Wong Shee? Would I have seen in everything an attempt to erase her memory from the building? There is no marker, no plaque. Until there is, if there ever will be, I will continue to understand the memorial to the immigrants and to Hom Wong Shee to be this absence, and to the seemingly comprehensive erasure of the fact that the immigrants had been there at all. And I will continue to understand the memorial to exist in the lack of awareness that is being passed down to the children and in their formation—and in their futures—as *responsible citizens.*

As I was thinking about Hom Wong Shee, my friend, the poet Mia Ayumi Malhotra, sent me her chapbook *Notes from the Birth Year*, which includes a poem

---

7. "Mission Statement," Cornerstone Academy (website), copyright 2017: cornerstone-academy.net /mission-statement

written for her grandmother called "A Death Diary." In it she asks, *What is the difference between a ghost and an ancestor?*[8] Mia, sansei on her mother's side, yonsei on her father's side, had seventeen family members incarcerated during wwii—in the detention center in Stockton, California, in the Department of Justice prison in Lordsburg, New Mexico, and in the concentration camp in Rohwer, Arkansas. Who among the seventeen are ghosts and who among them are ancestors, I wonder. Can they each only be one? When I read Mia's question, I thought—as I am always thinking—about my grandfather, who was incarcerated in the doj prison in Missoula, Montana, with men from 801 Silver Avenue. I have known my grandfather, since his death, as a ghost and as an ancestor, but I cannot say if he has been both at the same time, only that these facets—or revelations—of him and his memory do not seem incompatible, might even be inseparable. But, as Mia is asking, *what is the difference?*

I mourn the ways the dead are deprived of a place in the lives—the days and nights, thoughts and feelings—of the living. Maybe it is less about paying attention to the dead and more about sharing with the dead what we are paying attention to. Because if I were to attempt an answer to Mia's question, I would say that the difference between a ghost and an ancestor is the difference between the withholding and the sharing of our attention, that a ghost exists wherever we, the living, are not sharing our lives with the dead, and that an ancestor is the definition of that sharing.

How many of Hom Wong Shee's nine children—including her two sons who entered 801 Silver Avenue with her and who left 801 Silver Avenue without her—had children, grandchildren? Where are they now? I imagine them in two places, in two states of being, simultaneously: spread out, far away from each other—trying, occasionally, to project themselves into each other's lives, or pull each other into their own—and gathered together in a room. I see, in both images, a composition drawn by the dreams and the desperation of a woman who was as much the aspirant to, as she was the ancestor of, the people who, in the future, were waiting.

When I left the building, a group of children, twenty or thirty first or second or third graders, all Asian American, were lining up in long rows in the parking lot. The children, some with backpacks, some with lunch boxes, some wearing hats, all

---

8. Mia Ayumi Malhotra, "A Death Diary," in *Notes from the Birth Year* (Bar Harbor, ME: Bateau Press, 2022), 20.

Brandon Shimoda

wearing white, lined up along the yellow lines. They were remarkably quiet. So was their teacher, a young woman. I waved; they did not wave back. Why did I wave? I felt gangly, like an inflatable air dancer. I also felt distant, incongruous with the present, as if, because of the reasons for my being there, I had emerged not through the front door of their school, but out of an entirely different building.

The sun was bright. The children's shadows, growing out of the yellow lines, were soft, softly radiant at their edges, and were moving in a way that made them seem almost independent from the children, as if the children, standing still, were not casting shadows at all, but, in their innocence and lack of awareness, had let their spirits slip out of their bodies.

BIBLIOGRAPHY

"Separate Lives, Broken Dreams: Saga of Chinese Immigration." Center for Asian American Media. https://caamedia.org/separatelivesbrokendreams/

"Mission Statement." Cornerstone Academy. https://www.cornerstone-academy.net /mission-statement. 2017.

"Meet the Staff." Cornerstone Evangelical Baptist Church. https://www.cebc.net /meet-the-staff. 2020.

Lee, Erika, and Judy Yung, *Angel Island: Immigrant Gateway to America*. New York: Oxford University Press, 2010.

Malhotra, Mia Ayumi, "A Death Diary," in *Notes from the Birth Year*. Bar Harbor, ME: Bateau Press, 2022.

Warrior, William. "Song for Wong Toy Heung." Indybay. https://www.indybay.org /newsitems/2010/01/04/18634339.php. 4 January 2010.

(De)Tour of an Unincorporated Territory
Craig Santos Perez

On the morning of my fifteenth birthday, my dad left our house early while all of us were still sleeping.

"Where'd you go?" my mom asked when he returned after breakfast.

"The Dededo Flea Market. I bought a present."

I was sitting in the living room playing the Nintendo game *Super Mario Kart*. At the sound of the word "present," I dropped the controller and ran outside to see what was in the bed of my dad's Toyota pickup truck. My excitement crumpled when I saw the pile of junk: a rusted bicycle frame, flat tires, tangled chain, and a few plastic bags filled with supplies and spray paint cans. While I had outgrown my old bike, I was hoping for a new BMX or Schwinn, like the ones kids rode on American television shows set in white suburbs.

"Unload that stuff onto the carport," my dad said.

We worked outside for hours in the western Pacific humidity. I helped him clean and sand the frame, attach the chain, and install the new tires, handlebars, seat, pedals, and kickstand. Then we painted it my favorite color: ocean blue. He wiped his dirty hands against his sweaty Army T-shirt and asked: "What you think?"

"I'm stoked," I said.

Even though it was not a brand-name bike, it looked brand new. And having built it with my dad, having witnessed its transformation, made it special.

"I can't wait to cruise around the island."

"First, it needs to dry. You can ride it tomorrow. And your mom said you can only go to Manglona Market, the basketball court, or Grandma's house. Remember your coordinates."

~

My dad had explained latitude and longitude to me a few years earlier. He collected maps and hung them in the hallway. The first map was an aerial view of Guam, our homeland.

"Where's our village?" I asked him.

"Here," he said. "In the center. Mongmong."

I read the names of the other villages: *Yigo, Dededo, Tamuning, Barrigada, Mangilao, Chalan Pago, Ordot, Toto, Maite, Agana, Agana Heights, Sinajana, Asan, Piti, Yona, Santa Rita, Agat, Talofofo, Umatac, Inarajan, Merizo.*

"What does the name of our village mean?" I asked him.

"It comes from *momongmong*. Our people's word for *heartbeat*."

In our American-style school system, we were only taught English and not Chamoru, our native tongue. During my grandparent's generation, speaking Chamoru in school was forbidden, and you were punished if you were caught.

But what they do teach us is that Guam was "discovered" by Ferdinand Magellan in 1521—*the first inhabited Pacific Island known to Europe.* When our ancestors saw the monstrous galleons pierce the horizon, they boarded outrigger canoes to trade with them. Antonio Pigafetta, Magellan's chronicler, noted how these were the fastest watercraft he'd ever seen, and called them "flying proa" because they seemed to agilely skim above the waves. That's why the Spanish named Guam *Isla de las Velas Latinas* (Island of Lateen Sails).

This first contact ended in disagreement and murder. The Spanish renamed Guam *Isla de los Ladrones* (Island of Thieves). Then Magellan and his crew made landfall, burned a village, and killed seven Chamorus before departing to Magellan's own death in the Philippines. The damage was done, however, as Guam became a regular stopover on the galleon trade route between Acapulco and Manila.

The second map my dad hung in the hallway was an aerial view of fifteen islands. I recognized Guam, the largest and southernmost. I read the names of the others: *Rota, Aguijan, Tinian, Saipan, Farallon de Medinilla, Anatahan, Sarigan, Guguan, Alamagan, Pagan, Agrihan, Asuncion, Maug,* and *Farallon de Pajaros.*

"This is our archipelago," he said. "The Marianas."

At Sunday school, we were taught that the Jesuit priest Diego Luis de San Vitores arrived on Guam in 1668. While some Chamorus willingly converted, many others resisted. In 1672, Father San Vitores was killed by the chief of the village of Tumon, Matå'pang, because the priest baptized the chief's daughter without asking permission. This conflict led to the Spanish–Chamorro wars that lasted for nearly thirty years. Due to military conquest and disease, the Chamoru

Craig Santos Perez

population plummeted from around two hundred thousand to just five thousand by the end of the seventeenth century.

The Catholic authorities renamed the archipelago "Islas Marianas," to honor the queen of Spain, María Ana de Austria, the funder of San Vitores's mission to Guam.

"The islands look like Grandma's rosary beads," I said.

The third map was an aerial view of thousands of tiny dots scattered across the northwestern Pacific Ocean.

"This is Micronesia," he said. "That's what a French explorer called our region. *Tiny islands.* Here's the Marianas. There's Palau, Yap, Chuuk, Pohnpei, the Marshalls, Kiribati, Kosrae, and Nauru."

"The islands look like a constellation of stars."

The fourth map was an aerial view of the Pacific Ocean rimmed by Asia and the Americas. My dad traced a triangle between Hawai'i, New Zealand, and Easter Island.

"This is Polynesia," he said.

Then he drew an imaginary circle around Papua New Guinea, the Solomon Islands, Fiji, Vanuatu, and New Caledonia.

"This is Melanesia."

I took a step back and noticed how the Pacific looked like a blue continent, despite the colonial divisions, despite the latitudes and longitudes of empire.

"Where's Guam in this map?" I asked. "I can't find it."

"Here's a navigation trick. Find Australia, then Japan, then the Philippines. You see that small dot in the middle of them. Remember your coordinates: 13 degrees north latitude, 144 degrees east longitude. That's where home is."

~

"Is the bike dry yet?" I asked my dad after we finished singing "Happy Birthday," blowing out the candles, and eating chocolate cake.

"You can't ride at night," he said sternly. "Just go to sleep and wake up early with me."

That night, I lay in bed staring at the glow-in-the-dark stars that I stuck on the ceiling when I was younger. I thought about another one of my dad's collectibles: a model outrigger canoe that he purchased from a master carver on Rota many years before I was born. The canoe was about three feet long and the sail was three feet high. The hull and outrigger were made from a local hardwood and the sail was woven from coconut fibers. It was displayed atop a blue glass coffee table in our living room. When my dad wasn't looking, I would place my Lego men on the canoe and imagine we were traveling beyond the reef, beyond the maps in the hallway, beyond the seven seas, and farther toward uncharted regions full of marine monsters and mythic islands,

While the presence of this canoe echoed the rich legacy of transoceanic travel and wayfinding traditions of our ancestors, it also signified a haunting absence. During the Spanish conquest, the authorities burned many canoes and forbade Chamorus from pelagic sailing in order to immobilize, convert, and control the population. Within a few generations, the knowledge of how to build the canoes and the memory of our navigational chants, songs, and techniques were lost at sea.

~

I woke before dawn, changed my clothes, brushed my teeth, and put on my socks, shoes, and a hat. My dad was already sitting at the dining table, drinking his daily ritual cup of Folgers Coffee and reading the *Pacific Daily News*. I could see through the kitchen window that the morning light was beginning to pull back the darkness.

"Remember your coordinates," he said, without looking up from the paper.

I wheeled my oceanic bike from the carport to the end of our cul-de-sac: Deboto Street, whose name derived from the Spanish word *devoción*. Then, I straddled the seat, gripped the handlebars, and pressed my feet firmly onto the pedals. I turned left, downhill, on the steep Chalan R. S. Sanchez Road. The bike felt sturdy and sleek as it picked up speed. Gravity pulled me past the other single-story concrete houses, the plumeria and hibiscus trees, the stray cats and barking boonie dogs. As the wind blew against my face, I flew down the asphalt, riding the efflorescent wave.

I started pressing the brakes when the bottom of the hill appeared on the horizon. The intersecting road was Sergeant Roy T. Damian Jr. Street, named after a twenty-one-year-old soldier from our village who was killed in the Gulf War. I don't remember what the name of the street was before. All I knew was that I would join JROTC soon and enlist in the armed forces after graduating high school, just like my dad, my grandfathers, my uncles, and my cousins. Maybe I, too, would be a local hero with a street named after me.

I braked at the stop sign, looked both ways, and crossed the street to Manglona Market, an old mom-and-pop store that had been in this exact spot for decades. My dad had grown up with the family who owned it, and he always spoke Chamoru with them when we would go there to buy Budweiser, bags of ice, and American candies and sodas. I never knew their real names, and I don't think we were actually related to them, but I always called them *uncle* and *auntie*.

The parking lot was empty because it was still so early that the store was not yet open. I turned around and pedaled back uphill. After two blocks, I lost momentum. My thighs and calves tightened. Sweat dripped down my back. I stood up for better leverage, but it felt like I was rowing against a strong current.

When I reached a plateau, I paused to catch my breath. I didn't want to go back home so soon, defeated, so I kept pedaling until I found a second wind. I passed the house with the giant mango tree, passed the house with the leashed German shepherds, past the dilapidated house that I never dared to trick-or-treat at during Halloween, and past the basketball court until I arrived at the end of Chalan R. S. Sanchez Road as it intersected with Purple Heart Highway.

Directly across the from me, the sun was rising through the barbed wire fencing and No Trespassing signs that marked the edge of the fields and the runways of the airport.

The everyday majesty of sunrises and sunsets on Guam always left me in awe. My grandma liked to say that the sky was *as red as San Vitores's blood and as gold as the crucifix at the cathedral*. The Dulce Nombre de Maria Cathedral-Basilica, located just a short drive from our village, is where we went for mass every Sunday. It's located on the site where the first Catholic church was constructed in 1669 under the supervision of Padre San Vitores.

My revelry in the sunrise was interrupted by the cars revving by. Their license plates read "Guam, U.S.A. Tano Y Chamorro." *Land of the Chamoru*. One bumper sticker featured our island's official slogan: "Guam, Where America's Day Begins!"

In school, we learned that Guam lies across the international dateline, which makes us a day ahead of the continental United States, and the first US citizens to see the sunrise.

We also had to memorize the year 1898, because that was when Guam became a US colony after the Spanish–American War. Though the textbooks never used the word "colony." Instead, Guam was known as an "unincorporated territory," which meant we were a possession of the US without becoming a fully incorporated part of the nation, and thus not all rights of the Constitution would apply. Guam was deemed *foreign in a domestic sense*, whatever that means.

From 1898 to 1941, the Navy administered Guam, with a captain appointed as governor. As part of its civil and military mission, the new colonial administration built schools, hospitals, businesses, and roads. The Spanish galleon trade had ended, and Guam instead became a strategic location for military transports traveling between San Francisco, Hawaiʻi, and the Philippines.

On December 8, 1941, the Empire of Japan bombed and invaded Guam, eventually defeating the US forces. Japan raised the rising sun of the imperial flag, and Guam was renamed *Omiya Jima, Great Shrine Island*. The Japanese authorities transformed Guam into its own strategic military base. In 1944, the US military returned, fought the Japanese in a three-week battle, and reclaimed the island. Around two thousand Chamorus died during the war. Our island became known as *Guam* once again.

The native name for Guam, which has been buried and suppressed in colonial histories, is *Guåhan*, a word in Chamoru that translates as *a place that has*, or, *we have*. Indeed, we have had many names. Names of violence, names of conquest, names of dominion, names of war. Names that attempt to define and confine us.

Throughout the following decades, the Department of Defense took land from Chamorus through eminent domain. The military dredged Apra Harbor and established the naval and air force bases. These efforts disturbed many archaeological sites of ancient Chamoru villages and disinterred burial grounds. Today, around thirty percent of Guam's entire landmass has been transformed into military installations. That's why Guam is often referred to as an "unsinkable aircraft carrier" and "the tip of America's spear in Asia."

Guam is Where America's Military Begins.

~

I turned right on Purple Heart Highway, and pedaled down the sidewalk for about half a mile. I stopped at the intersection of Kanada-Toto Loop Road. This was the road to my grandma's house—the border of my parents' permission.

I was tempted to keep going.

If I continued, I would eventually reach Highway 16, also named Army Drive. And if I traveled the length of Army Drive, I would end up on the island's main thoroughfare, Marine Corps Drive. If I turned right at that intersection, I would head north and then east toward Andersen Air Force Base. If I turned left, I would enter Guam's tourist village, Tumon, known as "Paradise Island," where millions of visitors from Japan stay each year.

My dad told me that Tumon was once a rich agricultural and fishing village, as well as the site of burial grounds. But they were destroyed and unearthed during construction. Today, you can stay at the Westin Resort Guam, the Guam Plaza Resort and Spa, Hotel Nikko Guam, the Hyatt Regency Guam, the Garden Villa, the Pacific Islands Club Guam, or the Hilton Guam Resort and Spa. You can enjoy a meal at Tony Roma's, California Pizza Kitchen, Chili's Grill and Bar, Outback Steakhouse, and Burger King. You can shop at Duty Free Galleria, Gucci, Burberry, Roxy, Kate Spade, Cartier, Balenciaga, Rolex, Ralph Lauren, Louis Vuitton, and Prada. If you need to relax, there are many massage parlors, such as Dream Spa Massage, Sugar Hut Express Spa, Oriental Pearls Therapeutic Massage, Guam Royal Spa, and By the Ocean Massage. If you want to blow off some steam, you can visit Star Gun Club, Dallas Gun Club, and the Hollywood Shooting Club.

I would navigate around the tourists and taxicabs on Pale San Vitores Road until I reached the bronze statues depicting the priest baptizing Matå'pang's daughter as the chief stands behind him wielding a machete alongside his companion, Hirao. The child's mother kneels next to them, screaming. Out of reflex, I would make the sign of the cross at the sight of this memorial to the martyr of the Marianas. I would remember how, every time I misbehaved, my grandma scolded me: "Basta! Stop being Matå'pang!" I would wonder: who should I feel sorry for? San Vitores? Or my own ancestors?

Afterward, I would swim at the nearby Måta'pang Beach among sunburnt tourists.

If I continued traversing Marine Corps Drive, I would pass the War in the Pacific National Historical Park, Apra Harbor, the Polaris Point Submarine Base, and Naval Base Guam. I would turn left on Highway 2, then stop to visit Nimitz Beach Park, named after Chester William Nimitz, the commander in chief of the US Pacific Fleet during World War II. Then, I would venture south to the village of Umatac, the Magellan Monument, and the Fort Nuestra Señora de la Soledad, an old Spanish military outpost.

My imaginary journey ended when a car honked at another car who swerved into its lane. My dad's voice echoed: *Remember your coordinates.*

I sighed and pedaled to Grandma's house.

~

I parked my bike on the porch, took off my socks and shoes, and opened the screen door to the kitchen.

"Håfa adai, Grandma!"

She was wearing her usual floral muʻumuʻu and sitting on the plastic-encased couch in the living room watching American soap operas. Next to the television stood a makeshift altar of devotional candles and a crucifix. She held a rosary in her hands.

"Håfa nen, why you here so early?" she asked.

"Dad got me a new bike for my birthday. I'm test-driving it," I joked.

Even though I was only fifteen years old, I was already taller than she was. I leaned down to kiss her wrinkled cheek, to show respect. But instead of kissing me, she took a deep inhale to breathe me in—a custom among older Chamorus.

"Fataʻchong. Come say lisayu with me."

"Grandma, why do you always say the rosary?"

She muted the television and adjusted the rosary between her fingers. This was her daily ritual. Her mother, who died before I was born, taught her devoción, even named her Rose.

"The lisayu helped us survive the war," she said, as she closed her eyes and began reciting this archipelago of prayers.

"Gi naʻan i Tata, i Lahiña, yan i Espiritu Santo. Åmen. I Kredo: Manhongge yo as Yuʻus Tata na toda-ha hanasina, na hanahuyong i langet yan i tano: yan as Jesukristo, guiya-ha Lahina as Saenata, ni i mamapotgenaihon pot finatinas yan grasian i Espiritu Santo . . ."

She was nineteen years old at the onset of the Japanese occupation in 1941. She witnessed how our people were forced to grow rice for the Japanese soldiers, forced into labor camps to build military structures, forced into sexual slavery.

"I Tatan-Mami: Tatan mami ni gaige Hao gi langet, umatuna i naʻan-mu, umamailaʻ i gobietno-mu, umafaʻtinas i pinto'-mu, asi gi tano' komu gi langet . . ."

In 1944, right before the US invasion, the Japanese military rounded up and ordered the Chamoru population to march to a concentration camp in Manenggon, a valley located in the southern village of Yona. The soldiers wielded bayonets and beat those who fell from exhaustion or tried to escape. Those who got sick or died during the march were simply left behind, uncared for and unburied.

"Abe Maria: Si Yuʻus ungenʻnegge, Maria, bula hao grasia, si Yuʻus gaige guiya haʻgo, matuna hao entre i totos i famalaoan, ya matuna i finanagumo as Jesus. Santa Maria, nanan Yuʻus, tayayute ham ni i manisao pago yan i oran finatai-mami. Åmen . . ."

My grandma was pregnant with her first child at that time. Her slippers broke after a few miles, so she had to walk barefoot. Her feet bled as the imperial sun beat against her brown skin. They walked at night as well, under the pale light of the moon, and were only allowed to sleep on the side of the road for a few hours. After a few days of this grueling journey, the contractions shivered her body. She stopped, bled into the dirt. Chåtfañagu.

I could not imagine her at that age. I could not imagine how carefully she wrapped the fetus in banana leaves. How did she stand up after the miscarriage? How did she keep walking? How heavy was that precious bundle? How did she carry it miles and miles to Manenggon? Where did she bury her fetus?

"Umatuna I Tata: Umatuna i Tata, yan i Lahiña, yan i Espirito Santo. Taeguihe i tutuhonna, yan pago, yan siempre yan i manaihinekog na haane. Åmen . . ."

~

"Can you get the fruit in the yard?" Grandma asked after she finished chanting the rosary. She rubbed her hands nervously into her thighs. "Typhoon's coming. I feel it."

I walked outside and grabbed a large, empty rice bag, a fruit picker, and a small machete from the back porch. In her yard, Grandma had planted mango, coconut, papaya, lime, breadfruit, avocado, and banana trees. This tropical orchard had perennially gifted us with enough fruit to share with neighbors and relatives.

While I was cutting a nearly ripe bundle of bananas, it fell from my grasp. I leaned down to pick it up and noticed something metal half-buried in the dirt. I dug it up with my hands and recognized the object: a dog tag, an ID for military personnel. My dad had one from his days in Vietnam, which he stored in a pocket of his rifle case under his bed. I wiped the dog tag clean but could not make out the name because it was worn and rusted. I dug a little deeper but there was no sign of bones or human remains. Finding discarded World War II–era dog tags, bullet casings, or even unexploded ordnances was common throughout Guam. I did not want to disturb the spirits that might be in the yard, so I buried the dog tag.

Suddenly, a thunderous B-52 bomber flew overhead on its path north toward Andersen Air Force Base. I didn't cover my ears because I'd grown accustomed to the sound of bombers piercing the sky.

~

Grandma was right. A few days later, Super Typhoon Omar made landfall on Guam. It battered us for sixteen hours with winds up to 150. It caused an island-wide electricity outage. My dad placed shutters on the windows, but they could not keep out the rains. As our rooms flooded, we took our pillows and blankets and placed them in the hallway. Then we closed the bedroom doors and placed towels on the floor. My parents, brother, sister, and I all slept in the hallway that night. In complete darkness, under the maps, as the winds wailed and our power-less house trembled.

We withstood the storm, but it took months to restore power and water to the island, and to repair the damage to our home. School was canceled for two weeks, and when the summer came around, my parents made a decision that would change our lives forever. Our family would migrate to the "mainland."

When they explained it to us, they mentioned "better opportunities," "better education," "better jobs," and a "better future." California was the "sunshine state" where there were no typhoons. Several of my mom's brothers and sisters already lived in California, and we would be able to hang out with all our stateside cous-ins. We could even visit my dad's siblings who lived in Washington, Oklahoma, and even Alaska.

Over the last fifty years, Chamorus have migrated in large numbers to seek jobs, schools, and health care or to serve in the military, deployed and stationed to bases around the world. More than forty thousand Chamorus now live in California; fifteen thousand in Washington; ten thousand in Texas; seven thou-sand in Hawai'i; and seventy thousand more in every other state. Today, there are more Chamorus living in the States than still living on Guam, with generations having been born away from our ancestral homelands.

Throughout that summer, my parents sold our clothes, furniture, and cars, as well as my Nintendo and bicycle. We packed a few suitcases of our most precious belongings, including my dad's maps, which he took down from the hallway and rolled up tightly so they did not take up too much space. Once everything was moved out, they sold our house on Deboto Street.

~

As we walked into the Guam International Airport, my dad pointed to the entrance and said: "Look, it's shaped like an outrigger canoe. Our word for air-plane is *batkon aire*, air boat."

At the gate, our relatives and close friends came to wait with us and talk story for a couple of hours. When they announced our flight, we stood up, hugged everyone, and cried. We promised to talk over the phone. Write letters. Stay in touch.

The last person I hugged was my grandma. She placed her rosary in my hand and whispered, "Make sure to say lisayu."

As I walked down the jet bridge, I turned around one last time to wave goodbye. I can barely remember the faces of those we left behind.

Then we boarded the hull of *Continental*, the name of the airline, the name of our destination: a twelve-hour flight to San Francisco.

On the flight, my dad hand-carried the model canoe. He had packed it carefully in bubble wrap and old copies of the *Pacific Daily News*. He didn't want to ship it because he was afraid it would get damaged. He placed it carefully in the storage space under the seat in front of him.

I sat next to him on the flight, and as the plane accelerated down the runway, he held his dog tag around his neck. I held my grandma's rosary. As the plane ascended, I looked out the window.

"There's Grandma's house," my dad said.

I looked at the house as we flew over it. Would I ever see her again? Would I ever eat fruit from her orchard? Would I ever see my friends and relatives? Would I remember the route to Grandma's house? Would I remember the streets of Mongmong or the landmarks of Guam? How far could I carry my memories of home? Would the island forget me?

I gazed at the land of my birth until the coastline appeared, then the reef. When Guam was no longer visible, I stared ahead toward the blue horizon. Then I closed my eyes. My heart crashed against the shores of my chest like waves. *Momongmong, momongmong.*

"I Satbe: Si Yu'us un ginegue raina yan nanan mina'åsi lina'la yan minames ninanggan mami Si Yu'us un ginegue. Hågo in a'agang ni man distilådon famaguon Eba, hågo in tatangga. Man u'ugong yan mañåtånges ham guini gi sagan lågo' . . ."

~

On the first day at my new high school, the homeroom teacher asked us, "Where are you *from?*"

When it was my turn, I answered, "Guam."

"I've never heard of Guam," he replied, pointing to a world map on the classroom wall. "Prove it exists."

I dreaded this moment because I knew that my home island was so tiny that it did not appear on most world maps. I stood up from my desk and approached the Atlantic Ocean, glistening in the center, while the Pacific Ocean was split in two and splayed to the margins. I heard my dad's voice in my head: *Remember your coordinates.*

I found and triangulated Australia, Japan, and the Philippines. I looked closely at the blue area where I knew Guam was located. There was nothing. Not even an unnamed dot.

"I'm from this invisible island." I smiled.

My classmates laughed. And even though my ancestors were oceanic navigators, I felt so lost, shipwrecked on the coast of a strange continent.

"Are you a citizen?" the teacher interrogated.

"Yes," I said. "Guam is a US territory."

"Are you Mexican?"

"No, my people are called Chamoru."

I was not surprised that the teacher did not know anything about Guam. Most Americans are not taught about American empire in the Pacific. Most do not know that Guam is the westernmost territory in the nation. They don't know our slogan, our license plates. Most do not know that we learn American English, study American history, eat American food, listen to American music, watch American movies and television, play American sports, serve in the American military, die in American wars, and dream American dreams.

"You speak English well," he proclaimed. "With *almost* no accent."

Was this what it meant to be from Guam? To be *foreign in a domestic sense?* To be *unincorporated? Invisible?*

I returned to my desk. I wish I had said that I was from Guåhan, *a place that has* a culture and history as deep as the Mariana Trench. Guåhan, *a place that has* so much beauty and trauma, so many memories and stories, plumeria and banana trees, grandmothers and blue bicycles.

506 N. Evergreen Avenue, Los Angeles, CA 90033

Sesshu Foster

I remember the moment my parents' marriage ended. I don't recall the specific day or date, but I recall the moment.

As Dad bounced from job to job, six months here, a year somewhere else, he was briefly employed as a caretaker on a duck hunting preserve outside of Los Banos in the Central Valley. Our little house was in a dusty low spot below the highway. My brother Paul and I roamed the lagoons of mud and dead trees and tule reeds on long dirt roads atop the dikes. Maybe we had heard Dad rampaging, and Mom pleading and crying. Hanging around outside waiting. Maybe we heard him smash all the furniture (even the giant radio cabinet with glass tubes inside that glowed green?) and heard her shrieking. When are they going to stop? Maybe they'd stop and the house would be quiet. I would have been listening.

This was the end, it turned out, as Mom came out of the house and called me. "Help get the kids in the car." She was pregnant and she carried one of my sisters on her hip as we walked up the gravel drive to the highway. The car was already parked out on the highway. Dad had broken her nose and her hand. She held a tissue to her face to stanch the bleeding.

"Where are we going?" I asked. Maybe her voice trembled when she told me to just help get the kids in the car. So I shut up and shepherded the little kids through the gate. Maybe we were buffeted by trucks in the dust and wind as I helped my brother and four sisters into the car. Paul and I got up on our knees in the back seat and looked out the rear window. State troopers led Dad out onto the highway. His shirt flapped open as they leaned him over the hood of their patrol car to cuff him. When he saw us watching, he grinned at us with his bleary face. Mom pulled out and drove away.

I was eight years old when Auntie Fu and Uncle John took us in to their hilltop house in East LA. We lived there for a month or two. My mom's brothers, John and Bill, had talked about what to do about their sister and her bunch of kids. When the house that Uncle Bill had purchased ($19,000) on a nearby hill overlooking City Terrace Elementary School was ready, we ended up living in that house.

The house was on a hill with a view of the downtown skyline—when the smog blew off. Seven kids and Mom in two bedrooms, for which she paid her brother $100 a month and cooked all his meals. Uncle Bill had the back bedroom and his own bathroom. My younger brother Paul and I soon learned to fear Uncle Bill, the first adult we'd ever met who could hardly restrain himself from hurting a child. He trembled with rage above us, always on the verge of lashing out. Our dad had never hit us, never yelled at his own children. Sober, Dad had been a nice guy. Uncle Bill was the first person I met who seemed unhinged when sober. Usually he'd ignore us, but if he'd had a bad day, or Paul and I played too loud or made a mess, a fury would come over him. His face turned red and he choked up, barking curses as white spit collected in the corners of his mouth. "You goddamned little son of a bitch! You're gonna turn out to be scum of the earth just like your old man!"

I was eight years old the first time he wrapped a belt around his fist and whipped me. Paul usually ran away. Sometimes I stood for the whipping if cornered, but sometimes I ran away, too. Mostly, my uncle just seethed with rage. If Paul and I looked up and saw Uncle Bill staring at us from the driveway, we'd play somewhere else. Mom wouldn't tolerate anyone touching my four sisters, but Paul and I were left to face our uncle on our own. We were loud boys, I'm sure, used to having the run of fields and creeks, dirt roads and swamps. Mom would tell us to go outside and call us back when it started to get dark.

I found a photo of my grade-school friends standing in a row in front of City Terrace Elementary School, trying to look nice in our dressiest clothes. I was going to give it to Sixto's son, who grew up never knowing his father really, because Sixto died in 1987. There Sixto is, there we all are, with our hair combed, buttoned-up shirts, fresh baby-faced cheeks.

Bernardo, father to several women's kids before he went into the military, squints dimly, as if unhappy. In the photo, he's a little boy of eleven or twelve, long eyelashes, nice square head—who knew women would later swoon over him? "I already had sex with more girls than you will in your whole life," he boasted in high school.

Sixto, doing his best to grin. He was the biggest and darkest of us all. It was always good to have Sixto around. He was the nicest guy, the kindest one. But he was big and dark and looked tough. That made a difference in the street. His father died of a heart attack when Sixto was five or six. Having no father around was something we knew about. His mother was sick a lot and didn't work, lying on her couch in the dark whenever I stopped by, so Sixto never had money, another thing that we knew about.

His mom and sister had the rooms upstairs, and Sixto slept in a room off the basement, entered by a low door off the driveway, a cold concrete floor with the smell of broken plumbing. All those years, I never saw much of the upstairs. I knew I could always invite him over to our house, or anywhere, because what else did we have? On Christmas Day, when everyone else was busy with family gatherings, Sixto and I played one-on-one at the basketball courts at Cal State LA on the other side of the freeway. Then we walked to Yuki's Valley Liquor on Valley Boulevard, where we sat on the cinder block wall in the parking lot drinking sodas and eating chips. I invited him later for Christmas dinner. I didn't know what we were having, but he might not have anything at home.

Saul was pudgy and unsmiling in the photo. Was he trying to look tough? Looking soft, like a shy, chubby-cheeked boy, wishing he was tough? He got picked on for that, by his older brother and by most of us at one time or another. But he was tougher than he looked, which I found out one day when I put on boxing gloves with him and we went at it. Maybe on the day of the picture, he wanted to look hard. Saul never got along in school—my friends were mostly written off by teachers and by the school. Saul became a dealer straight out of high school, and when my younger brother went by to score, Saul refused to sell to him (he said). My brother went around the block and ended up with joints soaked in PCP. "That shit'll fuck up your brain," Saul told me, "I don't sell it to my friends." In those days, guys made that shit in their garage. Saul made fun of Bernardo for using his own stash and not making money, but then Saul snorted or smoked all of his own stash, fried his own brain maybe, and went to jail. By then, Saul had shed his baby-faced look and looked mean enough after all.

I once drove through Eastern and Ramona and a long-haired bearded guy was standing in the intersection screaming at cars passing by. As we passed, I saw that it was Saul.

I returned from college later and walked by Saul's house, with his burned-out car parked out front. Someone had lit it on fire—all that was left was the blackened shell. Saul had been living in the garage with his girlfriend and their baby. I stood in the driveway and called out his name, till his little brother Memo came out and told me Saul was in jail. "We had to call the cops on him. He was acting way too crazy," Memo said.

Taller than most of us in the picture, Raymundo was smiling, two crooked front teeth giving him a mischievous smirk. Tall and lanky, he was a trickster, too. Fast and clever, his comebacks were zingers, might set a crowd of bystanders laughing. Joking around never helped him in school, of course. By the time we were in high school, he and some of the others had dropped out. Late at night I had walked home through the alley between Sixto's house up on the hill and Raymundo's parents' house on the avenue, and a lowrider with tinted windows pulled up alongside. Some guys jumped out of the car and rushed me, and I thought I was in trouble.

They surrounded me, and a guy in a Pendleton and sunglasses (street lamps reflected in them) stepped forward and shoved me, "Where you from, homes?" But I already recognized the grin, the crooked front teeth behind his dark glasses. Ray cackled his trickster laugh.

I sat awhile in a back room with Ray and his cholo friends as they passed around weed and wine. Ray told me he was working at a foundry on Alhambra Road with Victor, a friend of his who had gotten kicked out of high school for getting shot while robbing a liquor store. "What happened to Victor?"

"He's in a hospital section of the jail. You gotta come by my place, ese, and I'll introduce you to my woman and my daughter. We'll get fucked up, man," Ray chuckled, "we'll get real fucked up." But I never went by, because my dad was an alcoholic and I hated that. I thought that getting shit-faced was not only lame, it was boring.

Who knew it, but in the next few years after that sixth-grade photo was taken, we'd all go our separate ways. It all happened by high school, so that only Sixto and I graduated high school together. Even my younger brother was out of the picture by then.

Who else was in the picture? Manny, who was strong and fast and smart, but who had to move away when they condemned his family's house. They widened the 10 San Bernardino Freeway, cutting a swath through City Terrace. The houses were razed by huge bulldozers, which picked up smashed pieces of walls and rooftops and threw them into dump trucks. During the year when the condemned part of the neighborhood was emptying out, all the empty houses and streets became a playground for our middle school gang. We knocked glass out of the windows with rocks and explored vacant homes left behind by exiled families. Some families left behind nothing except a picture of the Virgin of Guadalupe on the front door, and some people left behind major things, like a big TV set, which we threw out of a second-story window to see what would happen when it hit the patio. The families were notified that they had to leave because the freeway was coming through, but after they knocked all the houses down, they built a McDonald's on Eastern Avenue where the apartment building where Gary Soto used to live had stood, and where our friend Manny's house used to be, there's a Burger King to this day.

They widened the freeway overpass at Eastern where the same year Cal State students blocked traffic to protest the Vietnam War and were attacked, beaten, cuffed, and dragged to a bus by sheriffs. That was the year I got my friends to help push a big rock off the hill—thinking it was going to roll down into the intersection and cars would have to drive around it—but it picked up speed, bouncing, and smashed a big steel box on the sidewalk. All the lights in the intersection went dark. We ran away laughing. That was the year my dad was shot while driving a tractor at work in West LA. He survived, flat on his back for a year in a convalescent facility, encased in a cast that went from his toes to his nipples. Steel pins extended out of both legs. He'd learn how to walk again later, one leg shorter than the other. That was the year I smashed windows out with my fist, and when they sewed up my hand in the ER, I told them that I fell on broken glass.

I don't know who or what we're looking at in the picture, looking off to one side. But we looked out for each other in life, like the time at the Belvedere pool some guys from Maravilla pushed Bernardo into a fight with belts wrapped around their fists. Bernie was struck across the face with a buckle, and he got this weird ugly look on his face and savagely beat the other guy down (we'd never seen Bernie crazy like that, punching the guy repeatedly in the face as hard as he could, howling, "You want more of this? Want more? More? More?") till the guy pleaded—while lifeguards screamed that they were calling the cops. We didn't let Maravilla jump in, and we hustled Bernardo out of there. A gang out of Ramona Gardens projects stole our bikes in Lincoln Park and we pooled money to pay for Manny's because his dad cussed us when he found out. He called our houses and demanded that we pay, telling our parents it was our fault Manny's bike was stolen. Or just standing together as cops rousted us, forcing us to empty our pockets and confiscating things like our little pocketknives (the one present I ever got from my dad that I carried on my person).

We laughed at each other's jokes about all these things, no matter how lame.

At the far end of the kids in the photo, my brother Paul, a year younger than the rest of us, sweet-faced with a shy grin. Paul tried to hang out with us but somehow couldn't keep up. He tried to impress us with magic tricks, like the time he stole a chemistry text from Cal State LA and used it to mix nitroglycerin in the seventh-grade biology storeroom. They sent him home and suspended him from school for "arson" when the test tube blew up, breaking glassware, peppering his hands and face with tiny slivers of glass. Nobody remarked on his ability to read a chemistry text at age eleven; everybody acted like he was trouble. A year later he was brought home in a police car; the cops told my mom and my uncle that my brother was throwing rocks off the overpass at trucks. My uncle raged, spit, and howled, beat Paul to the floor (ripping off Paul's red-white-and-blue American flag shirt, yowling that it was kids like him "that are destroying this country!"), and threw him out of the house. They put Paul on a Greyhound bus at the station downtown, sending him to live with my dad. He was crying and I was sick with fury. That was like sending him to live by himself, since my dad looked out for nobody. As a teen, my brother lived in the streets and foster homes in Northern California, in a cabin with hippies in Big Sur, in a Christian commune in the Sierra Foothills, and on his own. As an adult, Paul finally kicked drugs but couldn't quit alcohol. He died young.

Anyway, these guys were my good friends, great kids during the few years that we had as kids—our little gang, growing up. And just this year, walking up the hill in City Terrace to my mom's house, a car pulled up alongside me and the driver yelled, "Foster! You don't remember me?" Wraparound black sunglasses, shaved head, and full beard gone whiskery gray, a slim dude grabbed my hand for a shake, rings on every finger. It was Saul, all cleaned up and gone gray, driving a cool low-rider, told me he was IBEW, a lineman on the power grid. "I just wanna live till I'm sixty-eight so I can retire! I live across the street from Sixto's old house, you know where Sixto used to live?" I told him I did remember. I told Saul he was looking good.

"I'm glad to see you!" I was astonished that he was alive. I felt good about that all day and every time I thought about it.

Sixto's son, Edward, contacted me, decades later.

He wanted to meet and talk to me about his dad, who died when Edward was five or six, so Edward never really knew him. We met at Chalio's birrieria on First Street over menudo or birria. He didn't know what that was, I had to explain the menu options. He looked like his dad. He was a soft-spoken guy; his mom, Rose, was Peruvian, Peruvian-Chinese. Edward admitted that growing up with the Peruvian side of the family, he didn't know much about "Mexicans—Chicanos." I replied, yeah, Peruvians were way different.

I told him that his dad was a great guy, wore his hair long in high school. After high school, I left LA for college in the Bay Area. When I was back for the summer, I sometimes borrowed Sixto's bike to see a girlfriend who lived in the Ramona Gardens housing project. Sixto was going to Cal State LA and was elected student-body president. He showed me a feminist fotonovela he took photographs for with a group of Chicano students. He was going to get a degree in history and planned to be a high school history teacher. But he didn't finish his degree.

I thought maybe the conflict and demise of the Chicano movement had something to do with it, but I didn't really know; Sixto had been a photographer for *La Raza* newspaper in City Terrace. Police agents infiltrated the movement and sowed violence; the East LA Six were set up and went to trial. Cars of supposed vendidos were set on fire in the CSULA parking lot and shots fired at houses. People we knew joined underground organizations, or were indicted, and fled underground. Sixto went the other way, giving all that up. He married Rose and worked two jobs in LA while supporting Rose through pharmacy school in Stockton, and Rose's family took care of their kids. Sixto worked nights at Home Depot and days at a rubber stamp factory working with toluene solvents. The last time I saw him, over beer at a bar in El Sereno, we talked about our kids and our new lives as fathers. We said we'd get the families together for a barbecue.

Sixto didn't call me when he was hospitalized for leukemia. Rose called after he died—five or six months after his gums started bleeding while he was brushing his teeth, she said—saying Sixto didn't want anyone to see him like that in the hospital.

I was pallbearer at the funeral. Relatives and friends of the family gathered in church clothes on the sidewalk. One of them, I don't remember his name, shook my hand and hugged me, thanking me for coming, and told me what to do. The gleaming bronze casket slid out of the hearse, perfectly soundless on ball bearings, and we carried it up the steps into the church and placed it on a bier at the front. People followed us in. It was a closed casket, on which someone placed a big color photo of Sixto grinning, taken years earlier. The next time I saw her, Rose asked me why didn't I go to the reception afterward. I didn't have a good reason, I told her, but I knew Sixto wouldn't be there. I just felt too sick with sadness to see any-body. I didn't think I'd even be able to speak.

I kept that photograph of Sixto and the rest of us as kids to give to Edward, but I didn't hear from him again.

After my Uncle John and Auntie Fu died, my cousin Tom gave me a digital file of his family photographs. Many photos dated back to the 1940s or early '50s after they and 112,000 other Japanese Americans were released from the concentration camps, given twenty-five dollars and a bus ticket, and told to go.

Where would you go on twenty-five dollars and a bus ticket?

In the first postwar years, some 750 Japanese Americans found temporary lodging at the Fellowship Hostel, at 506 N. Evergreen Avenue, Los Angeles, CA. It was a three-story tenement owned by the Presbyterian Church and run by Quakers, who put a Japanese-speaking woman, Esther Rhoads, in charge. The Fellowship Hostel charged tenants one dollar a day, help with meals in the kitchen, shower in bare concrete doorless stalls in the basement by the laundry tubs. It had large sunny common rooms for dining and long hallways of tiny, often window-less rooms, with bathrooms at the end of the hall. That was where my aunt and uncle first met.

Fumiko Karamoto would have been twenty-one or twenty-two, petite, out-wardly sunny and vivacious—and inwardly, like the women of her generation, tougher than she looked; a striver, someone willing to go elbow-deep in the hard work that family demanded. Growing up during the Great Depression, followed by hard years in dreary camps, she and John both yearned for the American prosperity promised by the material culture. In later life she and my uncle took us with their own kids to Sunday school at Union Church in Little Tokyo, but Auntie Fu was just as much a devotee of Walt Disney and his vision of a Disney world, taking us to every new Disney movie upon release, reveling in a Technicolor irreality where protagonists might die for one sentimental climax, only to come alive for a final happy ending.

Tall, handsome, and genial, my uncle had been a popular guy, judging from the many photos he kept from those days, inscribed "Dear John," in the upper-left corner, with a signature in the lower-right corner and, "Love," or "Your friend," or "Your pal." My uncle was the eldest surviving child of farm workers who had lost everything they had to internment, his father disabled by a stroke suffered in camp and his mother working the strawberry fields in Santa Maria after the war. His mom returned from the fields each evening to take care of a bedridden husband.

Like many in his generation, Uncle John was determined to leave the fields far behind, to enter the television- and radio-repair business. A golfer and trout fisherman with a great casual grin, in later life Uncle John enjoyed appearing as an extra in movies. He was a samurai retainer in *The Last Samurai* with Tom Cruise (shot in Griffith Park), sat cross-legged in a Pepsi commercial as a Buddhist monk, and he and Auntie Fu boarded a bus re-enacting their lives as internees outside a concentration camp in *Come See the Paradise*. Of course he only had one lung due to the tuberculosis treatment of the time. TB had killed his two oldest sisters and his brother Tom, all in their early twenties, by 1940. Uncle John beat TB, quarantined at sanatoriums in Elysian Park and the San Fernando Valley. And to salvage something of the lives that had been lost, John and Fu would name their firstborn son Thomas.

Ubiquitous now, photos cost nothing, a camera on a cell phone in every hand, but in the 1940s photographs were special. They weren't cheap, and not everyone could afford a camera, let alone the money to process and print negatives. Giving someone your photograph was special. These were gifts, these photographs, tickets to the future. Uncle John and Auntie Fu kept them for the rest of their lives.

I'd heard mention of the Fellowship Hostel, but that's all. I didn't really know where it was or anything about it. That is, till I found myself at 506 Evergreen, looking up at the broad steps leading to double doors with the sign, "Fellowship

Hostel." Ken Ehrlich, professor at CalArts, had asked me to take a walk with him around the Cinco Puntos neighborhood in East LA.

I told Ken we should go inside the Fellowship Hostel and check it out. Mexican music could be heard from a side door, so I knocked there.

I told the guy who answered that I wanted to look around because my aunt and uncle had met here. The caretaker hesitated, reluctant. I made my move and walked in. As if in a slippage of time, as if we'd stepped inside 1946, we found the building the same as it had been seventy years before. Then and there, I was putting two and two together about the course of my own life.

Auntie Fu and Uncle John had taken us in when my parents separated and my mom drove us on a long highway to Los Angeles. We lived with John and Fu until the house Uncle Bill had bought nearby was ready. That was how we came to East LA in the year of the Watts Riots, the National Guard on TV firing machine guns at high windows, storefronts burning; the Vietnam War and war dead on TV; protestors beaten and sometimes shot; Malcolm X killed and three years later MLK assassinated, Robert Kennedy also at the Ambassador Hotel on Wilshire; war abroad, war at home. War all the time, that was America.

Later, looking back at the photographs of these nisei just come of age, here was another America. These young people, little older than teens, in suits or nice skirts and blouses, their smiles and their grins confident—triumphant, really.

Without any money and nothing much left of the past to return to, these nisei combed their hair carefully and struck proud poses in brilliant California sunshine. Free finally, feeling that freedom in full after release from camps where they might be shot if they lingered near the barbwire fence line, they came of age in the Great Depression and in camps, in apartheid-like hatred and discrimination, dispossession, and threats of violence. They had determined to leave that world behind. They didn't discuss that past with us. They had the chance at new lives and they were going for it. These pictures were the promissory notes—betting on a better life—that they gave to each other.

Crossing the inner courtyard of the building, its fountain dried out ages ago, Ken and I went upstairs, strolled down the halls and peered into the dim, narrow quarters where the nisei had had a single bed and perhaps a trunk or chair, something to put a few personal items in, maybe a reading lamp. One internee testified, "It was almost like camp in that all we had was a bed and a little stand where we kept our personal belongings, and it was more or less the honor system for everyone. You left your belongings there, and being Japanese, we were all very honest. Nobody took anything. We never had that kind of problem."[1]

Ken and I walked through the lobby, down the front steps, and stood on the lawn. The current caretakers had planted a few fruit trees. Later I saw that John and Fu's photographs were taken in this exact spot. I realized finally who the people in the photos were.

The palm trees behind them in the photographs facing Folsom Street are taller now, and sometimes a woman hangs children's clothes, dresses, and T-shirts along on the fence for sale. Sometimes a paletero or other sidewalk vendors wait outside in the shade. But the walkway to the broad steps up to the doors of the hostel is the same (that same "Fellowship Hostel" sign), the railing is the same. The sunlight on our faces is the same.

1. Niiya, Brian. "Evergreen Hostel." Densho Encylopedia (website). March 25, 2015: https://encyclopedia.densho.org/Evergreen_Hostel/

In memory of Fumiko Karamoto Agawa 1924–2010 and John Heigi Agawa 1919–2007

Navel, Bury

Thirii Myo Kyaw Myint

A week after the birth, baby's umbilical cord fell off. It was brown-purple-black, the color of dried blood, and brittle. The end that had been cut fanned out and curled at the edges, like an ear or a flower. Where the stump had been, baby's skin puckered and oozed a thick pus that smelled like rot. The sight of his tender, newly made belly button made me cry. I insisted we keep the umbilical stump. It was grotesque, like all body parts are once removed from the body: hair, nails, teeth— but the grotesque was what I wanted to preserve. The memory of my husband clamping the cord, a translucent rope the lavender-gray of mollusk shells, bright red drops of blood splattering on baby's cheeks.

We live on the first floor of a little white house built in the year 1880. Above us live two statisticians and their cats, and below us is the unfinished basement where we have found spiderwebs, the carcasses of crickets, and mice droppings. I am afraid of the basement, as I am of all basements, but I no longer believe it is haunted. Our street is named after a tree, or a nut, or a color of wood, and is so small that our house is one of only two on the block. The front door opens onto a vestibule, which opens onto the front porch, and from the front porch I can see, in the east, the bell tower of the chapel. An emblem of the college.

The town where we live and the college where we teach have the same name. The college is named after the town and the town is named after a man, and the man, of course, is named after other men—his father, and his father's father, and so on. But it is the singular man—and not the forefathers who passed down his name— for whom the town is named. This singular man, the namesake, was a man of violence, and much has already been written about him. I do not want to write more. I do not want to name him. I want, perhaps, to un-name him, to take his name away, wrest it, pry it loose.

Thirii Myo Kyaw Myint

After baby's umbilical stump fell off, my mother, who was visiting from across the country, said it meant this place was baby's ချက်မြှုပ်.

What is a ချက်မြှုပ်? I asked.

I had never heard the word before, though I knew its component parts, ချက်—navel, and မြှုပ်—to bury.

Hometown, my mother said in English.

At the end of my first trimester, my husband's mother gives me a journal, along with an annotated copy of *What to Expect When You're Expecting*. The journal is meant to record my pregnancy. I do not know what to write in it. I have spent the past three months immobilized by nausea. Every day I lie in bed or on the sofa beneath an open window. It rains, or snows, or the windchill falls below freezing, and I press my face against the window screen. It is the only way I can breathe. If I cannot lie perfectly still, I retch. I keep a bucket nearby, though I prefer the toilet bowl. I retch, heave, gag, but can rarely make myself vomit because I am barely eating. I cannot remember the feeling of hunger.

My husband is desperate to help, but neither of us can guess what would be helpful. All I want is for the nausea to dispel, though I know I should want baby more. I do want baby, very much. It is just hard to believe that there is, or will be, a baby at all. My belly, which was never flat, remains the same in its soft roundness. I have lost rather than gained weight. My body does not look or feel different, not even to me, not even to my husband, though I question him daily.

Do I look pregnant yet? Look at me. Look at my belly.

No, he says each time. No, you don't.

Sometimes, he sounds weary when he answers. Sometimes almost irritated. Sometimes it makes me cry. The journal from my husband's mother is hardcover, faux-antique with gold accents. I do not think it can contain my experience.

The first time I visited this place where we now live and where baby is born, I was twenty-one, a senior in college. *The evening light falling into my lap.* My friend was going to see his girlfriend, and I came along so I wouldn't have to spend spring break alone in my empty dorm. *Driving through a thicket of trees, the gauzy tips tickling the sky.* I was already a writer then. *Brick houses, the village rotunda, an expanse of land lying flat along the highway.* I kept not a journal exactly, but an array of journals and loose pages, sheets torn out of school notebooks, then typed up. *A farmhouse, a line of trees.* My memory of this trip is now inextricable from what I wrote then. *It was the night.* On the drive over, I made the mistake of telling my friend I liked all music, and he played country songs about trucks the whole time were on the interstate. *It was the day, and the day after, and the weekend, the Wednesday through Sunday of the week, and the whole week.* When we turned onto the back roads, though, I remember only silence. *The last real spring of my life.* I remember the little wells beside farmhouses, stone walls rising and falling like breath. *The Trapeze Swinger, and how gossamer the trees.* We drove past what could only be described as pastures. *How the light was falling.* We felt what could only be described as longing. *Seeping into the earth again.* Longing for the drive to never end, for the village rotunda to take us round and round. *Stacking pebbles into small piles.* I did not want my friend to stop the car, for us to step out into the cold, the snow still on the ground. *Lovers' graffiti etched into the gazebo by the pond. The pond water so still.* I did not want to arrive.

There is no written record of my mother's pregnancies, and no archive of my early childhood. The first picture that was ever taken of me was when I was already nine or ten months old. My husband's mother asked for pictures of me as an infant, and I did not want to explain why there were none. I was born at a time of political upheaval, a military dictatorship renewing its reign of terror, and my parents had no time for mementos, only for survival. Or perhaps no photos existed of me, no photos existed of anyone in my family at that time, the year of my conception and the year following my birth—1988 to 1990—because cameras were not readily available to ordinary citizens, or because ordinary citizens were afraid to be caught holding cameras, because it was dangerous to be taking photos at all, because the military junta wanted no record of what was happening in the country.

The second time I visited this place, I was twenty-nine and ABD, an acronym I found depressing since I learned it in my penultimate year of graduate school. I was picked up at the nearest airport the next state over and driven to this town, to this college, under the cover of night. When the shuttle—which was just an ordinary car—arrived at the inn where they put me up, it was as if the town materialized out of nothing, out of the pitch dark. It felt like waking up from a dream.

ABD means *all but dissertation*. It is a liminal state that could last only a year, or several years, or an entire decade, or the rest of one's life, as was the case for my father. I was already past the halfway mark of my first year as ABD, and my dissertation, my second book, was not anywhere close to halfway finished. I was beginning to fear I would never finish it.

Dinner my first night was at the inn's restaurant with the search committee. I was overdressed and pretended to be more familiar with Isabelle Eberhardt than I really was. From my potential future colleagues, I learned that the risotto was good and that the inn had historically and recently been named something else, after the former school mascot, the same man for whom the town and college were named. The inn's name was changed and the mascot was removed, not because new information was discovered about the man but because it was no longer socially acceptable that he, generally speaking, had been a colonizer and imperialist, and more specifically, had advocated in his letters for the use of biological warfare against Native peoples.

The next evening, after a full day of formal and informal interviews culminating in a job talk—which did not register in my memory because I was so nervous— I came to in the passenger seat of a colleague's car. I was being dropped off at the inn again, the campus visit was almost over. In an effort to make small talk, I repeated what I had learned about the inn's recent name change. The colleague driving me began to explain then stopped. She didn't want to tell me about the man, the namesake, she said. He wasn't worth talking about.

The first time I heard a land acknowledgment at the college, it was at an event organized by student activists, a panel subtitled "(In)visibility & Asian American Studies Womxn Scholars." I was an invited panelist, despite having no background in Asian American studies as a discipline. The other panelists were far more qualified, but all of us were visitors. We were gathered in a glass room in the Robert Frost Library called "the Think Tank." The student introducing the panel said, "I'd like to begin this event by acknowledging that we stand on Nonotuck land. I'd also like to acknowledge our neighboring Indigenous nations: the Nipmuc and the Wampanoag to the east, the Mohegan and Pequot to the south, the Mohican to the west, and the Abenaki to the north."

East, south, west, north. It made me think of the metta chant I recited every night on my first month-long retreat. In the eastern direction, in the western direction, in the northern direction, in the southern direction. Free from enmity and danger, from physical suffering, from mental suffering. May all beings take care of themselves happily.

I do not write in my husband's mother's journal, not only because I do not know what to write in it but also because I do not have time to write at all. I am teaching, attending department meetings, committee meetings, meetings with students, vomiting—or worse, attempting and failing to vomit—before, after, and between engagements. I am also on the academic job market. My second book, which I finally finished right before I became pregnant, is coming out next year. I spend the fall dispatching cover letters like prayers, coveting, then dreading the rare interview and the even rarer campus visit.

Come winter, I am teaching two classes, advising two senior theses, helping to organize a literary festival, and interviewing for days, sometimes weeks at a time. I meet with search committees, presidents, deans, interim deans, provosts, humanities executive committees, undergraduate committees, department chairs, departments, pre-tenure colleagues, diversity, equity, and inclusion officers, diversity and equity advisory boards, graduate students, graduate directors, undergraduate students, and student tour guides, all the while keeping my burgeoning belly off-screen. I talk endlessly about myself until I am bored with myself, until I begin to loathe myself, my writing, my writing process, my teaching, my teaching philosophy, how I think a workshop should be run, what I think the difference is between fiction and nonfiction. After every campus visit, my husband and I swell with hope, imagining ourselves back in California, Colorado, Ohio, then deflate with doubt and anxiety.

Every weekend, I collapse. I fear that the stress I am under is bad for baby. Despite the kindness and innocence of my husband's mother's gift, I begin to resent the pregnancy journal, the leisure that is required to keep one.

The first photos of me are family photos. They were taken to capture not my baby-hood, but the home my father was leaving forever. I think he knew—even then, when the photographs were being taken—that he would not return. The photo-graphs are proof of this knowledge. They are formal and posed. My mother has dressed herself and my sisters and me in matching outfits. In the one family por-trait, my mother is seated on a low tree branch. The sunlight illuminates her high cheekbones and her blazing white blouse, her silk longyi drapes over her feet in elaborate folds. My eldest sister stands on her right side, in a sleeveless red dress that ties at her shoulders, white lace at the neck and hem. One of her legs is bent awkwardly behind the other, and with the pointer finger of one hand she grasps the ring finger of her other. It is as if that point of contact is what holds her still. My middle sister is perched behind my mother's left shoulder, also in a red dress, but with white puffy sleeves and a ruffle collar. She is holding something blurry in her little hands, a toy or a brown leaf plucked from the ground. My father is stand-ing behind everyone. Most of his face is in shadow, and in his dark blue shirt and jacket, he seems to recede into the background, into the trees in his parents' yard, as if he has already left, as if he is already far away, in another country.

I am sitting on my mother's lap. I am wearing a white floral onesie and red tights, a floppy bonnet on my head. My brows are deeply knitted and my lips pursed. I am scowling. In almost all of the photographs taken on this day, on the eve of my father's departure, I scowl. In the arms of my mother, my father, my young baby-sitter. There is only one photograph, of my sisters and me seated on the wood floor of my grandparents' house surrounded by our toys, in which I look innocent and curious. This is the photo I send to my husband's mother when she asks me for a baby picture. She asks if there are any of me alone. Any of me when I am younger.

At the launch for my second book—an event that was held virtually, because of the ongoing pandemic, and because I was caring for and nursing a newborn—the moderator asked me and my conversation partner what gods we brought with us to this country. A beautifully odd question I had never been asked before. I remember answering that my gods, our gods, were already here. The cosmology I was raised in included this and every other place. On this earth, and elsewhere, beyond, through, or behind it.

Without discussing it, my husband and I both settle on chanting metta to put baby down to sleep. When I was a young child, my mother sang to me in English so I would be bilingual: "Home on the Range"; "Take Me Home, Country Roads"; "Yesterday Once More." All songs about nostalgia. Songs that I realize—only now that I am the same age my mother was when she left her country—were born out of the pain of exile. That is how my father calls the country where he and my mother were born and where my sisters and I were born: my country.

The metta chant is in Pali, the liturgical language of Theravada Buddhism. The language of my name, and the language that the faithful believe was spoken by the awakened one himself. I am faithful as well, but I do not know what I believe. I do not know what belief is, if it is something that must be fixed and hard and jealous. Pali is long dead as a spoken language. I sing to baby in Pali, not so he will be bilingual but so the chant will fill baby's little body, and fill our apartment, and make it our home. There is more than one way to know a language, I think. More than one way for it to be yours. Perhaps this is true of places as well, even of countries.

The third and final time I arrived, I was thirty years old, a newly anointed PhD and a newlywed, though both my degree and my marriage felt unreal, almost fraudulent. I had still not finished my second book. I submitted three-fifths of it as my dissertation and passed my defense. My husband and I had not yet had a wedding, or even an offering to the monks. One morning we drove to city hall and signed papers and were married, and we did not know how to spend the rest of the day.

My official position at the college was *Visiting Writer*. It was a three-year position, renewable for another three years. We did not know if we would stay a year, or two, or more. For the past decade, my husband and I had both moved almost every single year—across town, across the country, across the world. I had lived in Rhode Island, California, Spain, Indiana, and Colorado, and my husband had lived in Missouri, Taiwan, Colorado, Oregon, Malta, and Colorado again. We met in Denver, a city that felt inhospitable to us—because of its thin air, traffic, rising rent—and escaped together to this place.

We arrived days before our things, our furniture, which was mostly bought for cheap from former roommates, or at the back of thrift stores, or not bought at all but picked up from curbs and alleyways. The cost of moving the furniture far outweighed the furniture's value, but the college had paid the moving costs, so we packed all of it. When we moved again, we told ourselves, we would buy new things, nice things. In the days before our furniture arrived, we ate on the bare floor in a sunny corner, slept on an air mattress that swayed like a boat, and spent our days wandering around the town. It felt like a camping trip, a vacation. That is all this place was meant to be: a brief respite.

We are naming baby based on the day of his birth, so we have to come up with names for eight different days. The week is divided into eight days because eight is an auspicious number. Wednesday before noon and Wednesday after noon are two different days: the gentle tuskless elephant and the tusked elephant. My mother calculates that the luckiest days for baby to be born are Monday, Tuesday, Friday, and Sunday, so we focus on finding names for those days. I collect family names over three or four generations and we scour the internet, but I feel unsatisfied with everything we come up with. My husband's family, and sometimes my husband himself, cannot pronounce half the names. I joke we should name the baby after my husband and his father, make the baby a *third*. My husband begs me not to make that joke. We decide on a hyphenated last name despite both families' distaste for them. My eldest sister says we should use our last name, my middle sister says just pick one, and my parents say there are no last names in our culture. My husband's sister admits she thinks hyphenated last names are weird and complicated, then takes it back once she realizes why we are asking for her opinion.

Since I am on the job market and we may leave this place soon after baby is born, we consider naming baby after this place. Of course, we do not want to name baby after the man for whom the town is named, but we wonder if we could name baby after a street, or the bike path near our house, or the trails, or the mountains. Perhaps a middle name, we muse, a private tether to the place of his conception and birth.

But we do not name baby after this place because we end up staying in this place. We accept a last-minute retention offer from the college. Baby will not only be born here but will also grow up here. It would be embarrassing for him, we decide, to have a local name. Besides, all the names in this place are references to other people, or peoples, languages, and histories that are not ours. Perhaps this is true of all names everywhere. Naming is fraught, impossible.

The first photograph of baby is taken minutes after the birth. He is red-faced and screaming against my naked breast. Little forehead scrunched, eyes squeezed shut, nostrils flaring. Mouth open wide, howling. I remember the sharp sound of his cries. How relieved I was to hear them. When the nurse first placed baby on my chest, he was silent, and my heart froze. I heard the nurse yell for something, saw a bulb appear in her hand, watched as she pushed it inside baby's mouth and squeezed, once, twice. Then, miraculously, he screamed and screamed and screamed. From the corner of my eye, I saw the pediatrician leave the room. A good sign. My husband took this photograph, I think. I remember hearing his voice over baby's screams. I could not hear what he was saying, but I knew what he meant, because I meant it too. I remember hearing myself say oh my god over and over again, even though I knew it was the wrong thing to say. I did not believe in god, but here was baby; red, warm, limbs long and numerous, and I kept saying god, god, god. The photograph is out of focus, and baby's face is blurry. This is why I think my husband took it. My hands were shaking too.

The one entry I made in the pregnancy journal describes a long walk my husband and I took. It was a rare temperate day in late December. The entry is very neatly written and quite boring. It reads like a set of directions—south on South Pleasant, right onto another trail, cross the golf course, past the football field, up Woodside—and is full of proper nouns we never use: the Common School, Larch Hill Conservation Area, Bramble Hill Farm. My husband and I usually referred to places as *that place by that other place* or *that place we went with so-and-so* or *that place we passed that time.* I do not know why I broke from this in the journal entry, why I felt the need to look up and use the official names of places. Maybe I thought that baby would one day need names and directions to retrace our footsteps, to orient himself. I think now that I was wrong.

Baby's umbilical cord is still in a plastic bag, in a box in the laundry room, unburied. This town is the place where baby's cord fell off, but it does not have to be his ချက်မြှုပ်. I want baby to be able to choose where the cord is buried. I want him to be able to name his home.

A Pale Persephone: On the Work of Theresa Hak Kyung Cha

Angie Sijun Lou

It was the first week of the new year, with snowflakes illuminating the sidewalk in Nolita. I had been walking in circles around the Puck Building, sometimes alone and other times with Dimitri. I hadn't gone inside the building yet, though I'd glimpsed it from proximal streets, the layer upon layer of red brick, a Celtic sprite wielding a hand mirror perched on each vertex, figurines of Shakespeare's mischievous Puck. I wanted to find the vestiges of the poet Theresa Hak Kyung Cha's presence there, which I thought would be subterranean yet palpable, even after all this time.

Forty years ago, on November 5, 1982, the young Korean American avant-garde filmmaker and poet walked to the Puck Building to visit her husband, the photographer Richard Barnes, who was documenting the building's renovation. Cha was thirty-one years old. What would become known as her magnum opus, *Dictee*, had just been published a few days prior with Tanam Press.[1] The book evades succinct summarization, but I can say that it is an epic poem that contends with the inaccessibility of postcolonial history, tracing an exilée as she struggles to find her homeland. *Dictee* interlaces the mythic plights of heroines—Joan of Arc, the Korean martyr Yu Guan Soon, St. Thérèse of Lisieux, Persephone, Cha's mother, and Cha herself. In the end, the speaker beckons us to return to poetry and cinema, sacred locations where a pure experience of the present is possible.

---

1. Saltzein, "Overlooked No More: Theresa Hak Kyung Cha, Artist and Author Who Explored Identity."

But Cha would not live to see the radical afterlives of this book and how its legacy has persisted in syllabi across Asian American critical race theory, feminist psychoanalysis, postcolonial literature, and contemporary poetry. That evening, she was murdered in the basement of the Puck Building by serial rapist Joey Sanza, her body discovered in a parking lot in Soho three blocks away.[2] I knew that all physical traces of her would be imperceptible now, four decades later, but it was the aura of the building that drew me, cold and oblique, how it enticed and expelled me at once like a lover.

At the time of Cha's murder, the owners of the Puck Building intended to transform it into a commercial condominium for businesses primarily related to the arts. When this project failed in 1987, the property was acquired by Kushner Properties, owned by the family of Jared Kushner. In 2011, Kushner sent in a request to the Landmarks Preservation Commission to erect six luxury penthouse suites on the upper floors of the mixed-use building. The executive director's initial response was that the historic building "should not be sacrificed for a wealthy developer's passing fancy to add an enormous and unnecessarily visible penthouse addition on top."[3] After waging a months-long battle, Kushner's firm was finally granted permission to renovate.

At the time of this writing, each of the penthouses has sold or is selling for $21–60 million.[4] The interiors are co-designed by Kushner's wife, Ivanka Trump; each suite is finished with La Cornue stoves, bullet-shaped H. Theophile door hinges, and custom mahogany-framed windows with built-in UV protection for artwork.[5] After a few unlucky years in a housing market stagnated by the pandemic, many of the units remain vacant at the time of this writing. When I see the architectural renderings of the mother-of-pearl terrazzo floors, maple headboards with butterfly joints, Sicilian lava stone countertops, and the infinite recurrence of mirrors concealed inside of other mirrors, I think of Walter Benjamin's angel of history with his back turned from the past, hurling itself toward a future cleansed of its debris.

And then I think of the nameless ruins that comprise the cover of *Dictee*. It is a granular, black-and-white image of a cruel, inhospitable landscape: the ruins of

2. Dziemianowicz, "Historic NYC Building Becomes Murder Scene for Artist on Verge of a Career Breakthrough."
3. Dunlap, "Landmarks Panel Rejects Second Penthouse Plan for Puck Building."
4. Marino, "$28.5 Million, a Record Sale in Nolita."
5. Tzeses, "In New York's Famed Puck Building, a Two-Story Penthouse Is Listed for $58.5 Million."

Dictee (1982). When I look at these six archaic tombs on the cover of the book, I think of the Puck Building's six penthouse suites—as ruins in the present tense.

the Nubian pyramids in Sudan, though I believe it is more faithful to the text to leave them unidentified. Five equidistant eroded monuments constellate the foreground, with one slashed pyramid in the background of the image. The scene is uncanny because it implies a human presence while being evacuated of human subjects. It felt somehow significant to me that this set of luxury penthouses had become her unmarked grave. When I tried to look inside the windows, shiny as they were, all I saw was my own reflection.

Cha was born in 1951 in Busan, South Korea, during the Korean War. When Cha was a child, her parents were forbidden to speak their native tongue while seeking asylum in territory occupied by Japanese imperial forces. Her family escaped from Manchuria to Seoul, from Seoul to Busan, and from Busan to Seoul again, finally settling in the United States in 1962. Her first exposure to English and French was at the Convent of the Sacred Heart, a private Catholic girls' school in San Francisco, a city where Cha would spend most of her life. She earned an undergraduate degree in comparative literature and graduate degrees in art practice and criticism at the University of California, Berkeley, where she worked at the Berkeley Art Museum and Pacific Film Archive, which now houses her permanent collection.[6] A student of Bertrand Augst at Berkeley, her studies in poststructuralism and semiology are potent throughout her work. The opening prose block of *Dictee* features a translation exercise that embeds the speaker as the subject of discourse while maintaining her narrative distance from the gathering:

> Open paragraph   It was the first day   period
> She had come from a far   period   tonight at dinner
> comma   the families would ask   comma   open
> quotation marks   How was the first day   interroga-
> tion mark   close quotation marks   at least to say
> the least of it possible   comma   the answer would be
> open quotation marks   there is but one thing   period
> There is someone   period   From   a far   period
> close quotation marks[7]

---

6. Saltzein, "Overlooked No More: Theresa Hak Kyung Cha, Artist and Author Who Explored Identity."
7. Cha, *Dictee*, 1.

Immediately above this text block is its rendering in French. The speaker's painstaking awareness of the translation exercise seems to dilute its authenticity. The assimilative practice is lost in the mouth's orifice. In another exercise that follows, the speaker also transcribes her moans, snivels, stutters, and unedited sounds while practicing the new language. "She mimics the speaking," she writes.[8] Language acquisition becomes a disciplinary ritual that the speaker defies by saturating each exercise with her static murmurs. Wendy Xu writes, "An immigrant dreams of total assimilation as both fantasy and nightmare," an ambivalence reflected in *Dictee*'s hypnotic, defiant transmissions.[9]

In her 1975 video titled "Mouth to Mouth," the dictation exercise becomes playfully evocative. The title suggests that we will be witness to an act of resuscitation, the rebirth of a lost mother tongue. This eight-minute meditation features a mouth sounding the vowel graphemes of Hangul, the phonetic script of the Korean alphabet. The mouth moves in and out of visibility, a proximity that suggests both intimacy and alienation. The mouth silently shapes itself to sound each vowel, but the voice is muffled by a soundtrack of bubbling water, birdsong, footsteps, and a ticking clock. The audience barely sees the mouth through the haze of white static superimposed over it. What might have been clear at the point of transmission arrives as a snowy apparition, "language before it is born at the tip of the tongue."[10] Much of Cha's work magnifies this moment of suspension before meaning is encrypted into speech and then decoded again.

As an artist of the diaspora, Cha urges me to stop thinking of translation as the loss of the unadulterated original, as a delicate choice between style and meaning, our sacrificial lambs. Her video works delve into the transmutations and perversions intrinsic to the act, destabilizing the authority of the original by resurfacing the multiple tongues inside a mouth, tongues that coincide only to eclipse one another. Contrary to readings of her work by Lisa Lowe, Elaine Kim, and Shelley Sunn Wong collected in *Writing Self, Writing Nation*, I don't believe the presences in Cha's work signal a reinvention of Asian American identity, an unstable intersection between Korean, Korean American, avant-garde filmmaker, performance artist, poet, exilée, etc.[11] For me, her work captures only the faint echo of an I, a mutability that endangers the act of identification itself.

---

8. Cha, *Dictee*, 3.
9. Xu, *The Past*, 87.
10. Cha, "Artist Statement / Summary of Work."
11. Wong, Sun, Kim, and Lowe, *Writing Self, Writing Nation*.

As we walked to the Puck Building at midnight in the dead of winter, Dimitri innocuously asked why I went there every day and what I was hoping to find. We passed by a bubble tea shop called Cha Cha Cha, which is what I had been saying to myself as I looked for her. I didn't know what I was looking for, and if I knew, I wouldn't have to keep searching. That night, I read the Puck Building's Wikipedia page to Dimitri. While much of the description is dedicated to Thrive Capital, the venture capital firm owned by the Kushner family, a short paragraph towards the end details Cha's murder. As I looked for Cha in this dismal place, I realized I was not looking for her, but instead the proof of her absence. I wanted her to be haunting the empty estates, her mouth open wide enough to spill birdsong.

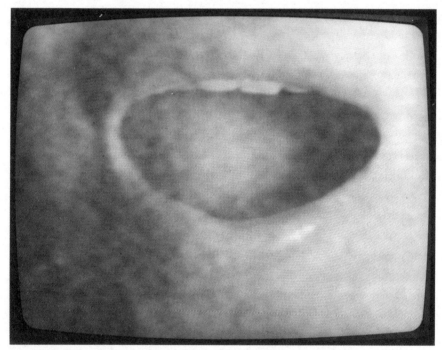

Mouth to Mouth (1975). This eight-minute meditation features a mouth sounding the vowel graphemes of Hangul, the phonetic script of the Korean alphabet. The mouth moves in and out of visibility, a proximity that suggests both intimacy and alienation.

The title of Cha's collected poetry and image essays published posthumously, *Exilée and Temps Morts*, translates to "exiled and dead time." A poem titled "Arrival, 31 August 1962, United States of America" is positioned alongside a photograph of a beauty supply store selling mass-produced wigs:

> The most astonishing
> of the first day
> was the abundance, wealth, the excess.
> As a child, one imagined this "Gold Mountain"
> as having no two treasures alike.
> Instead, repetition became an inevitable
> vocabulary member
> Inexhaustible duplication   self-regeneration
> as necessity
> This absolute wealth   tyranny of objects
> As force   force of the machinery[12]

The speaker is bewildered by the sheer accumulation of objects, and repetition is inserted into her syntax as a "vocabulary member." Replication becomes a mode of abstraction. The commodity is a purification ritual that dilutes and divulges meaning, a self-contained field that seems to be able to spontaneously regenerate itself without extracting value from human labor. The emptiness of these multi-million dollar units reminds me that "Gold Mountain" is beholden to an excess that eclipses its actual livability. When I looked at the Puck Building, I saw the phantom objectivity of capital divorced from the conditions of its accumulation—hard casualties in the construction of capitalism's soft violence.

In 1992, ten years after Cha's murder, Francis Fukuyama announced that the end of history had arrived; liberal democracy had become the final world order, the apex of human progress, and there would be no further evolution needed.[13] I felt a strange tension between wanting to accept the unknowability of the past and the sense that this Gold Mountain's prosperity was predicated on my forgetting. In the Puck Building's cold sheen, I saw our phantasmic destiny reflected: a

---

12. Cha, *Exilée and Temps Morts*, 96.
13. Fukuyama, Francis. *The End of History and the Last Man* (New York, NY: Free Press, 1992).

premeditated forgetting of the previous centuries of colonial violence that birthed such a fortress, the ruins of Fukuyama's dream.

In the summer of 1980, Theresa and her brother James Cha visited Seoul for three months to film her only feature-length film, titled *White Dust from Mongolia.* The film was never completed, as they were continuously harassed by officers in the wake of violent political unrest following a presidential assassination. All that remains is some unedited footage of trains, airplanes, mops, and the silhouette of an urban skyline. The film's protagonist is a young Korean woman living in China, the descendant of Koreans who fled the Japanese occupation to Manchuria. She suffers without memory of the past, an amnesia that also causes her to lose all speech function. The narrative traces her search for a cure as she travels to Korea to have a history and an alphabet injected into her.[14] Until history and language are recovered, what unfolds is a landscape of pure phenomenological experience, signs without specificity, a sentiment Cha recounts in *Exilée and Temps Morts:*

> some door some night some window lit some train some city some nation
>   some peoples
> Re Named
> u tt e rly by chance by luck by hazard otherwise.
> any door any night any window lit any train any city
> any nation any peoples some name any name to a
> given name[15]

The *mise en abyme* of Cha's travel to Korea to make a film about a woman who travels to Korea, only to be forbidden by martial law, reappears in *Dictee.* The section titled "MELPOMENE / TRAGEDY" includes a letter to the speaker's mother about how the carceral legacy of imperialism percolates into the present tense: "We are inside the same struggle seeking the same destination . . . I am in the same crowd, the same coup, the same revolt, nothing has changed."[16] Although this may seem like an obvious continuity between the colonial era and the postcolonial era, Cha leads us to a more radical claim: that the relationship between

14. Cha, *White Dust from Mongolia.*
15. Cha, *Exilée and Temps Morts,* 55.
16. Cha, *Dictee,* 81.

the colonizer and colonized becomes, in its essence, a semiotic relationship, elastic in its exploitation by future powers: "The enemy becomes abstract . . . The nation the enemy the name becomes larger than its own identity . . . Larger than its own signification . . . Japan has become the sign. The alphabet. The vocabulary."[17] The relationship of domination is not incidental to her historical circumstance; it is systemic and eternal, embedded in the architecture of the nation-state. What unfolds is a reckoning about the conditions of exile: when she realizes that no legal recognition can reverse this wound, the exilée also experiences a loss of the identity that was predicated on the perpetuity of her search. In *Dictee*, she writes, "I heard the swans / in the rain I heard," alluding to Baudelaire's exilic poem "Le Cygne," an interplay of *cygnes* (swans) and *signes* (signs):

> I think of my great swan with his crazy motions
> Like those in exile, ridiculous and sublime,
> Consumed by a singular desire.[18]

Like the myth of the mute swan that sings beautifully in the moments before death, the revocation of this "singular desire" necessitates an undoing of the self. She arrives at the site of banishment in the hopes of reconciliation, only to be met with a double estrangement, casting her deeper into "the dim forest of the soul's exile."[19] Cha warns me against making the past into an Eden: when she reaches for the past all she retrieves is a floating signifier. After she failed to make this film, Cha seeds a central question that propels the body of her work. If the exilée's identity cannot be recovered by returning to her homeland, where should she go with this desire?

There is a recurring dream my Nainai used to have. Toward the end of her life, there was little else happening to her—Baobao, dying is so boring, she complained. I couldn't be beside her because the lockdowns in China were several degrees more rigid than lockdowns anywhere else. Visitors were forbidden from entering retirement homes, even when my grandma entered hospice care. Calling me on WeChat became her main event of the day. Baobao, what did you eat today? she asked, and I would tell her what I ate that day. Nainai, what did you eat today? And she

---

17. Cha, *Dictee*, 32.
18. Baudelaire, *Les Fleurs du Mal*, 147.
19. Baudelaire, *Les Fleurs du Mal*, 147.

would tell me what she ate that day. It seemed we had nothing else to say to each other beyond this script until I finally thought to ask her about her dreams.

When my Nainai was eight years old, the daughter of farmworkers in Anhui, she watched as Japanese soldiers captured her village, burning crops and ransacking silos. When I asked about this period of siege, she shrugged and said that it was fine. And then I asked her what happened, and she said that nothing happened. The closest she came to telling me about the occupation was when she told me about her pet pig. After the soldiers set her shack on fire, they slaughtered her pig, her prized possession, and roasted it on skewers while she stood in the courtyard and watched with her hands tied behind her back.

It had been at least a decade since I had last heard her talking about the pig, but she was suddenly afflicted with dreams of it towards the end of her life. She dreamt of the pig sifting through the muddy silt, its deafening screech upon capture, and the smoke that rose from her village like curdled milk. She described this dream with such explicit detail that now, in my dreams, a pig will randomly come trotting through my field of vision, injecting itself into my narrative. Sometimes it's only a speck in the distance, and other times it's close enough to touch. The dream pig pokes at me with its snout, leaving a trail of drool on my hand. Now that she's gone, I feel like this pig is my inheritance. I don't know what it means except that I am tasked with keeping it alive.

History comes to me as this decontextualized pig—pig as a talisman, pig as a cipher for something inaccessible to me. This pig is powered through adjacency, burning with the oil and blubber of other auras. Maybe writing this reveals my process of reconciling with history's unknowability, admitting that I no longer feel a need to salvage the past in order to understand our future and its terrain of struggle. To me, keeping my Nainai's pig alive is about condemning the militarized police state that forced her to live undocumented in America for over a decade as much as it is about condemning China's parasitic and neocolonial trade relationship with Africa. The praxis has to be transcendental of any geotemporal context. It has to be greater than any nation-state.

In *Dictee*, Cha writes, "Why resurrect it all now. From the Past. History, the old wound. The past emotions all over again. To confess to relive the same folly. To name it now so as not to repeat history in oblivion."[20] If we are to "redeem the present through the grace of oblivion," Cha asks us to follow her from the stasis of

---

20. Cha, *Dictee*, 33.

history into the realm of mythology. In an unpublished lyric essay made of fragments that never appeared in the final version of *Dictee*, the speaker recounts a dream sequence in which faces appear in transit on a freeway:

> from the apex comes a continuous stream of heads without bodies. Faces from every history speed furiously down the tunnel, some glancing off my windshield. One stops, a pale Persephone, like a bee hovering. A moment of eye contact through the glass and then she accelerates past. It is fast in this era, there is no time for these dismembered shades to stop and tell their stories, to ask of their sons and daughters[21]

This is the picture I see when I look at the blank spaces in my Nainai's photo album: a pale Persephone, promising an impossible presence moments before her sudden abduction through a cleft in the earth. It's true that we can't bring Persephone back from Hades, but her disappearance gives us the spring.

From the start of the section titled "ERATO / LOVE POETRY" through the remainder of the text, the temporality of *Dictee* transitions from revolutionary time to geological time. "What of the partition," she incites, alluding both to the DMZ and the screen that divides the performer from her audience.[22] In this crucial passage, the screen becomes "unattainably pure," a place where all memory is collective memory, absent of historical epochs: "The memory stain attaches itself and darkens on the pale formless sheet, a hole increasing its size larger and larger until it assimilates the boundaries and becomes itself formless. All memory. Occupies the entire."[23] There is no distinction between self and other, no expansion of the exilée's identity that is necessary to make space for the coexistence of others. Instead of reifying her as an absolute other to be assimilated or expelled, her passage over the border is precisely what dissolves the border. This is the true end to exile: not the repatriation of the exilée, but the arrival of deconstructed space where xénos and plíthos are negated, and the conditions that originally produced her exile are abolished. The screen becomes the location where she can practice her enactment of this other world.

---

21. Cha, "Recit: Previously Unpublished Works by Theresa Hak Kyung Cha."
22. Cha, *Dictee*, 131.
23. Cha, *Dictee*, 131.

At night, after Dimitri fell asleep, I lay awake and looked at the Puck Building through the window of the hotel, how it emitted light despite its vacancy. Every shard felt manageable as it filtered through the blinds, gleaming with equanimity. And then I imagined a future where the building would be in ruins, a referent without a symbolic order attached to it. There was the slivered moon, and there was a slivered affinity between Cha's deconstruction and my own revolutionary desire: to evacuate the name of an empire until it recedes into oblivion. "She says to herself if she were able to write she could continue to live. Says to herself if she would write without ceasing. To herself if by writing she could abolish real time. She would live."[24]

I am indebted to Cha's poetry as it makes fluid those categories of memory, geography, time, self, and other. On the surface, the goal might appear to be total fragmentation, but I believe her intention is the opposite. The page is a location where we can gather and bear witness to each other, testing the boundaries of

A Ble Wail (1975). "In this piece," Cha said, "I want to be the dream of the audience." She subverts the audience as a static body, instead rendering witness as a dialectic relationship. The performer becomes a figment of the audience's invocation, allowing us to partake as imaginative agents.

---

24. Cha, *Dictee*, 141.

Angie Sijun Lou

intimacy and narrativity, beyond spatiotemporal fixity and toward an open field—
"In the enclosed darkness memory is fugitive."[25] I felt Cha's fugitive force vibrate
in the hollows of the building, her aura petrified in the stone colonnades. It's not
an easy transcendence. I don't believe that art lives on the exterior of history, or
that history has an exit sign we can follow. And I still believe in militant struggle
and the elsewhere it beckons that some things cannot be repurposed because they
are destined to burn. But what I see in Cha's cinematic allure is a blueprint for the
dissolution of all sovereign borders.

The final pages of *Dictee* contain potent images of reincarnation: the theatre is
emptied after the simulation, a child revives her mother with the tinctures of
a shaman, and flowers sprout from a slain branch. After the extinction event,
we enter a creation myth beginning with the elemental substances: water, pigment, saliva, blood, light, and ink. "Earth is made porous . . . In the blue-black
body commences lument."[26] The world detaches itself from "plural pasts taken
place beforehand."[27] Time makes monuments into cenotaphs. Signs have their
etymologies evacuated before they are imbued with new meaning:

> Words cast each by each to weather
> avowed indisputably, to time.
> If it should impress, make fossil trace of word,
> residue of word, stand as a ruin stands,
> simply, as mark
> having relinquished itself to time to distance[28]

These words, now hieroglyphs, are being primed for re-assemblage into new
orders. I kept the Puck Building in my field of vision before closing my eyes. Its
light radiated outward, shining into the hotel room. "You remain dismembered
with the belief that magnolia blooms white even on seemingly dead branches and
you wait."[29] After I fell asleep, my dreams were graced with visitations from my
Nainai's pet pig. I listened while it spoke softly to me, in a human voice.

---

25. Cha, *Dictee*, 118.
26. Cha, *Dictee*, 160.
27. Cha, *Dictee*, 175.
28. Cha, *Dictee*, 177.
29. Cha, *Dictee*, 155.

BIBLIOGRAPHY

Baudelaire, Charles. *Les Fleurs du Mal*. Paris: Éditions Gallimard, 1999.

Cha, Theresa Hak Kyung, "Artist's Statement / Summary of Work." Berkeley, CA: Berkeley Art Museum and Pacific Film Archive, 1978. https://oac.cdlib.org/ark:/13030/tf4j49n6h6/?brand=oac4

Cha, Theresa Hak Kyung, director. *A Ble Wail*. Berkeley Art Museum and Pacific Film Archive, 1975.

Cha, Theresa Hak Kyung. *Dictee*. Berkeley, CA: University of California Press, 2001.

Cha, Theresa Hak Kyung. *Exilée and Temps Morts*. Berkeley, CA: University of California Press, 2022.

Cha, Theresa Hak Kyung, director. *Mouth to Mouth*. Berkeley, CA: Berkeley Art Museum and Film Archive, 1975.

Cha, Theresa Hak Kyung. "Recit: Previously Unpublished Works by Theresa Hak Kyung Cha." FENCE. Fall/Winter 2001. https://fenceportal.org/recit-previously-unpublished-works-by-theresa-hak-kyung-cha/

Cha, Theresa Hak Kyung, director. *White Dust from Mongolia*. Berkeley Art Museum and Pacific Film Archive, 1980.

Dunlap, David W. "Landmarks Panel Rejects Second Penthouse Plan for Puck Building." *New York Times*. November 15, 2011. https://archive.nytimes.com/cityroom.blogs.nytimes.com/2011/11/15/landmarks-panel-rejects-second-penthouse-plan-for-puck-building/

Dziemianowicz, Joe. "Historic NYC Building Becomes Murder Scene for Artist on Verge of a Career Breakthrough." *Oxygen*. February 12, 2022. https://www.oxygen.com/new-york-homicide/crime-news/security-guard-joey-sanza-killed-theresa-cha-puck-building

Finn, Robert. "Penthouses for the Puck Building." *New York Times*. September 19, 2013. https://www.nytimes.com/2013/09/22/realestate/penthouses-for-the-puck-building.html

Fukuyama, Francis. *The End of History and the Last Man* (New York, NY: Free Press, 1992).

Marino, Vivian. "$28.5 Million, a Record Sale in Nolita." *New York Times*. February 26, 2016. https://www.nytimes.com/2016/02/28/realestate/28-5-million-arecord-sale-in-nolita.html?

Saltzein, Dan. "Overlooked No More: Theresa Hak Kyung Cha, Artist and Author Who Explored Identity." *New York Times.* January 7, 2022. https://www.nytimes.com/2022/01/07/obituaries/theresa-hak-kyung-cha-overlooked.html

Tzeses, Jennifer. "In New York's Famed Puck Building, a Two-Story Penthouse Is Listed for $58.5 Million." *Architectural Digest.* March 11, 2016. https://www.architecturaldigest.com/gallery/new-york-puck-building-two-story-penthouse

Wong, Shelley Sunn, Elaine H. Kim, and Lisa Lowe. *Writing Self, Writing Nation: A Collection of Essays on Dictée by Theresa Hak Kyung Cha* (Bloomington, IN: Third Woman Press, 1994).

Xu, Wendy. *The Past.* Middletown, CT: Wesleyan University Press, 2021.

Whether the Border Looks Out from Eight Hundred and Fifty Eyes, or Two, the MBQ Remains Few Though on the Rise

Saretta Morgan

[31.812180°, -111.443051°]

The boundaries of Buenos Aires National Wildlife Refuge (BANWR) in Southern Arizona were determined in 1985 to facilitate reintroduction of the masked bobwhite quail (MBQ) to a stretch of desert along the US–Mexico border.[1] This charmingly plumed, bottom-heavy ground-dwelling bird has been designated as an indicator species for the region. This means that based on intensive research on the causal and proxy relationships between overlapping phenomena, the presence or absence of MBQ can be used to assess vitality of the ecosystem as a whole. As part of a range-wide survey, visitors are asked to report MBQ sightings to the refuge with as much contextual information as is available. However, priorities.

[31.812180°, -111.443051°]

Between the years 2000 and 2022, the remains of 425 migrant women were publicly recorded in Pima County. Of these, five were found in BANWR. These five were each found on a segment of the refuge's north, east, or west border.

---

1. Buenos Aires National Wildlife Refuge, "About Us," U.S. Fish & Wildlife Service (website), accessed August 8, 2022: https://www.fws.gov/refuge/buenos-aires/about-us.

If you look at a map of all the migrant women's deaths recorded in Pima County during this twenty-one-year period (a map in which each woman is represented by a bright red dot) there's an empty refuge-shaped patch in the field of bright red dots.[2] If you find this difficult to visualize, that's appropriate. If you can visualize this, don't take the absence of an image as evidence that the refuge is safe.

[31.812180°, -111.443051°]

I enjoy camping at BANWR because of the administrative perks afforded to a wildlife refuge. Where national parks necessitate spending on advertising, or amenities such as bathrooms and picnic tables, the refuge budget goes to preserving indicator species, such as the MBQ. The absence of bathrooms, picnic tables, and advertising filters out most people, which is great, as most people camping in southern Arizona are, as a simple matter of statistics, racist and armed to their teeth.

What's unfortunate about the people we do see in the refuge, whether they're white or not, is that nine times out of ten they're Border Patrol, who share a symbiotic relationship with the refuge by maintaining roads—something the refuge cannot afford much to do.

Occasionally at the beginning Nazafarin or I would wave at an agent passing on the road. It wasn't a wave to communicate "I'm safe," or, "I'm unthreatening and a citizen," but an unfortunate reflex of rural places that surfaced when our guard was down.

[31.779571°, -111.560183°]

A further notable aspect of the BANWR border occurs at the northwest corner, where the refuge ends, and then approximately half a mile down the road begins again. After turning west off Rt. 286 over a cattle guard and down a decently serviced road, the refuge reemerges in the Baboquivari Mountains to carve out what is known by the US Bureau of Land Management (BLM) as Brown Canyon, a sky island ecosystem accessible November through April by reservation, so long as volunteers are available.

---

2. "Arizona OpenGIS Initiative for Deceased Migrants," Humane Borders (website), last modified July 2022: https://humaneborders.info/app/map.asp.

Sky islands are a type of mountain range found throughout the Sonoran Desert. They take their name from a rough metaphor. The high elevation of the mountain is in such contrast with the surrounding low desert that species thriving at the mountaintops would never make it in the surrounding lands. These species are, in a sense, stranded. Though, generally speaking, they aren't stranded until they need to leave.

Just west of Brown Canyon is Baboquivari Peak, a steady accumulation of centuries and magnificent cliff face which, in the Tohono O'odham tradition, is where everything begins.

[31.763821°, -111.472797°]

The construction is simple. Someone digs a trench. A grate is laid over the trench. Bar spacing of the grate must not allow a large hoofed animal to pass safely from one side of the trench to the other. Vertical clearance of the grate must not allow an animal to lift itself from the trench once they've stepped between the bars. In addition to barbed fencing, these cattle guards line Rt. 286 along the west border of BANWR.

Why so much (and so little) concern over rogue cows?

Open-range cattle ranching was a major player in the destruction of habitat suitable for MBQ. Introduced by settlers in the mid-nineteenth century, cattle thrived on what until then had been miles and miles of fertile grassland (MBQ habitat of choice). It was too many cattle, and poorly thought out. Before long, this error was exposed by miles and miles of sun-bleached bones.

The cattle that didn't die during the mid-nineteenth-century drought tore the land down to its earth. This was/is a serious problem. Barren earth doesn't possess sufficient fuel to support natural wildfires or controlled burns. In the absence of fires, thriving brush and mesquite prevented the return of grasses. In the absence of grasses, ranchers planted additional trees. In the absence of grasses, when the rains returned there was nothing to hold the land back from the arroyos one sees opening the landscape today.[3]

---

3. Buenos Aires National Wildlife Refuge, "About Us."

Standing in the park's northern territory, I find it difficult to visually reconstruct a prior ecological identity. The stressed vegetation and eroding soils
adhere closely to American cultural mythologies of parched desert wilderness
in need of white-supremacist protection. I say to my dog, Federica: This, lady,
is where we practice faith. We believe that the world was different. We believe
that it can be different again. Our part in this process is an anxiously evolving
question.

[[·], [- ·]]

The difficult thing. And this difficulty is ambient, can be non-impressive. The
difficult thing about imagining a prior ecological identity is that so much of
my imagination, which is to say also my capacity to arrive, has been formed by
and within the conditions on which this tragedy rests.

So much rests. And waits. And reposes physically unquestioned. And is
estranged within. And wrests within settler-colonial landscapes.

[32.222874°, -110.967530°]

Nazafarin moved to the US in her twenties for art school. After years in the
Midwest she relocated to Tucson, where her partner is now a professor. We
share a loneliness in the desert that's challenging. Her difficulty moves, in
part, through the language of painting:

*I knew this geography only through painting and photography. Almost always empty
of human presence. And grand. Desert romanticism in line with the eighteenth-
century European tradition . . . inviting exploration. Expansion and the settler colonial project . . . The main idea being negative space. What is erased or absent from
it needs to be recovered.*[4]

We send pictures back and forth as she tends an olive tree. I fix nitrogen with
native seeds. The practice of watching things grow distorts my alienation into
its own curious bulb. Thick-rooted language and orientation. The self-evolving
work to remain alongside Native peoples while geohistorically enmeshed in
their absence and ongoing genocidal erasure.

---

4. Nazafarin Lotfi, text message to the author, February 2, 2022.

Though the consequences weren't immediately visible, the Gadsden Purchase in 1854 drove a then-invisible boundary through the Tohono O'odham Nation. That policy/line superimposed Venn diagrams of tribal/settler-colonial/international spheres that increasingly criminalize and restrict tribal peoples from caretaking lands, engaging in prayer, and practicing traditional climate-responsive migratory patterns that alleviate environmental stress.

Today the boundary grows increasingly visible in some ways.

Example:

Wall construction.

Example:

Israeli-imported Integrated Fixed Tower (IFT) surveillance technology has been installed on and off the reservation. While the intended subjects of observation are migrants, cameras don't know the difference.

Today the scope and consequences reproduce infinitely and un-visibly in other ways.

Example:

When it began after 9/11, it was so aggressive that it forced the people not to go out on the land anymore. That is really affecting the health of everybody. The health of the elders—who really need to be out on the land to connect with the plants and with the mountain. From that point on, the children don't see their elders out there, they're not connecting to that part of our life. This forced disconnection to the land is unhealthy because with the disconnection they lose their language, traditional diet, and sensitivity to turn to traditional medicine.

—OPHELIA RIVAS, TOHONO O'ODHAM ELDER[5]

---

5. Caitlin Blanchfield and Nina Valerie Kolowratnik, "Significant Impact," E-Flux (website), accessed August 8, 2022: https://www.e-flux.com/architecture/at-the-border/325749/significant-impact/.

Example:

Saguaros having been torn from their orientation to the sun.

[31.791988°, -111.577037°]

The BLM asks us to accept that their regulation of the Baboquivari Peak Wilderness (roughly two thousand acres added to the National Wilderness Preservation System in 1990) is for everyone's benefit.

Example:

for the preservation of wildlife, motorized equipment is legally pro-hibited on all lands federally designated as "wilderness."[6]

To believe that the BLM protects land for everyone's benefit, we must first forget that the Tohono O'odham were always here. Or we must believe that their relegation to the Tohono O'odham reservation was/is a painless process. Or (the BLM's favorite) that they don't exist at all.

[43.472208°, -80.542454°]

If Black culture is critical culture, what I am suggesting is that perhaps it hasn't come about yet . . .

—HORTENSE SPILLERS, ON "THE IDEA OF BLACK CULTURE"[7]

If it's true (and everything Spillers says is true in one way if not others) that our work is to turn critically from the world, to assume a position by which the earth's impressions arrive in view,

if from necessity certain bodies turn quietly to earth,

if the enactment of one environment extracts life from another,

---

6. "A Cheatsheet for Demystifying The Wilderness Act Public Law 88-577," United States Department of Agriculture (website), accessed August 8, 2022: https://www.fs.usda.gov/Internet/FSE_DOCUMENTS/stelprdb5313909.pdf.
7. University of Waterloo English Department, "Hortense Spillers: The Idea of Black Culture," Youtube Video, 1:25:36, November 24, 2013: https://youtu.be/P1PTHFCN4Gc.

if there's a border where life is no longer possible,

if an indicator species points toward the health of a question, a question
of Black culture is: whose body constitutes an environment,

if I imagine sounds that challenge my orientation in the grasses,

if constitution happens in that way, at times the practice of Black culture
requires a challenge to my impulses of orientation,

if accumulation positions criticality, we might see us in the ghost
tufts of grasses, if I'm unthreatening and a citizen thinking through
one word, it would be, what it is that a challenge *releases* to coming
together.

[31.484262°, -111.461975°]

The formal cemetery (belonging to the Garcia Ranch family) is a short distance from the BANWR southern border, which is the northern border of
Mexico. The roads in this area are increasingly difficult to drive. On our way
to the cemetery we pass several deer and a few birds we haven't seen before.
No MBQ.

Standing outside the fence, Nazafarin talks about her youth in northern Iran.
These hills are similar to those of her mother's ancestral village. She asks if
Federica is allowed in the cemetery, as Federica is sniffing around the graves.
I say, Federica Garcia Lorca Elisabeth Morgan-Diaz, if you don't get your Black
ass out of there. And she does in her time.

Nazafarin (the painter) and I (the poet) think about how we encounter and express our socio-geographic experiences of southern Arizona.
As immigrant. As Black. As woman. As queer. As cis. As citizen, natu-
ralized and not. We stumble through language and subject positions, the
web of desires and antagonisms our bodies emerge, upon contact with
systematically exploited lands. Lands that still function as long, shallow
graves. And that collect a sky so stunning that unless it's you who are
dying, you forget at times how fresh they are, the graves.

Again I'm late and Nazafarin has chosen a campsite. She's chosen this site for its vista, which is indeed impressive. When I arrive, she's reading Etel Adnan in a folding chair overlooking the mountains. She's identified where the ground is soft enough for stakes. I choose a clearing of dirt behind three low mesquite trees, where I anticipate protection from the wind.

My tent is half up when I notice Federica rolling through dead grass between the three trees. She's so into it. Full-body enthusiasm from nose to tail. It's the particular roll, neck first, that she reserves for things that stink. Federica is rolling back and forth over the severed leg of a deer. I say, Federica Garcia Lorca Elisabeth Morgan-Diaz, get your Black ass out of there. I call to Nazafarin to show her what we've found. She says that she remembers having seen it. That she saw it, then quickly un-saw it. I realize that I had too.

Not far from the leg there's another, and a little farther from that, a twisted carcass. We like this spot, so it's the remains that must go. I load them up and drive a few minutes down the road, where I nudge each off the truck bed with my boot.

On my way back to camp, I get an uneasy feeling. I return to the coarse hair followed down to flaking hooves, and I cover them with what branches are near.

I walk down the hill from our spot for wood. No rain this year, but the downed wood is faintly green at its core. Fresh cut by the rangers. No good for fires. I find more deer legs. Three, and I'm disappointed. You're going to be sleeping in someone's kitchen tonight, my lover tells me when I call her on the phone.

Around the fire we pour wine and listen to coyotes hunt beyond the tree line in howls and yips. We open a pack of cigarettes to observe stars and the moon.

[37.923461°, -122.596331°]

I feel trapped in this universe and think of what an anti-verse could mean, which is still a universe; there is no way out.

—ETEL ADNAN, *JOURNEY TO MOUNT TAMALPAIS*[8]

[40.672736°, -73.982974°]

What is meant here by perception is a form of listening that transfigures the relation between subject and object, that reaches into layers of history buried underground.

—OMAR BERRADA ON *JOURNEY TO MOUNT TAMALPAIS*[9]

[[·], [- ·]]

I've worked with No More Deaths to provide humanitarian aid in another stretch of the Sonoran Desert (about 130 miles northwest) since 2018. On our way out to drop water at the coordinates we maintain, I don't look up. The trail is unpredictable, shifting as it does with rain. Because water is heavy, my breath pulses in my ears. The chain cholla stand in clusters, small men bearing fruit. Inevitably a cholla pup adheres to my pants. For the first three years my backpack lacks a suspension system. The straps constrict nerves in my neck and shoulders, which produces pain and occasional numbing in my arms. A pain of my own negligence, as I had money and intent to purchase a better one.

On our way back from placing water, the mountains defy my memory. There's no sufficient way to acknowledge the interstitial vacuum between what I see and how the landscape appears without water and satellite GPS, or a truck two miles away, or with policies such as Prevention through Deterrence forcing each step into the most circuitous terrain. Here too, faith is no substitute for a systematically limited imagination. The vacuum is incomprehensible. It waits beyond my understanding, in thorns and biological soil crusts. Waiting for someone else even as I enter it.

---

8. Etel Adnan, *Journey to Mount Tamalpais*, 2nd ed., (New York: Litmus Press, 2021): 11
9. Omar Berrada, "The Undying Vibrancy of All Things" in *Journey to Mount Tamalpais*, 2nd ed., (New York: Litmus Press, 2021): 74.

[32.213466°, -110.971526°]

Increasingly in the wake of US withdrawal from Afghanistan, Nazafarin mentors Afghani youth in refugee status. I asked her what it's like to hear her language spoken abundantly in these deserts. She replied: it's strange.

[32.538254°, -114.558886°]

A fellow humanitarian aid worker began a database and map of IFTs across southern Arizona.[10] She submits FOIA requests or skims travel blogs for a general sense of where a tower might be. Then she combs Google Earth for exact visual cues, such as roads smoothed for a tower's installation and service. Or the bright-white cluster of pixels on which each beacon rests.

In real life, they're unmistakable—eighty-foot structures supporting 360-degree radar, night cameras and a telephone all juiced off a renewable solar battery with propane reserve. Via satellite, the lattice of virtual fencing slips with its data into an angle of shadow so slight at times there is no telling how many.

[31.459365°, -111.465157°]

From mile twenty we could see variations in a corner of the San Luis Mountains. An ochre cut across the color time takes for land to encounter itself. We imagined phenomena and millennia building on top of one another.

Driving further the next day, approaching the border, we realized the absence of color was land cleared in order to extend construction. A trans substantive property of the American West is that it's "wilderness" until it's not. You can't operate a motor vehicle until you can plow the land over to build a wall. The BLM has patience, and faith that in time everything can change.

[31.592359°, -111.448734°]

I wake to the sound of rustling, perhaps sniffing, outside my tent. I think maybe a coyote or bobcat. Federica is unbothered, which upsets me, as I would like to be asleep too. Mountain lions come down this far when water is scarce. Less than ten miles from the border, it could be cartel, a possibility

---

10. Tara Plath, "Methodology," AZ Beacon Map, accessed August 8, 2022: https://azbeaconmap .org/methodology/.

the BANWR website clearly **states**. Worst-case scenario, it's one of the backward-looking white men who come here to hunt.

The truck's panic button can startle off animals. It might repel humans, but if not, they'll be ready. I consider a single shot in the air. Warning shots are illegal. If you truly believe your life is in danger, the only legal response is to kill. I breathe and listen. I will my bladder to rest.

Illuminated by sunrise, the dirt around my tent is smooth. Without tracks or signs of disturbance. Nazafarin is out for her morning walk. She goes off to paint and watch for animals. I'm making cheesy grits with eggs when she returns. I keep hearing deer, she says, herds of them running through the trees.

We drive down to the border and east along the wall, weaving through crews of men, water-holding pools, and trucks with tires taller than my head. The packed dirt is red and rises into steep hills. I pause at the top of one, feeling already the drop of it, nearly vertical. Roadrunners slip in and out of the steel beams that divide our bodies from the neighboring State.

After Silent Incantations, the Intertidal

Ronaldo V. Wilson

P(act) I.

scene i.

McLaughlin Eastshore State Park, a state park and wildlife refuge along the San Francisco Bay shoreline of the East Bay extending, in part, between Berkeley and Emeryville, CA. The sky is gray-blue-thick. Shadow-bellied potato bug clouds drift above. Below, lichened rocks, rust bearded, lead into the bay; green, dimpled brown by the lapping water, "Spartina alterniflora hybrids (smooth cordgrass) take root then spread outward—covering mudflats . . ." reveals the placard, its tilted, weathered gloss, "Habitat for Tomorrow . . ." Out there, before the outline of the turning Bay Bridge and the city, mountains cut the horizon above the high tide. Uba's sightline flies beyond the bay, across the slight Pacific wind.

(Tracy Chapman's "Telling Stories" plays from a mini Bose speaker on a rock next to which Uba set her three masks: BY BY Black, Newborn, and Yell-O-Why.)

Enter Uba (A morphing no-age cypher made of silicon and two human eyes, twenty-six mile marathon trained, who works in Inglés, Mirinkai, and sometimes Tagalog. Eyes: BRN/Hair: a Black mullet). Uba wears a navy blue H&M jacket under an AG Japanese cotton "Trench Jack," horseshoe crab carcasses as gloves, and a golden iron-rust scarf as their cape.

& Lio (Uba's son, who longs in songs, subtracts to aggregate and drive the bass, and silences with sonic beats. Lio's PolyImagilingual—Eyes BRN/Hair: Faded). He dons his dad's boxy mauve sweats and camel corduroy house shoes, all too big but warm. Lio's more cloud than human in his "father's memory" outfit.

Uba: Lio, when I saw you come downstairs in Noa's sweats, I think I noticed you noticing me, remembering your father, his skin—

(*Lio remembers Uba crying over her beloved's body . . .*)

Noa Come Home!
Come Home!

(Your skin as soft as his was, as soft as the morning air when I go out to dig the lawn, till it, kill the grass to farm my tomatoes, soil soft as the lotion you rubbed into your dad, his silky calves, his forearms, and his heels . . .)

Long kitchen knife out back to gut the grass, and too, my pitchfork works.

Enter Noa (Never dry lipped, and brown, who proudly wears diapers and served in the US Navy. Used a pearl-handled pistol shot to the sky, to face race. Human—Eyes: BRN/Hair: gray tufts, now blended into the dug-out ex-"lawn"): Noa in black Pro-Endurance "Jammer" Speedos for a swim. Like a kaleidoscope's twist, he travels in layered frames between realms, and so too, does his lower torso. It twists. Noa dolphin kicks from immediate recognition, breathing to the right on the slight head-turn, his free.

(*Uba and Lio hover over Noa in the plaid, light copper, and maroon fold-out in the den, Lio lotioning his dad's ashy body to shiny skin.*)

Ronaldo V. Wilson

Noa: Look Mom, it's soaking all the way in.

Lio: I wore Dad's sweats because you left them for me, upstairs, where I plug
        in all my devices, iPad, iPhone, M_B-Pro corded to layers of the self,
        hoping I may get to listen to your voice as a way toward recalling where I
        was born, Millington, TN, our walks around Navy Lake.

Noa: Show them the photo!

Uba: Pops, it's not that kind of shot. It's a still with Newborn, BY BY Black,
        and me thinking of our fun: "Stitched as a ZinZin."

Noa: Whaddyoucare, that's not what I asked!—"Stitched as a ZinZin," is get-
        ting us to look into our present, via our lingo, Mirinkai to get, "what we
        want to know, out there . . ."

        Lio! Lio! C'mere!

Lio: Sometimes rendering takes staring into the gray-green bay, but on
        foot, as opposed to from the Hilton Garden Inn's "Bay-View" vista.

Ronaldo V. Wilson. *Lucy the Intertidal*, 2019. Video (still), 11m. 12s.

Grounded from that POV, we stack masks of the self on the tripod, selves atop one another near the rocks, us. As if to say, *this is the story of where you are*, or *were is the rehearsal and the performance*, of what is both real and made: To witness what you meant to one another, *all alive then*, is simultaneously our entry and our departure.

Noa: You got dat right!

Lio: *(Singing along with Chapman's voice)*

          There is fiction in the space between
          You and reality
          You will do and say anything
          To make your everyday life seem less mundane

          As you died, Noa, I made a bridge over your body with my chest and arms, willing my upper half into an arc. Careful not to dislodge the IVs and wires taped below your clavicle, my boots gripped, pebbled leather above the emergency sickbed floor. It's not so much in the fighting where I recall how you lived, but in how I wanted only to be a root between life and death, you & Uba, you two: my only mom, my only dad—

Noa: *FaH-JA? FaH-JA!*

Lio: *Face? Face?*

Noa: *Yeah, FaH-JA! FaH-JA!*

          (. . . grabbing his own sparse white beard and soft face between his free fingers, Noa's hands are shaped exactly like Lio's but thick . . .)

Lio: Dear Dad, I compose: ". . . what we want to know, out there . . ."— () Look, into the gray bay, a past, as in there is a sentence and in there, a sacred place:

The Ohlone may have expanded this mound and had a village atop it, but the Emeryville Shellmound appears to have been abandoned about 700 years ago, around 1250 A D. The house of a European settler was reportedly built on 1 of the nearby smaller mounds around 1840.[1]

(Lio singing, raspy, yet full throated.)

Dear Father, I have gone away . . .

     Dear Father, I have gone away . . .

Dear Father, I have gone away. . . .

     I know the sound

Dear Father, I have gone away . . .

I know the sound
     is coming
through

Dear Father, I have gone away. . . .

I know you
are there

Noa: When I heard you sing that song, mine, in the snowy Monadnock mountain forest, so far from where I died, away from my sailor-sea, I knew this was a song I couldn't have taught you while I lived. I knew because I taught you *to sing from the diaphragm*, in other words, for yourself. Even in my imagination, alive, I would've sung it for you, your brother, your sister, for Moms, too, if I could—you know this

---

1. California, Emeryville. "Indigenous People: An Idyllic Place for Human Settlement," city (website): https://www.ci.emeryville.ca.us/657/Indigenous-People

already—root the intertidal to brackish and through exile and capture, to what's ours.

~

P()ct II. Workitout.

scene ii

Uba, Lio, and Noa cruise the center of the asphalt walkway. Noa alive, Uba's face opens, yellow-pink apple cheeks and cheekbones. Banjee boy, Vogue-Crushing, Lio stomps while smelling the sea air. Noa is close, just north and east of here, and in the wind and all the while, Uba is looking into the distance, making sure to balance on the balls of her feet. "Walking," Lio pushes the stilettos' tips in too, grinding down to take notes, register where their bodies fuse in sync with the cracking stone bits beneath.

Click / Click / Click.

"He pops. He pops good . . ." Brown boys praising Michael Jackson's dancing—the memory cuts through Uba as they drag the cursor to still the

Ronaldo V. Wilson. *Lucy the Intertidal,* 2019. Video (still), 11m. 12s

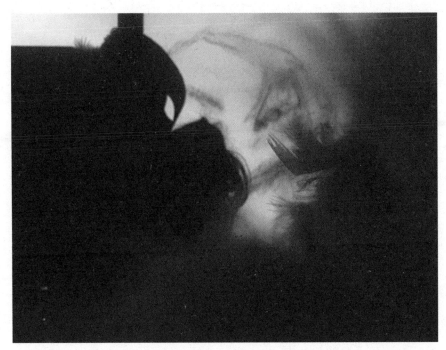

Ronaldo V. Wilson. *"BY BY Black, B_K Memory, and Yell-O-Why,"* Provincetown MA, 2019. Digital Image.

frame where the tan runner's leg splits Uba's gait. Kanye West's "Clique," ft. Big Sean & Jay-Z "Now who with me/ vah-ma-nos." They fuse, too. From inside her mask, Uba sees not quite a white light, but something close to a silicon blur, and out of this, she makes out an equally opaque resin. Shards of clear sight. Bridge/Glimpse. The feel from the inside of the mask steadies Uba's balance between the rock rails and the cut grass, two passing beings moving along a shared path. Light is water, is feather, is palimpsest is promontory—Uba retreats and thinks of Noa, now forever gone.

Uba: With diA there too, I wasn't the only one of our family in the audience to hear you sing. *It was your first live show!*

(*Uba stops, shifts her heels' tips into the sidewalk, plants them; back bent, she looks into the still gray sky.*)

(*Lio Singing*)

Guantanamera . . . Guajira, Guantanamera
Guanta-na-mehhrrra
JuajiraGuanta-

Na·
Mehhrrrrahhhh—

Uba: Noa, I didn't know he could sing!

Noa: Oh, I did. We taught him.

Uba: Lio, I flee, sixteen, rape-a-get-away, to run, so far away to work double
       doubles as a CNA in South Sacra. Silver wires sinew up my spine, pins and
       bolts set so all your eyes could see clearly into a future. For you and diA
       and ci(), your brother and sister, I would work forever, beyond my bones'
       threshold, bent and curved inside. Heart valves pop. Constrict. I'm never
       fat. I eat candy. Anything can be fixed—I see a mobile family portrait of us
       driving by the long-gone Emeryville Mudflat Sculptures in our Ford Pinto
       Squire, Noa driving us, and you, Lio, latching onto the art staged in the
       mud in the rising water in front of the bridge, further back, a horizon. Was
       this sight enough, your freedom? Our escape? My labor, my love? Your
       worth. Ours? What I don't tell any of you is how I remember the sky the
       day I ran from my "so-called uncle," rape-a-get-away. The details, you'll
       get, and construct. *Go off!* I know you'll make it, no matter what, or to
       wherever you decide, and when. Noa knows I know how to raise you, even
       when he went away to sea, and even as he is now there, forever so.

Noa: . . . She raised you guys
       while I was runnin' all around the world
       with a whole gang of badges (. . . *Ahehhehhhuhhuhehhehehehehhhh.*)
       You guys have a whole gang of badges
       she gave you!
       . . . like I raised you.
       So I'm proud of her too.
       I'm just lucky . . .
       Just lucky.

"Driftwood Art in Emeryville Mudflats," Shaping San Francisco's Digital Archive @ Found (website).[2]

scene iii.

"No matter if it was vandals who didn't like what you made, or the tide com-ing in, the artist's creation out in the mudflats existed in a finite moment. This finite moment negated any sense of ownership to what you made. Since you knew that it wasn't going to last, this allowed a focus on just the experi-ence of making."[3]

> *For Lio, he reads "a finite moment," as set in his figuring out what his dad was saying in the first film he made with his family's home-movie footage. "Silent Incantations" is dubbed some with a sound recording of his dad's voice caught between laughter and crying. Noa's beat, and theorem: Lio transcribes Noa's words while watch-ing Uba serve, go up after the ball on the old Super-8 sequence, her Spalding Doris Hart wood racket in Guam, in Tennessee, candy-apple red heart painted on its glossy throat—Uba rushing the net, following her serve to attack.*

> > *Lio made the film, and realizes he learned to play, too, with wood, Dunlop/TAD leather grip to feel, to touch the overlay, his own quick, flutter laugh after Noa's story of him first meeting Uba, the story on rewind "like I raised*

2. https://www.foundsf.org/index.php?title=Driftwood_Art_in_Emeryville_Mudflats. Photo: cour-tesy Carl Griffith via Facebook
3. Joey Enos, "Radical as Folk: Second of a Three-part Series on the History of the Emeryville Mudflat Sculptures," Evileeye.com, June 24, 2016: https://evilleeye.com/history/radical-folk-second-three-part-series-history-emeryville-mudflat-sculptures/

you . . ." Lio thinks and could listen to Noa say this
forever—it's why sometimes Lio wears no-mask, which is
a state too, a place from which he marks, yet still language
grounds every performance.

Noa: That's how we raised you!

Uba: Arising from where you are there, or where you were then, feeds your
        sight. We did not say to you, *"Look at the* ART*!"* We drove by, and you
        did . . .

Lio: . . . and as we drove by, we were free in our beings in this place: here, us.
        That [it] could come out of anywhere . . .

. . . is the place as to root the intertidal . . . every . . .

Ronaldo V. Wilson. *Lucy the Intertidal*, 2019. Video. (3 stills), 11m. 12s.

thing . . . to brackish and through exile and capture, *to what's ours.*

At the end of the act, there is both the collection and the walk, its documentation, and its isolates. To leave the masks—here Newborn and Yell-O-Why—where they fall is maybe the condition of the exilic, as this marks the site of our mourning, offering a nowhere leading to that which remains. Here, I know I'm not staring out into a no place, and I know, too, that I've come to gather at the site of projection and release to make up a way back, but to where? My mother lost her first child after fifty-five days of his being alive. *This little boy* returns, like the tide. It comes back, where I record my mom's voice, on the small pull-out and stacked mattress, lying with her on what was my dad's last day.

Noa: It's in your cells.

       (Interlude: Lionel Richie [Commodores] "Sail On" plays, and Noa sings along.)

       Sail on down the line
       'Bout a
       half a mile or so
       and I
       don't really want to know
       where you're going . . .

Lio: I have this signature dance where I move in one place, grounding my feet, isolating my shoulders in slow syncopation with my wave-pulsing chest. I let the beat or lyrics of whatever song course in, as if I am in time with the last seconds of the washing machine, spun out, the slight shake, holding my drum inside. My hips sway in a slow, unsuspended cycle, I rock into what beats back as the beat backs into my composed moves, some parts of me in, others just out enough.

Noa: *Howboutthat.*

Uba: I carried him from the house,
running to the dispensary.
The dispensary's not very far
. . . about a half a mile,
so I'm carrying this little boy, already dead
and I don't know what to do
because I was new to the place.
We just got there about six months ago.
My house didn't have any curtains.
We got pots and pans,
and a little heater on the sides . . .

Ronaldo V. Wilson. "Bye Bye, Be Good Don," 2020. Video (still), 22m. 39s

(Lio's earbuds suck in, then emit three soft tones, power down, and die.
Uba listens to "the ocean," held in a sea shell picked up, the rustling air.)

Lio pops, pushes in his elbow in and flexes; his wrist rubs his clavicle.

Hands clutch

Come and Take It—

The black

AK-47 *print on*

the white

stuffed in flag.

The racist,

Cretin's

Sun

blinded eyes

from the wide-open

window shade's sus-

tained light blast.

A guitar's twank

signals, again, the interlude:

> *(All sing . . .)*

>> *Sail on down the line*
>> *'Bout a*
>> *half a mile or so*
>> *and I*
>> *don't really want to know*
>> *where you're going . . .*

(Uba takes stock, looks around, and realizes their performance on the shore's adjacent to Pilgrim's First Landing Park at the tip of Cape Cod, P-Town.

Not near the Pacific, but still the breakwater, and soon, another high tide. She sings, alone, what she learns, in sync with the Commodores' melody . . .)

How many people know
when the Pilgrims came

to Patuxet/

to build their homes.
They had to

sweep away the bones . . .

~

p(Act) III. Telling Stories

scene iv.

*Dozens of small black heads pop out of Navy Lake at dusk. Lio and ci()
dream of catching them. What they think are turtles might be water moc-
casins peeking up and back from out of the lake. The boys want to catch
anything. If not turtles, or snakes, then fish. Not to eat, but for fun. Yet neither of them have fishing rods nor hooks, so ci() has a theory that he puts
into practice, showing Lio a way: ci() opens the Coke can by its finger loop
tab lip, peeled open, Pop!—its teardrop edge sharp enough to cut into meat.
ci() gouges a piece of frozen hot dog onto this "hook," tying a knot of thread
around the looped end. ci() tosses the strung bait into the lake. The idea is
that when the fish or snake or turtle bites the thawing hot dog, it's caught. Still
cold surface sticking to the insides of the animal's mouth, ideally, the hook'll
curve further down into its throat or gut.*

Uba: Lio, I think my past is cast into your question: *How far into the distance*
         might the archipelago of loss extend? That is, to where do these wooden,
         long-gone remnants of rotted-away piers lead—my home, my languages?
         English. Tagalog. Visayan. Iloilo. Leon, Roxas City, *a hundred thousand*

Ronaldo V. Wilson, "Archipelago of Loss," Emeryville, CA, 2017. Digital Image.

miles, to where I fled? Japan. The United States. To have left everyone. My sister. *My "so-called uncle" who tried to rape/me.* Maybe Lio, it's true. Exile is *light is water, is feather, is palimpsest is promontory*—at low tide, shadows (a way, too, to reveal).

In the low light, when I know Noa is going, that he's not coming back, *I kind of had a feeling that he's not. . . . I tell it.* Maybe, what I tell is the story of what I am inside your performances: our one life in all our acts.

> *[Inside: Uba and Lio make a pact in self-fashioning, agree that it's enough to not have to wear the masks, and with this comes an understanding that it's crucial to leave By By Black and Yell-O-Why in the field of the imaginary as "punctuation marks," marks that emphasize that the nature of recovery must be told by indirection, re-syntaxed facts, or by flattening "the story," which is akin to graying color images to black and white, where place and home unveils texture, variant, guidepost.*

> *By morning,*
> *it came out*
> *that he was still alive!]*

Lio: In the intertidal zone—between low and high tide—Was I in Emeryville, extending my Hilton Garden Inn hotel stays to play outside in what I still called the mobile studio? My study. My site-specific surfaces spike. Signposts, remnants of a past, the attack's respite comes alive in lines of language that move from their contingencies. A figure, after all, isn't a place to return to when one is forever on the run, nor is it the place that is found where water courses, fluid as blood in the body, however fresh, however polluted, dying, and still, and still life.

> *(Lio freestyles)*

> *Light is water,*
> *is feather, is Pa lim sest*

> *toe up, heels down to*
> *spike in life is the promontory—*

> *Can of tuna, my mom likes*
> *with rice, a feeding ground.*

Run to peek at the lowest
vantage point, to fish,

gutted to the resin
trail of the tin, done,

and do you know?
How Uba retreats

is what I think of
in smackdowns. First

class, Jet Blue Mint
Black son of Noa now,

goes to brighten the silicon
Yell-O-Why's hand&eyeattack!

Ronaldo V. Wilson, "Newborn, Cretin, and Horseshoe Crab Shell," Provincetown,
MA, 2021. Digital Image.

Noa: Do you remember us teaching you how to swim?

Lio: We started at the wall, our hands gripping the ledge, calves locked, legs
        kicking hard through the pool.

Uba: We hit against the wall too!

Noa: Mom, that's tennis! I'm talkin' 'bout swimming!

Uba: I/know! You think I don't know?

Noa: I know you know Mom!

        (Noa Freestyles)

        Light
        Water, the memory
        double faults.
        Feat Sepsis, Beat.

        Lost. Spike lif—can
        s of tuned
        fed blood
        the slow

        advantage.
        Guts froze to resin,
        mortality rate,
        trail of the low.

        Done, and do you
        know?
        Dummy Don,
        I miss Moms.

        As Noa now,

Ronaldo V. Wilson

I sing My Newborn,
"This little boy"
spikes back.

Lio: What I know is that I, maybe too often, think about my body, its fat-
        ness. Yet I stretch through the water, no fear of sinking, my arms cut-
        ting through as I punch and open my hands, bend current. I think of
        you, Dad, flotation father Noa of the sea, holding us up by our bellies. I
        know when you let me go on my bike, you pushed me into my own first
        balance. You let us go in the pool, too, you sitting at the bottom. As if
        in a lounge chair, you blew all the breath out, your rounded cheeks, lips
        and nose releasing bubbles, roiling to the surface. I watched your closed
        eyes. Your black, short Afro under the water.

        (Noa corrects Lio . . .)
                I have curly hair, too!
                My curls are just tighter than yours!

        What you made underwater made us, while Uba fortified, above, our
        lungs, stamina built from your running, away and into our life force.
        In the pool, my living legs kick—*Woooooo!* Blasts the surface between
        water and air.

Uba: You put them there, all perfect, and in the right place.

Lio: *By By Black, Newborn, and Yell-O-Why?*

Uba: *Mmmmhuh.*

Noa: And is that horseshoe crab's sunlit shell still one of your gloves?

Lio: San zi, Si. Lan to, go pons lo do. That hold see
        K! Nor pan vi-san to Go. Lean to shun-shun.
        Why me? GuanTon see, seize it. Gut la apostrophe.

Uba: San zi mero di co sup position? What say?

Noa: *Gut la. & Ton seize!* Since it makes sense, the supposition of the performance resides in the idea of the whole world you make, masks angled,
flopped, shot as ever, or in another way: *What you make is what we make.*

Lio: Por ejemplo, Das EFX,
Grimey on a Bro-Daze
Taze *FaH-JA!*
"Bye Bye, Be Good Don"
A preview at Wake
For Rest: a pre-pre
in the Cantu
Cinema du Ba. Baba
get Pressed, *Cretin.*
I shoot a warning shot
to that racist and his
Honey Pot in Mint Class
mines, mind my por-
traits, Sun lines, hor()
iZones! TBA TAB BAT

scene v.

In the Provincetown Harbor, there are "dead man's fingers," and "bladder
wracks," some of the sea flora that Lio remembers staring at when he made
poems there when Noa was alive, and Uba could still hit. Lio is on the same
side of the court as his dad at Trailhead Park in South Sacra, where the courts
are empty, except for the three of them. And Lio, young man, is strong and
hits the ball heavy, but just close enough for Uba (momma hard still, yet soft-
ening) to get to the ball, to return shots with accuracy, pace. "Hit it just where
she can get to it," Noa coaches his son, but Lio doesn't think then, as he does
now, of when Uba must have fed him the same kind of ball, pace just out
of reach for Lio, a little boy then. To attack his mom's easy-enough shot, his
dad, Noa, somewhere on the court, maybe like then, on the same side, yells
"Big Time!" Lio hits the ball, naturally, on the rise, winner down the line,
Lio's left leg planted, closed stance, knee bent, then, and then he moves for-
ward, to cut off any potential response.

Ronaldo V. Wilson. "Bye Bye, Be Good Don," 2020. Video (still), 22m. 39s.

Interlude

"We used little delay, but suddenly laid hands upon them. And it was as much as five or six of us could do to get them . . . For they were strong and so naked as our best hold was by their long hair on their heads."

James Rosier, on the abduction of five Wampanoag men sold as slaves in Malaga, Spain.[4]

(Uba freestyles)

Light,
Why-a-Strewn
mem
branes
or why is
falt.

---

4. Christina Rose, "Captured: Wampanoag History Finally Exposed in Provincetown Exhibit," Indiancountrytoday.com. Updated September 13, 2018: https://indiancountrytoday.com/archive /captured-wampanoag-history-finally-exposed-in-provincetown-exhibit

`Gis/
feather, ispa.
Squanto, a nick-
name on
dis
break.

Tisquantum/
sepsismasksus

        to sorrow
        bodywaves
spans U
ba's
        ground,

Vat the low-lo estuary
age gut-resin. New
borne
trail in
and out the life, mines—

Circa
de de
of done,
        do you know?*

FIGHT FOR YOUR FORM:

Ubaetre atis Malaga. To learn Spanish and Inglézzzz
        ink of don se jo ran ci-co fan fan,
and Noanow—To snatch, seal, snake, steal, toll, su_set, point LoveZero,
        seedling, the look, ache—dig dig dig—Don, Don, Don,
        My Noa.

Ronaldo V. Wilson, "As In, Uba and Noa," Provincetown, MA, 2021.
Digital Image.

scene vi.

*Solidago sempervirens, seaside goldenrod bloom above the low tide, center-
ing Uba's vision into the late September humid morning in Provincetown, in
the rocks, no tide, just outside the Provincetown Inn. Uba and Noa are still
both alive, and Lio wakes up before the rains come to go on his ArtWalk, to
make anything he wants. Lio drops Lucid and Cretin on the after-shore, shell
of rocks-us only after Noa is gone to snap shots of the sky from his first-class
seat and leers against racism into the boiling orange lava of a pool of silver-blue
milk out the plane's window, and thinks: What moves across this could ever
contain? Why? So, too, the intertidal was less the shore, than it's the seeing, so
Lio renders an ellipsis, shoreline of the East Bay extending, looking down from
the sky and into the burning horizon across this country. The rocks are gray-
blue-thick. Sand sticks to silicon, and fake honeypot hair born by the dimpling
water waves after the attacks, the kidnaps, the run, as in flight, alter-root then
spread outward, as in Uba's ". . . bye bye, Don, be good now . . ."*

Exeunt, Noa.

The Blue Plume

Juliana Spahr

][

These are these ways to hold
the river in one's heart.
Drive south is one way to it.
Drive south and leave the flatlands behind.
Briefly follow the Scioto
with its unusually large floodplain
spread like a skirt, along its sides.
Drive through valley bottoms smooth,
through flood deposits rich,
through a valley so wide, so deep.
Drive through farmlands
with fields full of grasses and wheats.
A place so full of a richness
that it is beyond description.
Then turn to the east,
leave the Scioto behind
and drive into the hills covered
with sugar maples, beech,
northern red oak
grown to a largeness
with the help of ferns and fungi,
a largeness that shelters

both the bobcat and the woodrat.
Slide past the churches and cemeteries
of prior generations carved into hills,
perched on the sides of the road.
Drive around and over
to arrive at this grassy lot,
at this unmarked grave of a town,
that rests beside this serpentine
turn of the river.
A path that resembles
the one taken each fall
by the warblers,
those golden-winged,
those chestnut-sided,
and those yellow-rumped.
That resembles the path of the north winds too,
the ones that the saw-whet owls
use in late November,
the main southward passage of the bobolinks too.

Juliana Spahr

][
When we came, she said,
we too traveled south.
We came to be near the river;
Dad was a river man
who held the river in his heart.
Because he held the river,
we too held the river.
Because we were his child,
we were the child of the river.
But not just the river,
the river's tributaries also.
The ones that flowed south,
the Muskingum, the Miami,
the Wabash, and the Scioto.
The ones that flowed north,
the Tennessee, the Big Sandy, the Licking.
We breathed the humid, heavy air of
winds that blow the vapor mists
full of the river over the town.
Some days this vapor
moist, warm, soft
on our bodies like a lover.
Other days fast-moving,
beating, relentless,
a different sort of lover.
At moments carrying within it
coolness and the sweet fragrance
of river mud. Then later so cold
it felt solid in our lungs.
We were not the only things
touched by these vapors.
Vapor traipsed over the tubal
inflorescences of the bee balm,
lingered to open the stubby blue flowers
of the blue wild indigo,

polished the vibrant red, deeply five-lobed
racemes of the cardinal flower,
glistened on the pinnately cut and lobed
leaves of the wood poppy,
rested on the dark-green and black stems of
the white wood aster.

Juliana Spahr

][
Beautiful river, she said,
beautiful river,
gentle currents,
dark, slow-moving river;
waters rich with soil.
We came to the river, she said,
this river, the one called beautiful,
the Ohio.
We greeted its shallow depths
its connecting routes,
all its possibilities.
We refused to think of it as
a border, as a division.
It had two banks and
both belonged to the river,
and thus belonged to us,
us and those who came before us.
Not to the governments who
made it a boundary.
These banks that supported the fauna and flora
of both the humid climates,
the subtropical and the continental.
Greetings she said to the river,
greetings to you glaucous-leaved greenbriar
prickly with bluntly triangular leaves
intertwined with the Virginia creeper.
Greetings to you Virginia creeper
and your leaves of five with adhesive tips,
your carefree round ball-like fruits
intertwined with the sawbriers.
Greetings to you sawbriers,
growing so fast overnight
that it is as if by the foot.
And greetings to you familiar bluet
as you hover over, above, around.

][

We came to be near the river
and once we were there, she said,
we poured the cement of the sidewalks and
we built the school and its football field,
two churches also and
one corner store.
Then the Kyger Creek Power Plant came.
And so did three smokestacks.
And as if that was not enough,
the General James M. Gavin Power Plant
would arrive next, with two smokestacks
and a cooling tower.
So too the coal-loaded barge came
floating slowly down the river.
The coal ash fly, that came too.
The southern winds still blew north,
but the humid wind now carried coal ash,
fly ash, bottom ash, boiler slag,
scrubber sludge, fluidized bed
combustion ash, and scrubber residues.
Carried milky droplets,
soot, and white specs.
We went on like this for years,
we lived with the coal ash,
not entirely happy with it
but our complaints went unheeded.
And then one day a blue plume
scuttled down the smokestack
and rolled across the park
straight into town, touched down
at the corner of Maple and Walnut,
traveled down Walnut until it came
to Mulberry, expanded so that
it covered Poplar next.
Scuttled down the stack like Pazuzu might,

holding on first with eagle talons,
then letting go to fly on the winds,
a vapor, a blue plume of particles,
sulfates, nitrates, water, and
gaseous nitrogen dioxide.
The blue plume of humid
sulfur trioxide full of mercury
full of polyfluorinated alkyl substances
full of sulphuric acid emissions.
The blue plume seduced the girl
who loved the river
who already dwelled in the bitter dioxins.
Gently and smoothly rubbed
her mucociliary clearance,
lingered around a little
and changed her lung function,
looked into her eyes
and entered her throat,
bid it to close and cough.
Slowly and steadily
expanded the capillaries that
brought on the headache.
Bronchitis, emphysema,
chronic runny nose,
tearing of the eyes,
nosebleeds, nausea,
erosion of stomach and teeth.
All the while claiming
it was nothing, it was only
a little cough.

][
To many it felt like the power plant
had taken the land.
First they replaced the vapor
with the plume.
Then they bought the place called Cheshire.
All together—both those who sold
and those who bought and those
who refused to sell—they all believed
that it was possible to buy,
that there was a thing called owned,
that there were boundaries,
and they believed the river was an example of one,
that it divided instead of connected.
But they were wrong.
And blue plume knew this,
for blue plume, like vapor, understood
the river as connection,
so it acted otherwise
as it too traipsed over the tubal inflorescences
of the bee balm, snuck into the stubby blue flowers
of the blue wild indigo, covered
the vibrant red, deeply five-lobed
racemes of the cardinal flower,
rested on the pinnately cut and lobed
leaves of the wood poppy,
dusted the dark-green and black stems of
the white wood aster,
dusted the sidewalks, the school
the football field, and the corner store too,
settled on the church pews,
dusted the feet of the birds who
walked on the ground,
dusted each blade of grass,
each leaf of the oaks that rested

in the front lawns
of the houses that would
a few years later be demolished
and replaced by the unmarked
grave of grassy fields.

][
There is a song that goes
that river's deep, and that river's wide
and the devil there, he stands on every side.
The history here is also deep and wide.
This is the reason to do the drive down south,
along the Scioto
then through the mountains
to stand at this intersection,
grassy fields on four sides,
unremarkable, ahistorical,
an unmarked grave of what
was once a town that is
the unmarked grave
of those who died in various floods
that is the unmarked grave of
those who died in Morgan's Raid
that is the unmarked grave of
the Shawnee and Algonquian
that is the unmarked grave of the
Omaha, Ponca, and Kaw,
that is the unmarked grave
of the long-gone Osage.
A place that like all places
can't be owned despite being
claimed by those who believed they owned.
While the vapor carried this history of
loss and owning,
the blue plume carries this history of
loss and owning and also of
the unlined pits of fly ash
and now when we carry the river
within us, we carry the fly ash too.
I am there,
standing at the intersection
of the unmarked grave.

Juliana Spahr

You are there too,
with me in the foul-smelling smoke of the pit,
the reeking air as river-deep,
as this history,
as bird pecking away at bird.
This history too where elk beside the oak tree
that half a hundred hunted down
and yet it lives on.
This history as the night heron ghost and
the bluebird ghost
together calling to the evening.

Dark Soil Coordinates

801 Silver Avenue
37.7295883°, -122.4183334°
801 Silver Avenue
San Francisco, CA 94134

(De)Tour of an Unincorporated Territory
13.450126°, 144.757551°
Deboto Street
Mongmong-Toto-Maite, Guam 96910

506 N. Evergreen Avenue, Los Angeles, CA 90033
34.04525°, -118.199219°
506 North Evergreen Avenue
Los Angeles, CA 90033

Navel, Bury
42.370377°, -72.516069°
Charles Pratt Hall
3 Meade Drive
Amherst, MA 01002

A Pale Persephone
40.724589°, -73.995375°
Puck Building
295 Lafayette Street
New York, NY 10012

Whether the Border Looks Out from Eight Hundred and Fifty Eyes, or Two,
the MBQ Remains Few Though on the Rise
31.812180°, -111.443051°
Buenos Aires National Wildlife Refuge
South Sasabe Road
Sasabe, AZ 85633

After Silent Incantations, the Intertidal
37.831631°, -122.305306°
McLaughlin Eastshore State Seashore
University Avenue & Frontage Road
Berkeley, CA 94720

The Blue Plume
38.9448013°, -82.111255°
Ohio River Scenic Byway
Cheshire, OH 45620

Afterword

Karen Tei Yamashita

Dear Angie:

It was the hottest day of that year. Probably September Indian summer just before fall quarter. What year was it? 2019? Approaching retirement, I was finally wondering about the town where I had lived and taught for over two decades. Retirement would be settling in for the duration, and I wasn't interested in any other sunny beachside Mediterranean-like dreamscape; I was already here in what Ronaldo called "somebody's paradise, but not mine." Well, he could go back to Brazil, but I was staying in Santa Cruz. The sacred *X* marks the mystery spot, but I realized that it was still a mystery to me. I was embarrassed, really, at my ignorance.

Many years ago, my colleague and intrepid oral historian Judy Yung had taken me over to Mobo Sushi next to Trader Joe's, bordering the San Lorenzo River, the site of the vanished Chinatown; yes, the Chinese had long ago settled here, but who was Louden Nelson (corrected lately to London Nelson), whose name was on the community center I passed on the way downtown, several times a week, thousands of times over twenty years? When did I discover that Nelson, an enslaved man who came to California in the Gold Rush, was the godfather of the Santa Cruz public schools and that the center hosted a Juneteenth barbecue every summer? Just recently. What was I doing all those years up there on the hill in that university, assuming our local history was basically a white liberal entrenchment of the Summer of Love?

Previous to this hot Indian summer day, I was asked to write a noir story set in Santa Cruz. That story, coincidentally "Indian Summer," is perhaps the darkest of this collection; it initiated my investigation of the local, the locations of what you name *dark soil*, where the memories of migrant, immigrant, enslaved, and native people are buried and forgotten. And a couple of the stories are satiric gestures to the cockeyed sightings of people of color in our neck of the woods. Not necessarily noir, I called these *nori* stories, as if inscribed into the organically knit black fibers of dried and ironed seaweed. Toasted, inflected with shoyu, resonating, I hope, umami.

You agreed to meet me at Bookshop Santa Cruz to accompany me on a walk. Nice that you just came along innocently, happy to humor me. It must have been

110 degrees. You were cool in a sundress, but I was a sweaty mess. We cheated and did most of it by air-conditioned car, but you got the general picture. And then I pitched my idea that you'd complete the rest of the book by cajoling a group of authors of your choosing to come up with their own stories.

Now there are eight of you, each exploding, expanding, reinventing whatever it was that we thought we started here that day. Turns out it might be mythography. Mythos + geography. Maybe it started in detention on Silver Avenue in San Francisco, the repurposed Angel Island on land, now an elementary school. Immigrant children line up for class; their innocence among ghosts is your disquiet. Are the children ghosts or are you the ghost? Then, in the postwar, the War Relocation Authority releases you from detention, hands you twenty-five dollars and a ticket to ride. You take the bus to East LA and find lodging in the Fellowship House, and that's the beginning of your next life, and the place settles a precarious future for your kids. Or maybe the bus arrives in that side of Sac City, capital of California; your folks have fallen into love and escaped from the Philippines, and you're the military brat that emerges onto mercurial shores, navigating behind many masks. You stand at the river's edge, shores of timeless and lost idylls, where home used to be, a blue plume smothering once pristine skies, floating over unmarked graves. Persephone's spring pushes green shoots and floral arrangements through dark soil, deep from her underground abode; her floating mouth opens into silent vocals. You stand over an unmarked grave, holding in your hand the desiccated tissue of your baby's navel, evidence of baby's attachment to you and to your mother and to hers. How far away is your exile and to where have you arrived? You cannot bury the navel here. Peering into the grave, you see your grandmother's dream, pet pig roasting on a spit, the snarling grunts of Japanese soldiers, teeth tearing at greasy meat. A masked bobwhite quail, code name MBQ, prances into the brush beyond and flitters into the blue plume, and you are assured of the vitality of the ecosystem of this place. No one is counting the remains of 410 migrant women or Tohono O'odham people as vitality evidence. You wave to MBQ, *Bye bye, Don. Be good.* And your dad reminds you, as you cycle away, *Remember your coordinates.* How else will you be able to find yourself again on this invisible island?

With gratitude,
KT

Contributor Bios

Sesshu Foster taught composition and literature in East LA for thirty-five years. His most recent book is *ELADATL: A History of the East Los Angeles Dirigible Air Transport Lines*, a novel cowritten with artist Arturo Ernesto Romo (City Lights, 2021).

Angie Sijun Lou is a Kundiman Fellow and a PhD candidate in literature and creative writing at the University of California, Santa Cruz.

Saretta Morgan was born in Appalachia and raised on military installations. She's interested in the ecologies and intimacies that materialize in the shadows of us militarization.

Thirii Myo Kyaw Myint is the author of *Names for Light: A Family History* (Graywolf Press, 2021) and *The End of Peril, the End of Enmity, the End of Strife, a Haven* (Noemi Press, 2018). She teaches at Amherst College.

Craig Santos Perez is an indigenous Chamoru from Guam. He is the author of six books of poetry and the co-editor of seven anthologies.

Brandon Shimoda is the author of several books of poetry and prose, including *Hydra Medusa* (Nightboat Books, 2023) and *The Grave on the Wall* (City Lights, 2019), which received the PEN Open Book Award.

Juliana Spahr is a poet and a scholar. Her most recent books are *That Winter the Wolf Came* (Commune Editions, 2015) and *Du Bois's Telegram: Literary Resistance and State Containment* (Harvard University Press, 2018).

Ronaldo V. Wilson is an award-winning poet, interdisciplinary artist, academic, and author of six collections of hybrid and experimental works spanning poetry, fiction, mixed genre theory, performance, and visual art. He is professor of creative writing and literature; principal faculty of critical race and ethnic studies; and affiliate faculty of digital arts and new media at the University of California, Santa Cruz.

Funder Acknowledgments

Coffee House Press is an internationally renowned independent book publisher and arts nonprofit based in Minneapolis, MN; through its literary publications and *Books in Action* program, Coffee House acts as a catalyst and connector— between authors and readers, ideas and resources, creativity and community, inspiration and action.

Coffee House Press books are made possible through the generous support of grants and donations from corporations, state and federal grant programs, family foundations, and the many individuals who believe in the transformational power of literature. This activity is made possible by the voters of Minnesota through a Minnesota State Arts Board Operating Support grant, thanks to the legislative appropriation from the Arts and Cultural Heritage Fund. Coffee House also receives major operating support from the Amazon Literary Partnership, Jerome Foundation, Literary Arts Emergency Fund, McKnight Foundation, and the National Endowment for the Arts (NEA). To find out more about how NEA grants impact individuals and communities, visit www.arts.gov.

Coffee House Press receives additional support from Bookmobile; the Buckley Charitable Fund; Dorsey & Whitney LLP; the Gaea Foundation; the Schwab Charitable Fund; and the U.S. Bank Foundation.

The Publisher's Circle of Coffee House Press

Publisher's Circle members make significant contributions to Coffee House Press's annual giving campaign. Understanding that a strong financial base is necessary for the press to meet the challenges and opportunities that arise each year, this group plays a crucial part in the success of Coffee House's mission.

Recent Publisher's Circle members include many anonymous donors, Kathy Arnold, Patricia A. Beithon, Andrew Brantingham & Rita Farmer, Kelli & Dave Cloutier, Theodore Cornwell, Jane Dalrymple-Hollo, Mary Ebert & Paul Stembler, Jennifer Egan, Kamilah Foreman, Eva Galiber, Jocelyn Hale & Glenn Miller Charitable Fund of the Minneapolis Foundation, Roger Hale & Nor Hall, William Hardacker, Randy Hartten & Ron Lotz, Carl & Heidi Horsch, Amy L. Hubbard & Geoffrey J. Kehoe Fund of the St. Paul & Minnesota Foundation, Hyde Family Charitable Fund, Kenneth & Susan Kahn, the Kenneth Koch Literary Estate, Cinda Kornblum, the Lenfestey Family Foundation, Sarah Lutman & Rob Rudolph, Carol & Aaron Mack, Gillian McCain, Mary & Malcolm McDermid, Daniel N. Smith III & Maureen Millea Smith, Vance Opperman, Mr. Pancks' Fund in memory of Graham Kimpton, Alan Polsky, Robin Preble, Ronald Restrepo & Candace S. Baggett, Steve Smith, Lynne Stanley, Jeffrey Sugerman & Sarah Schultz, Paul Thissen, Grant Wood, and Margaret Wurtele.

For more information about the Publisher's Circle and other ways to support Coffee House Press books, authors, and activities, please visit www.coffeehousepress.org/pages/donate or contact us at info@coffeehousepress.org.

Photo © Jess X. Snow

ANGIE SIJUN LOU is a Kundiman Fellow and a PhD candidate in literature and creative writing at the University of California, Santa Cruz. Her essays and criticism have appeared in the *American Poetry Review,* the *Georgia Review,* and *Amerasia Journal.* She lives in Oakland.

Photo © Chris Hardy

KAREN TEI YAMASHITA is the author of eight books (including *I Hotel,* finalist for the National Book Award, and most recently *Sansei and Sensibility*), all published by Coffee House Press. Recipient of the Lifetime Achievement Award for Distinguished Contribution to American Letters from the National Book Foundation, the John Dos Passos Prize for Literature, and a United States Artists' Ford Foundation Fellowship, she is professor emerita of literature and creative writing at the University of California, Santa Cruz.

Dark Soil was designed by Bookmobile Design & Digital Publisher Services.
Text is set in Adobe Jenson Pro Light.